FOR YOU
I
Will

FOR YOU I Will

DONNA HILL

HARLEQUIN® KIMANI ARABESQUE®

For You I Will

ISBN-13: 978-0-373-09139-3

Copyright © 2014 by Donna Hill

HARLEQUIN®
www.Harlequin.com

Printed in U.S.A.

Dear Reader,

Thank you for joining me once again as I venture into the town of Sag Harbor. You'll come across some old friends like Desiree and Lincoln. Melanie Harte also makes an appearance, in addition to Layla Brooks from *Touch Me Now*. Sag Harbor welcomes two newcomers in *For You I Will:* Dr. Kai Randall and Assistant District Attorney Anthony Weston. Both are driven individuals with totally different goals, plenty of emotional baggage and a chemistry that neither can deny.

I had a great time researching Sag Harbor and creating two characters that I know you will love as much as I do. Anthony, on the fast track to being district attorney for New York, has a four-year-old daughter and a troublesome ex-wife. His life is in Manhattan. Kai Randall has had her fill of the harsh, fast-paced life of the big city and big-city hospitals. Her life is in Sag Harbor. Hmm... Someone will have to give in if their relationship is ever going to work.

Be sure to read the other books in the Sag Harbor Village series: *Dare to Dream, Heart's Reward* and *Touch Me Now.*

You can always follow me on Twitter @donnahill and on Facebook at facebook.com/donnahillfans.

Until next time,

Donna

Dedicated with love and appreciation to all of my readers who have supported this wonderful job of mine for 23 amazing years! Thank you!

Prologue

The air over Sag Harbor was charged and ready to joust with the storm that loomed on the horizon. A blanket of gray and white hung over the treetops and roofs of the homes that dotted the landscape. The residents of Sag Harbor were accustomed to the sudden spring storms and after two years away from the frenetic pace of New York City, Dr. Kai Randall had gotten used to them, as well. So well in fact that she no longer closed herself inside her quaint home during these outbursts but welcomed them, capturing nature's power from behind the lens of her camera.

For Kai, picking up stakes and leaving New York Presbyterian Hospital wasn't a matter of a simple getaway; it was to save her own sanity. The bureaucratic pressure, the fourteen-hour days, and being a constant witness to pain and suffering had begun to take its toll on her physical and mental well-being. And after ten years on the front lines as chief of the E.R., she packed her stethoscope, her skills as a surgeon and returned to her ancestral home on Sag Harbor in the neighborhood known as Azurest. Kai's great-great-grandfather Isaiah Randall had fought side-by-side with Warren M. Cuffee, a soldier in the black regiment of the Union Army who championed the liberation of blacks from slavery. Isaiah built his home on Azurest when he married Kai Seneca, a Native American who was said to have stolen Isaiah's heart with one look from her luminous black eyes. Decades later, Kai was named after her great-great-grandmother whose name means "willow tree."

Kai had visited the two-story family home with the wraparound porch that faced the water, off and on during her childhood and fewer than a dozen times as an adult. Her hectic schedule didn't allow for much downtime. And even then, she could never be too far away from the hospital in the event of an emergency. Finally deciding she needed a better quality of life, Kai sold her condo on the Upper East Side, traded in her Lexus for a Ford Explorer, her scrubs for jeans and flip-flops, and planted new roots in Sag Harbor Village. It took her a while to grow accustomed to the quiet and the slower pace, to realize that businesses closed at dusk and all the residents knew each other by first name and they didn't text all day long but actually had conversations and made phone calls.

Now, more than two years later, Kai Randall was a fixture in Sag Harbor Village. With the urging of Melanie and her own restless need to "fix things," Kai had converted her detached garage into a small medical office, complete with state-of-the-art equipment, from X-ray machines to nebulizers to sonogram machines. She ran the place herself. There wasn't much need for a staff. Actually, most of her doctoring was done in house calls. That was Melanie's doing as well. She referred all of her clients, family and guests to Kai, who was more than happy to pay them a visit when they were under the weather.

It was a good life. Easy. And for the first time in longer than she could remember, she was able to pursue her other passion of photography. She took real pictures, the old-fashioned way, and developed them herself in the attic that she had converted into a darkroom. She'd even donated a few to the Grenning Gallery in town, and Desiree Armstrong, a renowned artist in her own right, had suggested that Kai put up a show of her own.

But Kai hadn't left the demands of the big city to get caught up in the demands of a small town. She liked things the way they were. No complications. No deadlines. No demands on her time or ability. Besides, most of the pictures that she took were of the people in the Village. She couldn't begin to imagine the headache that would come as a result of needing people's permissions to use their images. No thanks. Life was fine just the way it was.

Kai stood in the archway of her front door, her eyes lifted to the darkening sky. She estimated that she had an hour, maybe two, before the rains came. She hurried up to her attic studio and gathered up her equipment.

It was a great day for shooting. While many photographers preferred sunshine and blue heavens, Kai did some of her best work during storms and overcast skies, capturing scenes in stark black and white juxtaposed against the silhouettes of buildings or crashing waves. Today was one of those days.

She packed up her equipment in her car along with her dog, Jasper, and headed into town. From the mouth of the town proper, Kai parked her car and took out her equipment. The outline of the businesses, turn-of-the-century streetlights and the masts of the sailboats docked at the pier set against the backdrop of the overcast skies formed the perfect composition. She shot a quick roll of film and then strolled down Main Street to capture the silhouettes of patrons beyond the glass windows, just as the rain began to fall. She put in another roll of film, snapped her final shots and hurried back to her car with Jasper hot on her heels just as the skies opened up.

After drying off, she went straight to her studio and removed the film from the camera. This was the part of the process that she enjoyed the most, watching the images come to life.

As she took the last photograph from the solution and hung it up to dry, she was once again fascinated by the transformation that happened in measured increments, an image coming to life right before her eyes.

All at once the profile of a man, with his head slightly bowed, his fist pressed against his forehead and seated alone in the coffee shop, emerged, and something inside of her shifted. She barely remembered taking the shot, but obviously she had. Her heart pounded as she looked closer. But it was more than his face through the plate-glass window that unsettled her. It was the aura of aloneness that wafted over him like the storm clouds. Everything within her wanted to fix him and make whatever it was that weighed down his spirit go away. *How ridiculous,* she thought. It was only a picture.

Yet, days later, she found that at the most inopportune moments, his image floated in front of her or that jumpy feeling in the center of her stomach wreaked havoc. At night she thought of him, and during the days she found herself hoping to catch another glance of him. But as the days turned to weeks and spring into early summer, Kai cataloged the image away.

Chapter 1

"You'll be fine, Mrs. Anderson." Kai snapped off her rubber gloves and pulled her stethoscope from her ears. "It's your allergies."

"Are you sure it's not the flu? I feel like it's the flu." She sniffed hard and blinked against watery eyes.

Kai's amber-toned eyes crinkled with humor. "No, Mrs. Anderson, it's not the flu." She handed her a tissue. "With all the rain we've been having and with the blooming flowers and grass, I'm surprised you haven't been bothered before. I'll give you a new prescription for your allergy medicine."

Mrs. Anderson almost looked disappointed. Kai tucked away her smile. "You can get dressed and then come to my office for the prescription."

"Are you sure?" she asked again.

Kai stopped at the door and glanced over her shoulder. "Positive."

Mrs. Anderson huffed and Kai closed the door softly behind her. When she stepped out into the small waiting area that was really only equipped to handle six people including her, she was stunned to see all the seats occupied. Mr. and Mrs. Hanson and their three children were huddled together as if they'd recently been washed ashore.

"Oh my goodness." Kai looked from one to the other and instantly saw the flush in their faces and the wan look around their eyes. "I'll be with you all in one moment." She started off toward her office but stopped when she remembered Mrs. Anderson, who already believed she had the flu. If the Hanson family had anything contagious she needed to get them out of the front room as soon as possible. Her triage skills from her years in the emergency room kicked into gear.

The office was small. She had three exam rooms, a tiny office and the waiting area. She quickly ushered Mr. Hanson into a room with the oldest son who was on the verge of turning six. Mrs. Hanson was placed in the adjacent room with the twin three-year-old girls. Today was a day she could use an assistant.

After getting them settled, she went to her office to write the allergy prescription for Mrs. Anderson and was just finishing when Mrs. Anderson knocked on the partially opened door.

"Come in." She tore the prescription from the pad and handed it across the desk. "Get this filled as soon as possible and I guarantee you will feel much better."

Mrs. Anderson took the rectangular piece of paper and placed it in her purse. "Thank you so much, Dr. Randall. I appreciate it."

"Of course. Never hesitate to come in if you're not

feeling well. It could have been something more serious, but fortunately it wasn't." She smiled.

"Thank goodness for that." She turned to leave. A wail from one of the twins pierced through the walls and halted her step. "Oh, my. That's some cry. Must be something terribly wrong."

Kai got up from behind her desk and ushered Mrs. Anderson out. "Kids cry. That's what they do," she said with a placating smile. "You be careful going home." She gave her a reassuring pat on the shoulder. Mrs. Anderson was a sweetheart but everyone knew she had the biggest mouth in the town of Azurest. If she even thought for a moment that an entire family was ill she would create panic in the streets of Sag Harbor before lunchtime.

Kai secured and locked the door and put her closed sign in the window then quickly went into the room with the wailing baby, who had in turn, gotten her twin involved in the symphony. Kai went to the sink and thoroughly washed her hands, put a disposable smock over her clothing and snapped on rubber gloves.

"Christine, I'm going to check out the twins first." She picked up one of the girls from her mother's arms and sat her on the exam table. "I can never tell them apart."

"That's Cara. This is Carmen," she said, indicating the baby in her arms.

Kai talked softly and soothingly to Cara while she made a game of placing the child thermometer in her ear. "How long has everyone been sick?"

"This is the second day. The only one who hasn't been sick is my husband, Mike. But I know taking care of a house full of sick people is going to catch up with him at some point."

"She has a slight fever." She tossed the disposable tip of the thermometer in the trash. "Any vomiting?"

"Yes."

"Hmm," Kai murmured deep in her throat while she checked Cara's ears, nose and throat. She listened to her chest and then did it all over again with her sister, Carmen. She pushed out a breath. "They both have low-grade fevers. And with the vomiting, I'm concerned about dehydration. When I'm done with my exam of Monty, I'm going to give my colleague over at General a call. He's a pediatrician. I'll see what he suggests. Okay?" She offered an encouraging smile. "I'm sure it's only a virus and it will run its course, but until it does, I want to make sure we're doing all that we can."

"Thank you, Doctor."

"Sure. I'm going to examine Monty and then I'll come back and check you out." She took off her smock and gloves and ditched them in the trash then went into the next exam room.

An hour later she sent the Hanson family to the local pharmacy and also advised that they get to bed early.

Kai went about cleaning and sterilizing the rooms and was ready to call it a day when the office phone rang. One of these days she might actually hire a receptionist, she mused as she hurried to the front desk.

"Dr. Randall. How may I help you?"

"What's up, doc?"

His corny greeting always made her laugh. "Dr. Drew."

"I'm calling to check up on my virtual patients."

She leaned her hip against the desk. "They should be on their way home by now and following your advice."

"Good. I so love doing business with you, Dr. Randall."

She could hear the laughter in his voice. That was a unique quality of Andrew Clarke. He was always upbeat and could make anyone around him feel the same way. It was probably why he was such an incredible pediatrician.

"I aim to please."

"The real reason for my call is that there is an author reading at the Grenning Gallery tonight. I know how much you love thrillers and mysteries and it's the mystery writer—Harlan Coben—that will be the guest."

Her eyes widened. "Right! I totally forgot. Harlan Coben is a favorite of mine."

"So...you'll go with me?"

She hesitated. They'd been out together before—casually—with a group of his colleagues from the hospital. But she always had the sense that if given the chance, he'd want more. This would be the first time they would actually be going out "together." Is that what she wanted? He was good-looking, and smart and funny and available...

"Sure. I'd love to go. I can meet you there—"

"Don't be silly. I can pick you up. I'm out of here early today for a change. Reading starts at eight. Maybe we can grab something to eat first or afterwards."

Oh, so this really was a "real date." "Uh, okay. I'll be ready."

"You want to grab something first or after?"

She was having momentary brain freeze. If they had dinner first then went to the reading it wasn't as romantic, whereas a late dinner gave off all kinds of signals. Didn't it? It had been so long since she'd been on a date, she really didn't know.

"I guess we could eat first."

"No problem. How 'bout I pick you up at six?"

"Works for me," she said, forcing cheer into her voice.

"See you then."

"See ya," she chirped. She slowly hung up the phone. Her right eyebrow rose ever so slightly. *A date*. Well, stranger things had happened.

Chapter 2

"You finally gave in to Dr. Feelgood. It's about damned time," Tiffany teased Kai as she sipped her iced tea during their etched-in-stone Wednesday afternoon brunch. They'd decided several years earlier that with their hectic lives they needed time for themselves and designated Wednesday afternoon for just that. They would always have brunch and when time and opportunity allowed they either went window-shopping or to a movie. Although Tiffany's import business of fine jewelry and fabrics often took her out of town to shop, she and Kai made it a point to keep their Wednesday afternoon dates. In the early days it had taken a bit of getting used to, with one or both of them often forgetting about their "date." But once they got into the swing of it, not hell or high water would keep them from getting together for some girl time.

Kai had hit it off with Tiffany Howard from the moment Tiffany had sought Kai's medical assistance when she needed a prescription for the morning-after pill. Tiffany was so warm, friendly and open that Kai had taken to her right away. They found themselves talking and laughing and finding more and more things in common long after the prescription had been written, and they hadn't stopped sharing confidences ever since.

Kai gave her the bug-eye. "Very funny." She cut her Caesar salad into smaller bite-sized pieces, and made sure that every slice of lettuce was sufficiently coated with dressing before putting it in her mouth.

Tiffany observed this ritual with wry amusement. "I swear you are the only person that I know that can actually make a major production out of eating a salad."

"Would you stop?" She cut up some more pieces. "What should I wear?"

Tiffany pursed her lips in contemplation. "Hmm. Gallery. Evening. First date. Famous author. Sexy doctor. I say wear the navy wrap dress."

"You don't think that dress is a little too low-cut?"

"Low-cut? You're kidding, right? Of course it's low-cut. It's supposed to be. That's the point. If you would ever come out of hospital garbs and sweat suits, you would know that."

Kai made a face. "I don't want him to get the wrong idea."

"And what if he did? Would that really be so bad? What would be so wrong with a handsome, sexy, intelligent man showing you how much he wanted you?"

Kai studied her salad. "It's just...I don't know if I want things to go that way."

"But you'll never know if you don't at least open yourself to the possibility. You said yourself that he's a really great guy." She smiled at her friend. "And he's been after you for a date for forever."

Kai giggled. "True." She released a long breath. Her eyes sparkled in the afternoon light. "I do kinda like that blue number and haven't had a chance to wear it."

"Now you're talking." Tiffany pointed a well-manicured finger at her friend. "And don't forget heels…the higher the better!"

"Girl, you are a mess."

After leaving Tiffany, who had an appointment with a client who wanted to buy some of her imported jewelry, Kai took a walk down to the nail salon and treated herself to a well-deserved and long overdue mani and pedi. She was enjoying the feeling of the warm sudsy water bubbling around her feet when pedestrians strolling past the plate-glass window caught her attention. She jumped up so quickly she splashed water all over the floor and the manicurist.

"Oh…I'm so sorry." Kai snatched up a towel and dutifully wiped the young woman's damp arms. "I'm really sorry," she repeated.

"Don't worry about it. Is everything all right?" She stared at Kai whose attention was glued to the window.

Slowly, Kai sat back down. In that split second of confusion he was gone. Poof, like an apparition. But she was certain it was *him*—the man she'd seen in the photo that she'd taken. She lightly shook her head and offered a half smile. "Thought I saw someone…"

The young woman continued to massage Kai's feet. "Must be someone important," the woman prompted.

"Just someone," she said absently, even as her entire body was consumed with an inexplicable heat from the soles of her feet to the top of her head, and it wasn't from the water. *Just someone.*

* * *

Kai took a final look in the bathroom mirror, dropped her lipstick in her purse and returned to her bedroom just as the front doorbell rang. Self-consciously she pulled on the deep V of her dress to no avail. She drew in a breath and went to the front door.

"Andrew," she greeted, pasting a broad smile on her face, a combination of nerves and more nerves.

For an instant his eyes widened with pleasant surprise. "Wow." He grinned. "You look…great."

Her face flushed. "Thanks." She swallowed. "So do you."

"Guess doctors can clean up pretty good, huh?"

"Guess so." She stepped aside. "Come on in for a minute. I need to get my purse."

Andrew came inside. Kai shut the door behind him. "Have a seat. I'll be right back. Can I get you anything?"

"No. Thanks."

"Be right back."

He took a slow look around the airy living area, which was dominated by a soft taupe-colored sectional couch with a bronze-and-gold stripped throw that looked like it had been meticulously hand-sewn. One wall held a bookcase filled with a cross-section of titles that included medical journals, British classics, contemporary thrillers, romances and a full shelf on photography. A flat-screen television was mounted on the wall. But what drew his attention was above the mantel. It was a near life-size black-and-white photo of the beach during a storm. The composition was breathtaking. Andrew could feel the fury of the surf as it roared toward the shore. Beyond the shoreline, the inky black sky was illuminated by a flash of lightning that exploded from an angry gray cloud and sliced through the horizon. He stepped closer to see the name of the photographer.

"Ready."

He turned and his heart knocked hard in his chest at the sight of her. She was so gorgeous. "Yep. Incredible photo," he said, hooking a thumb over his shoulder. "Who's the photographer?"

She gave a shy smile. "Me."

"What!" He chuckled. "You. Are. Good."

"Thanks." She gave a slight shrug of her right shoulder.

He crossed the gleaming wood floors to stand a few feet in front of her. "How long have you been taking pictures?"

"Years. It was always a hobby of mine, but with patients, working at the hospital for an inhumane number of hours a week, there wasn't much time to indulge in my little hobby." She drew in a breath and smiled. "When I moved here and my life slowed down…" She shrugged again.

"Well, you definitely have skills, doc."

"Thanks."

They stood facing each other in an odd moment of silence.

"Guess we better get going," Andrew finally said, snapping them both back to the moment.

"I'm looking forward to meeting Mr. Coben."

"You have quite a few of his novels on your shelf."

"Ya think?" she teased as they walked to the door and out.

Andrew held the door for her and she slid onto the smooth leather of the Mercedes-Benz CLK. The interior still smelled showroom-fresh and she briefly wondered how long he'd had it.

"I made reservations at Drummonds, the new place on Main. Have you been there yet?"

"No, I haven't." She settled herself in the car and fastened her seat belt.

"Good, it'll be a first for both of us. A colleague from the hospital said the food was great and they usually have live music."

"Really? Sounds great."

"I can't remember the last time I've been out for dinner where I could simply relax and enjoy myself. Dinners always seem to invariably revolve around business, patients, and hospital administration." He cut a quick look in her direction as he pulled onto the narrow two-lane road. "So I hope you won't mind if we don't utter a word about anything that has to do with patients and health care."

Kai laughed lightly. "Fine by me."

They drove for a few moments in silence. "I'm really glad you decided to go out with me," Andrew said, his normally assured voice laced with a hint of uncertainty.

Kai stole a look in his direction. His profile was set against the backdrop of the darkening sky. "Thanks for asking...*again*."

They both laughed at the obvious implication. Andrew had lost count of how many times he'd asked Kai out and she'd always found a reason to gently say no.

"Had I only known that all it would take to lure you out was a Harlan Coben book signing, I would have found a way to get him here long before now."

Kai laughed. The dimple in her right cheek deepened. "Was I really that bad?"

"Yes. Good thing I have a healthy ego or I would be permanently scarred."

"I doubt that very seriously." She relaxed in her seat, glanced briefly at the crest of the horizon beyond her passenger window then turned slightly toward Andrew.

"Do you even like mysteries?"

He gave a slight shrug. "I'm more of a Stephen King kind of guy."

She gave a fake shudder and a little frown. "Horror! Really? I would have never thought that in a million years."

"Why?" He stole a quick look at her and was delighted to see the amusement in her eyes.

"Hmm, I'm not sure. I guess I figured you for a history or a biography buff."

"Real straight, no rough edges."

"Not exactly but…"

"I get it. I totally get it. That's why it's more important than ever that you get to know the real me. I'm much more than a pretty face and brilliant mind, you know."

Kai tossed her head back and laughed. "That's to be determined."

Drummonds was everything that Drew had said and more. The circular tables were draped in brilliant white linen, with sparkling crystal glasses and gleaming silver. One entire wall was smoked glass from end to end and looked out onto the pier, giving view to the gently flapping sails of the docked boats undulating on the water. The circular bar was a mixture of chrome, dark red wood and marble. Every stool was taken.

"Welcome to Drummonds. Do you have a reservation?" the slim hostess donned in all black asked.

"Yes, two for Clarke," Andrew said.

The hostess checked her reservation list, looked up

and smiled. She took two menus from the rack. "Right this way. Your table is ready."

Andrew placed his hand at the small of Kai's back and guided her behind the hostess who wound her way around the tables, dance floor and up one level to their table in front of the window. She placed the menus on the table. Andrew helped Kai into her seat then took his.

"Can I get you anything from the bar before your waiter arrives?"

Andrew looked to Kai with a questioning rise of his brow.

Kai glanced up at the waitress. "A glass of white wine."

"Anything for you, sir?"

"Why don't you bring us a bottle of sauvignon blanc?" He gave Kai a quick look of inquiry.

She offered her assent with a shadow of a smile. "Please."

The hostess tipped her head. "Right away."

Andrew turned his full attention back to Kai.

"I had no idea Drummonds was anything like this," Kai said.

"Very Upper East Side Manhattan," he joked.

She laughed. "Exactly. I mean the restaurants here are very nice but mostly quaint and cozy." She gazed around in appreciation.

The waiter arrived with their bottle of wine and filled each of their glasses then took their dinner order before leaving as quietly as he'd arrived.

Andrew lifted his glass. "To a wonderful evening."

Kai lightly tapped her glass to his.

"So tell me some more about your photography." He took a sip of his wine then set his glass down.

Kai wrapped her long, slender fingers around the stem of her glass and gazed into the crystal depths of its contents. "I suppose I always had a thing for seeing things in parts."

"In parts?"

"Yes. This may sound a little quirky but…" She pushed out a breath. "To me, I see things in pieces, not as a whole. It's like looking at what's in front of me in…frames. I compartmentalize." She looked at him from beneath her long lashes.

A line of concentration etched itself between his brows. "All the time?"

"Pretty much."

He thoughtfully sipped his wine. "So you're not the 'big picture' kind of a girl."

Kai grinned. "Nope. Guess not." She sipped her wine. "What about you when you aren't doctoring?"

Kai listened while Andrew talked about his love of the outdoors, the yearly camping trips with his college buddies and the marathon that he ran every year. She listened, nodded and "mmm-hmmed" in all the right places and wondered if she could ever put Andrew into one her compartments and label it "her man," "significant other," or "husband." For whatever reason, she simply could not see him fitting into any of those spaces in her life. Maybe she had been out of the relationship game for so long that she no longer knew how to play.

When Kai and Andrew arrived at the Grenning Gallery there was a line waiting to get in.

"Looks like it's going to be pretty crowded in there," Andrew said as he guided Kai onto the line.

"This is so exciting. I can't wait to meet him."

"You and a lot of other fans."

They inched along on the line and finally made it inside. Andrew was right. The Grenning Gallery was packed, upstairs and down. The reading and signing were set up on the upper level. The lower level was for appetizers and refreshments. The crowd was an eclectic blend of the die-hard fan and the curious, garbed in everything from jeans and sneakers to evening wear.

"Can I get you something to drink?" Andrew asked, leaning close to be heard over the mild din.

"Hmm, sure. A glass of white wine."

"Stay put. I don't want to lose you," he said and flashed Kai a look that gave his words much more meaning.

Kai held her small purse to her chest and took in her surroundings. It had been a while since she'd been to the gallery, partly because she'd totally run out of excuses why she would not exhibit her photography and couldn't bear disappointing the owner again. She'd donated a couple of her photos months earlier for a fund-raiser and the owner had been after her to do a show ever since.

Hopefully with all the people at the gallery, they wouldn't cross each other's paths.

Her gaze slowly moved around the room, capturing images of the art, the people and the movements, and forming a montage of sorts in her mind. With each blink of her eyes, another image was snapped. Then there was a big hum in the air, the buzz of excitement that always preceded a major event. The author had arrived, accompanied by his publicist and a photographer. The surge of the crowd moved her along in their wake.

The bevy of guests began taking cell-phone pictures as Harlan Coben made his way through the throng, smiling and shaking hands along the way as he was led upstairs.

Kai peered over the sea of heads and shoulders trying to locate Andrew when her gaze landed on him. Heat rushed to her head and her heart banged in her chest. *It was him.* He was partially turned in her direction. His profile was identical to the one she'd snapped months earlier. He was turning in her direction. Something or someone drew his attention and he turned and walked in the opposite direction.

"There you are." Andrew had come up behind her. "Thought I'd lost you to the crowd. Did you get to see him before he was swept away?"

She glanced over her shoulder at Andrew. Her cheeks were hot. "Oh…yes. Just for a minute," she said.

Chapter 3

"Mr. Weston, your wife is on line three."

Anthony Weston's dark brows tightened across his forehead. He didn't know how many times he would have to tell his secretary, Valerie, that Crystal was the *ex*-Mrs. Weston. Maybe Val couldn't or wouldn't get it right because he was still wrestling with that reality nearly two years after their divorce.

He pressed the flashing light on his phone. "Hey… Crystal. What's up?"

"How are you?"

Her voice still flowed through his veins like good brandy, warm and fluid, and could sneak up on him and knock him out when he least expected it. "I'm good. You?"

"Fine. Trying to get everything together for Jessie's trip…and mine. She's so excited."

"I'm looking forward to it."

"I wish I'd had the chance to see where you'll be staying, Tony." The hint of censure in her tone caused his jaw to tighten.

"I wouldn't take our daughter anywhere that you or I wouldn't stay. The house is beautiful. The locale is safe and she'll have a ball."

Crystal pushed out a breath. "I'll drop her off in the morning?"

"Sure, or tonight if you want."

"No. I want us to have one more night together."

"You make it sound like she's going away forever. It's just a couple of weeks. With her father," he added a bit more harshly than necessary.

"I know that," she snapped.

Anthony squeezed his eyes shut. It never ceased to amaze him how their conversations could go from zero to sixty in a flash, and that was not always a good thing. "What time is your flight tomorrow?"

"Two."

"Do you want me to pick up Jess and take you to the air—"

"No," she said, quickly cutting him off. "It's not necessary."

Anthony was silent for a moment. He knew what that meant. Gordon Russell was taking her to the airport and more than likely traveling with her on the Caribbean vacation. It stung, but not as much as it once did. Crystal had stopped mentioning anything about Gordon after Anthony's last "another man around his daughter" tirade. He knew he'd taken it too far. He'd allowed his ego to run roughshod over his common sense. It took his and Crystal's amicable though cool relationship to an arctic freeze and it was still in the throes of unthawing.

"Hey, no problem. What time are you dropping Jess off?"

"About eleven."

"See you then."

"Bye, Tony," she said in the way that he remembered.

The phone clicked in his ear. Slowly he returned the receiver to the cradle, leaned back in his chair and absently massaged his chin. Two years. It was still hard for him to swallow the reality that he had failed at something. It wasn't in his makeup to fail. Whatever he took on—from a "friendly game" of basketball to the courts of justice—he won. Decisively. It's what he did. It's who he was. He was driven to achieve excellence. The divorce had rocked him, unmoored his foundation and forced him to question himself. There were moments, like now, that made him feel as if the ground were slowly shifting beneath his feet.

His intercom buzzed and jerked him away from his brooding. "Yes, Valerie?"

"Mr. Blumenthal wants to see you."

"Thanks." He shook off the remnants of his dark thoughts and returned his focus to the task at hand, dealing with his boss, the district attorney for New York, the man whose job he would seek come fall.

Anthony took his jacket from the hook by the door, slipped it on and walked down the corridor to Harrison Blumenthal's office. He nodded to Blumenthal's secretary, who smiled and waved him in. Anthony knocked lightly on the partially open door and stepped inside.

"Shut the door, will you," Harrison grumbled in his trademark no-nonsense grit-and-gravel voice.

Harrison removed his half-framed glasses and rested them next to a stack of files on his desk while Anthony unbuttoned his jacket and took a seat opposite him.

"I'll get right to it. I don't like the progress or should I say the lack of progress on this Warren mess."

"His lawyers say he won't take a deal."

"Make them take it. We can't win this case. You know it and I know it."

"I don't agree."

Harrison's bushy right brow rose to an arch. "I can't afford any of your cowboy antics in court. I have no intention of tallying up any losses. Especially now." He gave Anthony a cool green stare.

"I won't lose. This is the type of case I'm known for winning. You know that as well as I do," he returned with the same purposeful stare.

Something rumbled deep in Harrison's chest before the words rolled out, like a train in the distance before pulling into the station. "There's a first time for everything, and my point is, I cannot afford to let this case be that first time. Our conviction record is solid."

"Thanks to me," Anthony interjected.

Harrison pursed his lips. "It needs to stay that way. For my sake as well as yours."

Inwardly, Anthony smiled. That was about as close to a compliment as he was going to get from Harrison Blumenthal.

"Find a way to make this case go away." He put his glasses back on, a clear indication that the meeting was over.

Anthony pushed back from his seat and stood. He buttoned his jacket. "I'll see what I can do...*when* I get back from vacation."

"See that you do. When are you leaving?"

"Saturday afternoon. Crystal is dropping Jessie off in the morning."

Harrison's rocky countenance softened. "How are things…with you and Crystal?"

Harrison was one of two people who knew how hard he'd been hit by the divorce. The other was his lifelong friend Lincoln Davenport. It was Lincoln who'd convinced him that he needed some downtime to think really hard about where he wanted his life to go, and a great place to do it was Sag Harbor. He could relax, spend time with his daughter, put the job on hold and enjoy the company of his friends. It had taken a lot of convincing, but Anthony had finally given in.

He'd gone to visit a few months earlier, really liked the place, and after having lunch with Melanie Harte—who was equally as eager to find him a new love as she was finding him a place to stay—he found a great house that was on the market, priced to sell, met all of his needs and would definitely give him a sanctuary when he wanted to get out of the city. He'd gone back a couple of times on weekends to get the lay of the land, check on the repairs of the house and even stumbled onto a book signing at the local art gallery during a last-minute trip a week earlier. He was really looking forward to getting out of Manhattan and "setting up house" with his daughter— even if it was only temporary.

"Better," he finally answered. "At least, as good as it probably will ever be." His expression darkened.

"Hmm. It gets easier. Take it from a man who's been through it…twice." He held up two long fingers.

"Yeah." The corner of his mouth curved into a half grin. "So you have reminded me." He headed for the door.

"Try to enjoy your time away. You know, when you get back, this office will be pretty much all on your shoulders as my campaign will be in full gear."

Anthony nodded. "Don't worry. I've been trained by the best," he said with a wry smile. "I can handle it."

"See that you do."

Anthony tucked in his smile and closed the door quietly behind him. He was lucky to have a man like Harrison in his corner, paving the way. Often the D.A. was a megalomaniac driven solely by ambition, political polls and winning at any cost. Sure, Harrison loved to win just as much as the next man, but it was more than that. He had a true passion for justice and doing the right thing no matter if it was politically incorrect. And he wasn't always looking over his shoulder to see who was trying to move up the ranks to take his place. If anything, he encouraged his staff to climb the ladder, which Anthony had done and secured the position of chief assistant district attorney through the mentoring of his boss. The world of crime may have hated Harrison Blumenthal but his staff worshipped the ground he walked on. His shoes were big ones to fill, but Anthony knew he was up to the job. After all, hadn't he sacrificed everything… including his family…to get where he was?

Chapter 4

"You still haven't explained to me why you won't get serious with Andrew. You said the date went fine," Tiffany said as the two friends walked up the winding path leading to Melanie Harte's house on the hill. The house and the front lawn sparkled with pinpoints of light, and music could be heard floating in the air.

Kai gave a light toss of her head. "Don't get me wrong. He's a great guy. Handsome. Funny. Smart." She paused, blew out a breath of frustrated confusion. "He's just not right for me. This may sound like a fairy tale or something out of a romance novel, but I want a man that makes my heart pound. Makes my skin get hot with just a look, gets my stomach to flutter when I think about him and has my vajayjay talking in tongues when I know I'm going to see him." She sighed with a faraway look in her eyes.

"Damn, girl, well, when you find him please ask if he has a friend, a brother or a cousin just like him."

They laughed in unison and stepped into the party that was in full swing.

"Mel sure knows how to throw 'a little get-together,'" Tiffany said, raising her voice slightly above the hum of conversation and the live band.

Kai gazed around at the crowd, recognizing some faces from town, a few from television and the rest she wasn't familiar with. "What I need to do is take Melanie up on her offer to find me the perfect man," she said in a pseudo whisper.

A waiter approached with crab and shrimp appetizers balanced on a tray. They helped themselves to the delicate treats and snagged the next waiter for two glasses of champagne.

"There's Lincoln and Desiree." Kai waved and started to walk over when she heard her name being called. She turned. "Andrew…"

"I didn't know you were going to be here," he said, giving her a light kiss on the cheek.

"Kind of a last-minute thing," she managed while wishing that the floor would open.

He studied her for a moment then turned to Tiffany. "Good to see you again."

"You, too."

"I would ask if I could get you ladies a drink but you have that covered. Looks like I'll have to catch up."

"I'm going to say hello to Lincoln and Desi. Oh, Maurice and Layla just came in. Be right back. Good to see you, Andrew." Tiffany darted off before the ice daggers from Kai's eyes could land in her back.

An awkward moment of silence dropped like a final curtain between them. Kai sipped her drink and stole a glance at Andrew from beneath her lashes. *This is so bad.*

"Drew…I'm sorry I haven't called you back. I—"

He held up his hand. "You don't have to explain. Really. I'm a big boy and I can take a hint."

"That doesn't excuse me being rude and for that I'm sorry."

He gave her a half smile. "True." He paused, as if relishing her wide-eyed look. "But...apology accepted."

She released a soft sigh of relief. "Thank you."

"And now that we have all that out of the way...I hope that we can still be friends."

"Of course. I'd like that."

"Good, let's go mingle."

He really isn't a bad guy, Kai thought as she watched him chat and charm everyone around him. He had a great sense of humor, was good to look at, had a solid career... but that spark wasn't there for her no matter how hard she tried, and to lead him on would be plain wrong. Andrew was deserving of someone who gave as much as he did and wanted him as much as he wanted her. She wasn't the one.

Kai wandered out back while Andrew regaled a small group on the antics in the E.R. when it was filled with kids and crazed parents.

"There you are! Are you enjoying yourself?" Melanie slid an arm around Kai's waist.

"Yes, very much. You've outdone yourself as usual."

"I feel it's my duty to put a little sparkle into this sleepy little town." She chuckled.

"Where's Claude? I was hoping to see him."

"Congressional hearings. He had to stay in D.C. with Senator Lawson. I hope he can get back next weekend or I may pay him a surprise visit, stir things up a little." She flashed a mischievous smile.

"Just make sure you don't wind up on the front page of the *Washington Post* with a coat over your face."

They laughed at the image.

"It's good to see Maurice doing so well," Kai said, watching Maurice dance with his bride.

"Layla definitely has that special touch in more ways than one. It wasn't Maurice's war injury that needed the healing, it was inside." She tapped the center of her chest. "I wish I could take credit for that arrangement," Melanie said, "but they did it all on their own. Mostly." She winked.

"I'm happy for them."

"Actually—" She lowered her voice. "There was someone that I especially wanted *you* to meet."

"Oh?"

"Unfortunately he couldn't make it. Didn't say why." Her brow creased. "Another time. He'll be in town for a few weeks."

"Mel…"

"Listen, everyone needs someone. And that goes for you, too. I think he would be perfect for you. In fact, I know he would."

Kai lowered her head for a moment. There was no debating Melanie when she decided that you were her "special project." She wouldn't rest until she found Mr. Right or, at least, Mr. Right Now. As CEO of the Platinum Society, Melanie Harte and her team were renowned for their matchmaking skills that found that special someone for everyone from corporate executives, actors, athletes, and politicians to the average girl and guy next door. Before there was eHarmony there was the Platinum Society.

Kai laughed lightly. "I'm sure he is." She checked her watch. "Listen, I'm going to find Tiffany and head home." She kissed Melanie's cheek. "Thanks for a great evening as usual."

Although the gathering was pegged as a simple get-together with friends, Mel never got people together for a reason as benign as that. She firmly believed that if you put the right people in the room together they would find each other. She was usually right. As Kai wound her way around the guests and through the rooms of the sprawling house in search of Tiffany, she could already see the results of Melanie's plan at work as many of the guests who'd walked around unattached earlier in the evening were now a twosome.

Kai stepped out into the backyard and spotted Tiffany leaning casually against a towering maple tree in deep conversation with a really good-looking guy. She waved to get Tiffany's attention and when she did, she mouthed that she was going home and that she'd call tomorrow.

The waning evening was absolutely exquisite, Kai mused, as she drew her oversize teal-colored silk scarf around her bare shoulders. The sky was a lush blanket of deep blue with brilliant splashes of light that flickered and danced against it. The most gentle of breezes blew in off the ocean, capturing the scents of the sand, sea and budding jasmine bushes and other flora. The sounds of light laughter and music hovered around her then grew more distant as she descended the winding walkway leading to the main road. A perfect night for a walk…*with someone you care about,* a distant voice mocked.

She glanced briefly over her shoulder as the house grew smaller in the distance. Andrew really wasn't a bad guy. Actually, he was a great catch. There was no doubt about it. Maybe if she allowed herself she could care about him as more than a colleague.

She turned down the street that led to her house. The truth...she didn't want to care about him as more than a colleague.

The one great thing about being self-employed was that you could call your own shots and make your own hours, which was precisely what Kai planned for her Saturday. Unfortunately, she couldn't turn off her internal clock. She woke at precisely 6:00 a.m. just as she did when she had her shift in the E.R. Some habits die hard, but one habit that she was glad she'd never broken was turning on the timer for the coffee machine at night. The heady aroma of freshly brewed coffee wafting through her home would give Starbucks a run for their money. After showering quickly and donning her supercomfy sweatpants and hooded sweatshirt, she made a beeline for her kitchen, where she was eagerly greeted by Jasper, her Yorkshire terrier, who was frantically scratching at the door and yipping around the kitchen.

"Take it easy. Take it easy." She bent down and scratched him behind his ears. "I'm glad to see you, too. I'll let you out in one minute." She went to the kitchen window and pulled the curtain aside. Sometime during the night, it had rained and the air felt and smelled crisp and clean like freshly washed laundry. The grass and tree leaves still glistened with beads of water and morning dew. *A great day to take some pictures.* After she let Jasper out back and had her coffee, she would get her equipment.

"Jasper, what is wrong with you today?" He was jumping up and down on the door again and yapping like crazy. "All right, all right." Kai opened the side door and Jasper raced out like a shot. She stood in the doorway for a moment, shook her head at her eccentric pooch, then went to the counter to finally pour her first cup of coffee. Just as she lifted the carafe and was ready to pour, Jasper went completely crazy outside. He was barking and whining in that high-pitched squeak that only little dogs can make.

Kai went to the door and opened it. She stepped out onto the porch. "What in the world is wrong with you? You're going to wake up the entire neighborhood."

Jasper continued to bark and whine and run in and out from under the house.

"Jasper! Come in here right now."

Jasper planted himself in front of the porch with his tail banging rapidly against the wet grass.

"So what are you now, a television dog? You trying to tell me something? It better not be a raccoon. I'm warning you, Jasper," she said as she climbed down the three porch steps. "What is it, boy?" That's when she heard whimpering and the hairs on her arms rose.

She bent down from the waist and caught a glimpse of pink fabric and a little slippered foot. "Oh my God." She scrambled down on her hands and knees and peered under the stairs. Tucked under her house was a little girl, curled into a tight ball. The full realization that a child was huddled under her stairs knocked her back on her haunches as if she'd been pushed. For a full minute, she couldn't think. A million crazy thoughts raced through her head, none of which stayed put long enough for her to make any sense out of it.

Jasper ran under the house and tugged at the pink slipper. The little girl began to cry in earnest.

"What in the…" She lay flat on her stomach so that

she could get a better look. "Sweetie, you need to come out, okay?"

The little girl briskly shook her head. Her thick pony-tails, covered in leaves and twigs, flapped back and forth.

"Can you tell me your name?"

Silence.

"My name is Kai. And this is Jasper. Say hello, Jasper."

Jasper barked uproariously and ran in a circle before settling down.

"I think you must be really cold…and wet. Do you want a blanket? Would that help?"

The little girl nodded her head.

"I'll be right back. I'm going to get you a blanket so you can warm up."

Kai scrambled to her feet and ran inside, doing a pretty bad imitation of Jasper as she spun around in circles trying to think—she'd suddenly forgotten where she kept the extra blankets. Her heart kicked against her chest. *Maybe she should call the police. No. Not yet.* Her medical instincts kicked in. The first thing she needed to do was to make sure that the little girl wasn't injured. *Right. Blanket.* She darted down the hall to the linen closet. She pulled out a light quilt, bunched it up in her arms and hurried back outside.

Jasper was standing guard. Kai got back down on her hands and knees and peered beneath the house. Bright, frightened brown eyes stared back at her.

"Here you go, sweetie." Kai extended the blanket toward her and wished that she was small enough to crawl under to get a better look at the girl. A little hand pulled the blanket and she was quickly hidden beneath it with only the top of her head and her pony tails visible.

"I bet you're pretty hungry," Kai said softly. She

thought she saw the child bob her head. "If you come out I can fix you something to eat and get you warmed up. How does that sound?"

No response.

Kai tried again. "My name is Kai. Would you tell me your name so I know what to call you? This is Jasper. Say hi, Jasper." Japer yip-yipped and ran in circles. "Your turn."

There was the barest murmur of a response. Kai's pulse raced. "Jessie? Is your name Jessie?"

"Yes."

Kai momentarily gave in to a moment of relief. "I bet that's short for Jessica. Is it short for Jessica?"

"Yes."

"My name is not short for anything. It's just short."

A soft giggle rose from under the blanket and Jessie pulled the blanket down below her nose.

"I was named after my great-great-grandmother. She was a Native American…an Indian. My name means 'willow tree.'"

"My daddy named me," came the tiny voice. "That's what my mommy said."

"He did a good job. Did your daddy and mommy bring you here?"

"Daddy did." She sneezed.

"Bless you." Kai had no idea how long Jessie had been hidden beneath her damp house, but she knew that the longer she stayed the more risk she had of getting sick or catching something. "Jessie, sweetie, now that we're friends, why don't you come on out before you catch a cold. I can fix you something to eat and then we can call your dad. Okay?"

Jessie sniffed, sneezed again but didn't budge.

Jasper ran under the house and began tugging on the blanket, trying to pull it out and Jessie along with it.

This was crazy! She stood up, paced, ran her hand across her hair. Her gaze roamed up and down the soft rolling hills and across the tops of the fewer than half-dozen homes in the area as if seeking answers in the gray clouds that moved across the sky. What in the world was she going to do? She needed to call someone. The child couldn't stay under her house indefinitely. She'd been trying to coax her out for nearly forty-five minutes. What kind of parent would let their child wander off like this? Her temper flared.

"I'm cold."

Kai spun around and Jessie was standing in front of her. Her breath caught for an instant at the sight of Jessie's tiny body that shuddered beneath the blanket, which was more on the ground than around her. Her wide, almond-shaped eyes were slightly swollen from crying. Leaves and twigs stuck to her hair, which was wet with dew and rain.

"Oh, Jessie, thank you so much for coming out." Kai knelt down in front of her. The moist grass squished around her knees. "Let's get you warm and fed, okay?"

Jessie nodded her head and didn't make a peep of protest when Kai scooped her up along with the blanket and hurried inside just as the rain began to fall.

Chapter 5

Anthony nearly tore the door off the hinges when he saw the black-and-white police car pull up in front of his house. He ran out to meet them as they walked up the path.

"Have you heard anything?" he lobbed at them the instant they were within earshot.

"Let's talk inside," the middle-aged officer suggested.

Anthony looked from one to the other. A wave of panic rose up in his stomach. "What aren't you telling me?" he demanded.

"Son, we're not telling you anything 'cause we don't have anything to tell."

The air was sucked out of him.

"Let's talk inside," the officer said again, more gently this time.

Anthony lowered his head for a moment then led them inside.

The younger officer, who looked more like a Boy Scout than a cop, closed the door behind them.

"I'm Officer Cobb. This is Officer Monroe," the older of the two said.

Anthony nodded impatiently. "Yes, we spoke on the phone. Now will you please tell me what you're doing to find my daughter?"

Officer Cobb waved his hand in the air as if to calm him down. "Easy. I know this is upsetting. My team is rounding up volunteers as we speak. I want to get a few more details from you, and a picture...of your daughter."

Anthony's stomach knotted. *A picture.* The very idea brought on a wave of nausea. No, this wasn't the Big Bad Apple, where terrible things happened every day and kids went missing like socks in the dryer. It was a small town where everyone knew everyone else, but as chief assistant district attorney who'd seen all kinds of depravity, he knew it happened in these Happy Hollow towns, too. Only, when it did, it was all the more shocking. But he couldn't allow himself to go down that road.

"You mind if Officer Monroe looks around while we talk?"

"No. No, of course not." He knew the drill. Monroe would be looking for any signs of a struggle or indications that there might have been a break-in. He also knew that *he* was their first and prime suspect. When children went missing right out of their own bedrooms, the parents were the usual suspects.

Officer Cobb took a seat at the kitchen table. He pulled out a notebook and a pen, flipped the pages and stopped when the one he wanted caught his attention. "So you said you put her to bed at ten last night."

"Yes. Ten. Then I came downstairs to watch some television. I must have fallen asleep. When I woke up it was about three. I went to check in on Jessie and she was in her room sleeping. I went to bed. When I got up this morning to wake her she wasn't in her room. She wasn't in the house!"

"And what time was that?"

"Seven, seven-fifteen." His impatient hand ran across his close-cut hair.

Officer Cobb slowly nodded his head, as if somewhat assured that the words in his notebook matched the ones coming out of Anthony's mouth. "And her mother?"

"I told you, she's out of the country. She left yesterday." He had no idea what he was going to tell Crystal. He'd tried her cell phone nearly a dozen times with no luck. Half the calls wouldn't connect and the rest either rang busy or went to voice mail. Maybe it was best. The last thing he needed right now was Crystal being hysterical hundreds of miles away.

"Did you say you had a picture of your daughter, Mr. Weston?"

He did. He had dozens of pictures of Jessie and they were all taken with his cell phone. "I have to print it out from the computer."

Officer Cobb gave him a look as if to say, *Young people, no wonder.*

Anthony excused himself and went into the next room where he'd set up a mini office with his laptop, printer and a box of files from the office. He sent the most recent picture that he had of Jessie to his email and then opened the picture in his email account.

Jessie's cherubic face filled the screen. Her smile dimmed the sun. Anthony's eyes stung. If anything happened to her... The knot in his stomach tightened. He pressed the print key and slowly the image of Jessie slid

out. He clenched his jaw, got up from his seat and returned to Officer Cobb.

"Here's a picture of Jessie," he said, his voice thick.

Officer Cobb took the picture. "We'll get copies out
to the other officers."

"How many officers do you have working on this?"

"The entire office. Five."

Anthony's stomach swam.

Officer Cobb stood and tucked the photo in his notebook. "As soon as we hear something, we'll call you."

"I'm going with you. I need to be out there looking
for my daughter."

"You need to stay here in case she comes back."

Cobb's cell phone rang. He pulled it out of his pocket.
"Cobb." His eyes widened for an instant. "I see. We'll be
right there." He disconnected the call. His gaze jumped
to Anthony's. "They think they've found your daughter."

"Do you want some more soup, Jessie?"

Jessie bobbed her head as she slurped up the rest of
the thick soup. Kai had gotten her out of her damp clothes
and put her in an oversize T-shirt and pink sweat socks
that pooled around her ankles. But at least she was warm
and dry. She'd groomed and towel-dried the thick hair.

While Jessie played with Jasper, Kai had placed a call
to the local police office only to be told by the secretary
that the officers were out on an emergency—missing
child. But when Kai advised her that she'd found the girl
they were looking for, she was told that the police would
be there right away.

Kai hung up the phone, only mildly mollified. They
should be there any minute and Jessie would be reunited
with her very irresponsible parent. Just thinking that anyone could have been so careless as to let a four-year-old

get out of the house caused her head to pound. Anything could have happened to her. It was only by the grace of God that Kai had found her and not some stranger that could have… She didn't want to think about it. Jessie was safe. No thanks to her father, whoever he may be.

Not more than ten minutes later, the sound of cars pulling into the drive drew her to the window. She pulled the curtain back. A police car and a black SUV.

Jessie was busy playing with Jasper.

"You wait right here." Kai went to the front door and pulled it open in unison with the car doors opening and slamming shut. She stood beneath the overhang to keep dry from the rain that had gone from a light shower to a steady downpour. Fog hung heavy over the trees and settled around the homes and rolling hills like a scene from an old English movie.

She recognized Officer Cobb from town, who was trudging up the walk through the rain and was nearly pushed aside by the man who'd come up behind him breaking through the fog.

Kai's chest constricted and held her breath in its grip. *It was him.* Him, the man in the photo, the man she'd seen walking the streets, then that night at the gallery. The one who'd invaded her thoughts and her dreams. Her lips parted but no words came out as he took the steps two at a time and was right on top of her.

Anthony's gaze ignited with hers and his forward motion froze. He blinked, started to speak.

Kai found her voice first. "She's…in the kitchen." She stepped out of the doorway, turned on shaky legs and led him into the house.

"Is she…is she all right?"

"She's fine. Sneezing a bit, and she has some bites on her legs. I put some ointment on them. Got her dry and cleaned up." She came to a stop at the entrance to the kitchen and turned to him. Her breath drew in sharply. Her heart pounded. He was staring right past her and into the depths of her soul. A shiver fluttered along her spine and for an instant they were locked in an invisible embrace.

"Daddy!"

The spell was broken.

Jessie scrambled up from the floor and leaped against her father's thighs. He snapped to attention and snatched her up in his arms. He pressed her against his heart, covered her cheeks and hair with kisses until she giggled.

"Jessie, Jessie," he breathed as relief swept through him. He looked over her head into Kai's wide gaze. "Thank you," he said on a rough whisper.

Her skin heated at the sound of his voice. "I'm not sure how long she was out in the weather." Her voice took on a chastising tone that Anthony didn't miss.

He momentarily glanced away. "Thank you, Ms.…."

"Dr. Kai Randall," she offered.

"Anthony Weston." He smiled.

Her stance softened. "Take care of her."

"I intend to."

"Dr. Randall, I'll need to get a statement from you," Officer Cobb said from the doorway while he shook the water off his hat and broke the tenuous thread between Kai and Anthony.

Kai folded her arms. "Sure." She led Officer Cobb over to the kitchen table and provided the details of how and when she'd found Jessie.

"Is it okay if I get Jessie home?"

"Of course, Mr. Weston," Officer Cobb said, closing his notebook. "Thank you again, Doctor."

She nodded and led them to the door. A crack of thunder seemed to shake the foundation of the house. Kai took an umbrella from the rack by the door and a jacket that she kept hanging there. She put the jacket around Jessie and handed the umbrella to Anthony.

"She doesn't need to get wet."

Jessie sneezed as if to confirm Kai's statement.

"And you behave yourself, young lady. No more leaving the house to follow squirrels. Promise?"

"Promise," she chirped then buried her face in the curve of her father's neck.

What would it be like to press her lips against his neck, inhale his scent?

"Thank you…again." The hint of a smile pulled at the corners of his mouth.

Kai ran the tip of her tongue across her bottom lip. She held the door open. The trio stepped out into the rain. Anthony glanced back once, then darted to the SUV.

She stood in the archway until the cars were only memories. It was then that she realized she'd been holding her breath or, at least, it felt as if she had. She pushed the door closed. Her thoughts tramped through her head as she tried to make sense out of the chaos that had come when she saw the man who'd only been something fleeting become real flesh and blood and stand in her house.

Back in the kitchen, she pulled out a chair and sat, her chin propped up on her palm. How incredible was that? If someone had told her this had happened to them, she wouldn't have believed it. It was the kind of thing that happened in Lifetime movies…no those were the ones where the woman always killed the husband or boyfriend. But…anyway, it was just hard to believe.

As if stung, she sprung up from her seat and darted upstairs to her attic. She flipped thorough the photographs that she'd mounted in a large book. Her pulse kicked. There was the picture that she'd taken that rainy afternoon....

She slipped the black-and-white photo out of the plastic sleeve and held it up. *Anthony Weston.*

"Crystal, she's fine. I swear to you. No...there's no reason for you to come back. Apparently she went out of the back door, wandered off and got lost. She wound up at a doctor's house of all places." He squeezed his eyes shut against his ex-wife's barrage. He deserved it. He still couldn't wrap his head around how it had happened. "As soon as she wakes up, I'll have her call you. Yes. She'll call. All right."

Anthony heaved a breath and disconnected the call. At least that hurdle was over with. Crystal had every reason to be furious, hysterical and accusatory. If he was hundreds of miles away and received that kind of call from her, he would have reacted the same way or worse.

He ran his hand across his face, then went into the room to check on Jessie. He stood over her sleeping form and slowly shook his head as the events of the day ran in his mind like an endless reel. His gaze lifted from his sleeping daughter and the image of Kai Randall emerged in front of him. His gut flexed. Jessie stirred, moaned softy.

Anthony shook off the sensation, tucked the light blanket around Jessie and eased out of the room, leaving the door open. The last thing he needed to have on his mind was a woman, even if she was the woman that rescued his daughter. What he needed to be thinking about was never letting what went down that morning ever happen again. He was going to have a long, serious talk with his daughter when she woke up.

* * *

"Well, I'll be damned, girl," Tiffany said before taking a sip of wine. She set the glass down on the coffee table and curled her bare feet beneath her. She stared at the photograph that Kai shared with her and the story of how it came to be.

"Tiff, it was surreal. Well, the whole thing was surreal. I mean how often do you wake up and find a little girl hidden under your house?"

"I'm saying." Tiffany shook her head. "But the kicker is that her dad is your mystery man. How crazy is that?"

"I know." Kai finished off her wine and refilled her glass.

"So what was he like up close and personal?"

Kai let a long breath. Her gaze drifted off. "F. I. N. E." She laughed and Tiffany joined in.

"I get that much. But that's not what I mean. What was he…like?"

"I don't know. I guess I was so stunned." She pressed her lips together in thought. "There definitely was something. I don't know how to explain it. A connection." She looked at Tiffany.

"A connection. I guess so. You just found the man's lost daughter."

Kai shook her head. "That's not what I mean. It wasn't gratitude. I mean, it was, but it was more than that." How could she explain that it was like a match being struck when they'd looked at each other and everything else receded into the background, blinded by the flame?

"The downside to Mr. Wonderful is that if there is daughter, there is a mama."

Kai's gaze slid in Tiffany's direction. She sighed with resignation. "True." She brought the glass to her lips. "Lucky woman," she murmured.

Chapter 6

The rain hadn't let up. If anything it had only grown more intense as the late afternoon slipped into early evening. There was a decided chill in the air, almost fall-like rather than midspring. Anthony was thankful for the fireplace, something he'd always appreciated but never had in his New York City home. This one was gas. Easy, flip a switch and you had a fire. He smiled in bemusement while he listened to the crackle of flames in the hearth and the beating of the rain against the window and then he noticed how dark it had become. The deep gray sky hung like a soaked canopy over the treetops and homes, while the fog rose and floated to meet it like lost spirits tossed out into the unknown.

He checked his watch. Frowned. It was almost four. Jessie had been asleep for hours. He pushed up from the couch and walked down the short hallway from the living room to Jessie's bedroom and stepped inside. Quietly, he went to her bed and sat on the side.

"Jess, Jessie," he said softly. She sighed. Her long, black lashes fluttered, but she didn't wake up. He gently brushed stray strands of hair away from her face. She felt warm as buttered toast. He adjusted her covers to give her a little more air, kissed her forehead and tip-toed out. She'd had a major adventure. He was sure she was exhausted. He knew he was. But the terror that he'd felt when he woke up and found her gone was enough to keep him sleepless for a very long time. The idea that he could wake up and Jessie would be gone....

He went into the kitchen to get dinner started. He knew when Jessie woke up she would be hungry. He checked the refrigerator and found a package of chicken that he decided would go along with baked potatoes. He knew Jessie hated green peas but she would eat string beans. As he walked by the kitchen stool, he inadver-tently knocked over the jacket that he'd tossed there when they'd returned from that sexy doctor's house. He bent to pick it up and he wasn't sure if it was his imagination or if the soft scent of her was really filling the room. He drew the jacket up to his face and the scent of her filled him. For an instant, his eyes drifted closed and he was standing in front of her in the kitchen, inches away from her very kissable lips and eyes that were as warm as heated chestnuts.

With a half smile, he hung the jacket on the back of the chair. It had been a while since a woman had made him think about her more than once. Since his divorce from Crystal, relationships had been put on the back burner. He filled his time with work and building his ca-reer, making sure that he was too tired at night to think about the empty space in his bed.

There'd been women, of course, from time to time if he needed a date for a big event or when the loneliness got to be too much, but it never lasted. He drew in a long, slow breath. He wasn't going to let the good Dr. Randall get in his head or under his skin. He'd already failed in a relationship at close quarters and he knew that long-distance wasn't his thing because he had no intention of giving up his Manhattan life or lifestyle.

His cell phone vibrated against his thigh. He reached in his pocket and pulled it out.

"Linc. How are you?"

"The question is how are *you?* I was out all day and I got back to hear that Jessie went missing?"

Anthony put the phone on speaker, turned back to the fridge and took out a bag of red potatoes. "Yeah, man. It was crazy. She must have gotten up just at daybreak and went out the back door. She said she was following a squirrel. Can you believe that?"

Lincoln bit back a chuckle. "With Jessie, yeah, I can believe it. I hope you put an extra padlock on the door and set the alarm. Just think, Tony, if she can slip out at four years old, imagine what she'll do when she's a teen."

"Thanks for the words of encouragement."

"I'm just saying," he teased. "Hey, the only thing that's important is that she's back and she's safe. Desi said that Dr. Randall found her."

"Yeah, she'd wandered all the way over there and hid under her house when it started raining."

"Man, you must have been going out of your mind. I don't know what I would have done. Thank goodness it was Kai and not some perv."

"Don't I know it." He turned on the water and rinsed the potatoes, lathered the skin with butter, and wrapped them in aluminum foil. "So, uh, how long has Dr. Randall been around?"

"Hmm, couple of years, I'd guess."

"So you know her pretty well."

"I wouldn't say *know* her. I've seen her at parties, run into her in town. She's pretty good friends with Melanie Harte, and Desi definitely knows her better than I do." He paused a moment. "Why?"

"Just asking. I want to know what kind of woman took care of my daughter. That's all," he added.

"Yeah. Okay. Well, since me and you go way back, and even though you didn't ask I'm sure you want to know…she's single. And from what Desi has mentioned a couple of times, Mel has been trying to find her Mr. Right, but Kai isn't interested."

"And you worked that all out in your head and figured I'd want to know."

"Of course. I got *skilz,* my brother. And I didn't need paper nor pencil," he said, miming the late Richard Pryor.

The two men broke out into laughter.

"Yeah, okay," Anthony was finally able to manage.

"But on a serious note, Jessie is fine. She's safe, and from everything that I know about Dr. Randall, she's a good person and not bad to look at either."

Anthony had to agree with him on that point. He could spend a lot of hours looking at the very sexy doctor with the warm throaty voice, who looked at him as if she would cut him a new one for letting his daughter get away from him. "Yeah, well, even if I was interested— which I'm not—I won't be around long enough to put any real time in."

"That's true, and with you planning on running for D.A.…." Lincoln let the unspoken words speak for themselves. "And since you're only going to be here for what…two weeks, we have to make some time to hang out."

"I'll have to work something out—a sitter for Jessie."

"No need for all that. We can hang at my place. Desiree loves kids."

Anthony heard the faint hitch in Lincoln's voice. He knew it was the one thing missing from his marriage. But Lincoln had known going in that Desiree wouldn't be able to have children. It didn't matter to him.

"We can have dinner, a few beers and catch up."

"Sounds like a plan. Let's make that happen."

"Cool. I'll check with Desi's schedule and get back to you."

"Thanks for calling, man."

"Talk to ya."

Anthony disconnected the call. He and Lincoln were frat brothers, both of them having attended Howard University, but on a deeper note, Lincoln Davenport was the brother that Anthony never had. Anthony didn't share parts of himself with many people, not even Crystal, which was on their list of marital woes, but he did share his life with Lincoln. Lincoln knew all about Anthony's devastating childhood, his personal struggles and his triumphs, and he never judged. They'd been there for each other. And it was good to be close again, like the old days, even if it was only for two weeks.

A crash of thunder seemed to shake the very foundation of the house. Its aftermath vibrated like the shockwaves following an earthquake. The lights blinked then focused themselves. At least he'd been smart enough to invest in a generator. This part of the Sound was notorious for losing power during bad storms. A brilliant flash of lightning lit up the sky, making it look like daytime.

He finished cleaning and seasoning the chicken, put it in a pan and popped it in the oven, then went to check on Jessie. He'd been sure that he would have heard her feet pounding down the hallway after that last blast of thunder.

He opened her door. This time he turned on the light and walked to her bedside. Immediately he knew something was wrong. Her saffron-toned skin was flushed red. Damp tendrils of hair clung to her forehead.

Anthony reached out to touch her and could feel the heat wafting up from her body before he put a hand on her. His insides tightened.

"Jess…Jessie, sweetheart, wake up, baby." He put his hand on her forehead and alarms went off. She was burning up.

Jessie whimpered softly. "Don't feel good," she managed.

"I know, sweetie. I know."

"Cold," she whispered.

Anthony pulled the covers up to her chin. *Cold, she was burning up.* His thoughts raced. What to do? The last time he was around Jessie and she was sick, she was an infant. "Be right back, baby." He darted off to the bathroom to check the medicine cabinet and was greeted with shave cream, deodorant and dental floss. Maybe Crystal had put a first-aid kit or something in Jessie's bag and he hadn't noticed.

He quickly returned to Jessie's room and took her suitcase out of the closet and checked all the zippers and pockets. *Nothing.* He tossed it back in and shut the door. Now what? Clearly he needed some medication for the fever and clearly there wasn't any in the house. Another roll of thunder moved over the roof of the house. Rain banged against the window, demanding to get away from the wrath of the thunder and lightning.

"Daddy," Jessie croaked.

He returned to her bedside. "Yes, baby?"

"Thirsty."

"Okay. I'll get you something to drink." He kissed her forehead and felt the damp heat.

He hurried down the short hallway to the kitchen and remembered the food in the oven. He reduced the heat in the oven and then went to the fridge for some juice. He poured, stood for a moment and stared at the contents. Maybe water would be better. He reached for the bottle of water and then grabbed the orange juice, too. He poured a glass of each and turned to go back to Jessie's room when the jacket that hung on the back of the chair caught his attention.

He put the glasses down on the counter, picked up the jacket and pulled out Dr. Randall's business card. He returned to Jessie's room with the glasses and the card.

"Water or juice, sweetie?"

"Water."

He helped her to sit up and brought the glass to her lips. Jessie took a few sips and pushed the glass away.

"Try to take a little more."

She shook her head and burrowed under the covers.

Anthony placed the glasses on the nightstand and took his cell phone out of his pocket. He walked to the doorway of the bedroom and punched in the numbers.

The phone rang as if it was struggling to make the connection.

"Dr. Randall…"

The sound of her voice sent a shot of heat running through him. His insides shifted. He cleared his throat. "Dr. Randall, I'm sorry to bother you. This is Anthony Weston, Jessie's dad."

"Yes, yes. Is anything wrong?"

"Actually, there is. Jessie is burning up."

"I see. How high is her fever?"

"I don't know. But it's got to be pretty high. I can feel the heat coming off her."

A clap of thunder boomed in the heavens.

He could hear her dog barking in the background and then silence.

"Hello. Hello." He looked at the face of the phone. The call had been disconnected. He tried dialing her again and got an error message that the call failed.

"Dammit." He tried again with the same result. And then his phone rang in his hand. It was a number that he didn't recognize. "Hello?"

"Mr. Weston, it's Dr. Randall. I'm on my landline. Cell phone service gets kind of sketchy in bad weather."

"Thank you for calling back."

"Of course."

"So what should I do?"

"Is she taking in any fluids?"

"Barely."

He heard her soft exhale on the other end of the phone and irrationally wondered if he could make her sigh like that. He shook his head to clear his runaway thoughts. Jessie was what was important.

"Give me your address."

"I couldn't ask you to come out in this weather."

"I'm used to it. I'm a doctor that makes house calls. A dying breed."

He heard the laughter in her voice.

"I'm sure it's nothing major, but I want to check her out for myself. You can't be too careful with a fever."

"If you're sure."

"Very."

He gave her the address.

"Hmm, give me about twenty minutes."

"Thanks, Dr. Randall."

"See you soon. Don't keep her too warm if she's hot. A light blanket should be fine. And try to see if you can get her to drink juice, water, whatever she likes."

"Okay. I will. And thank you."

The call disconnected.

Anthony stood there with the phone in his hand.

Chapter 7

Kai's heart thumped against her chest as she quickly moved through her office and collected her medical bag. What she should do was call Andrew. He was the pediatrician, not her. But Anthony Weston hadn't called Andrew; he'd called her.

Her cheeks flooded with heat. All afternoon she'd replayed the moment that he'd come into her line of sight, the sound of his voice, the feel of his hand in hers, the smell of him, the way his body moved with the grace of a panther. The man she'd thought she'd never see was real, and he'd been standing in her kitchen.

She hadn't been able to shake the effects of seeing him up close and personal. Now she would see him again. *In his home.*

This was business, she reminded herself as she slipped on her raincoat with the hood. Lightning slashed across the sky and the lights dimmed. She was going to do what she was trained to do—heal the sick. That was it. And, as Tiffany said, there was certainly a baby's mama around somewhere.

Jasper ran circles around her legs.

"Not now, boy." She reached down and scratched him behind his ears. The lights flickered again. She hesitated a moment, then darted to the back room and got his carry bag. Jasper jumped up and down like a show dog. "Take it easy," she gently warned and picked him up, then tucked him in his bag. She grabbed her medical bag, car keys and headed for the door, just as the lights went out.

When she stepped outside it was like stepping into the abyss. All of the lights along the roads were out, along with houselights. The entire town was enveloped in pitch-blackness. The only light was the intermittent flash of lightning.

Kai ran to her Explorer and was drenched by the time she got behind the wheel. The frigid rain seeped straight to her bones. Jasper whimpered. She wanted to whimper, too, but instead she turned on the car and put the heat on blast and then flicked on her high beams. She could see about ten feet in front of her. The rain was falling crossways and the wipers, though working overtime, did little to help with visibility.

"Okay, Jasper. Hang on, here we go." She shook off a chill, crept her car out of her driveway and, driving at a crawl, she headed in the direction of Anthony's house on the edge of Azurest.

The ten-minute ride, which she'd estimated would be twice as long today, took nearly forty minutes of slow and cautious driving. Not only did she have to maneuver around fallen tree limbs, but she had to take several detours because of flooded roads. The last thing she needed was to get stuck in a ditch.

Finally, she made it out to his house up ahead, or at least what she hoped was his house. It was one of the few homes on the lane that had lights. Her pulse kicked up a notch. She eased the car up the driveway and as close to the front door as possible. She turned off the car, grabbed her bag and Jasper, and darted for the front door.

No sooner had she put her foot on the last step than the door was pulled open. The light from inside the house outlined his long, lean frame. Air from her lungs knotted in a ball and stuck in her throat. She felt as if the world has suddenly come to a standstill as his gaze held hers and his devastating smile cinched the corners of his dark eyes.

He stuck out his hand and pulled her to shore. At least that's the way it felt.

"Come in. Come in. Thank you so much for coming."

Jasper yipped from the confines of his bag. "Sorry, I didn't want to leave him."

"Not a problem." He grinned and a dimple flashed in his right cheek.

Kai crossed the threshold and the door closed behind her.

"You're soaked. Let me take your coat."

She put her bags on the floor and he helped her out of her wet coat. His hands grazed her shoulders and the chill that she'd felt for nearly an hour simmered away.

"Where's our patient?"

"Right down this hall." He led the way.

"I haven't seen it this bad in a while," she said, as she tried to concentrate on putting one foot in front of the other and not stare at the way the soft gray sweatpants hung low on his hips. "You're lucky you have power. My lights went out just as I was leaving."

Anthony glanced over his shoulder. "Melanie advised

me to get a generator when I bought the place. I'm glad I did."

"You know Melanie?" she said, her voice lifting in surprise.

"Doesn't everyone?" he said, tongue in cheek.

Kai smirked. "True."

"Right here." He opened the door to Jessie's room. "Hey, sweetie," he said, approaching his daughter. "Look who's here to see you."

"Hey, Jessie." Kai came to the side of the bed and placed her hand on Jessie's forehead. A slight frown creased her brow. She sat down on the side of the bed and opened her medical bag. "Looks like you're not feeling too well," she said. "I want to take your temperature. Can you open your mouth for me?"

Jessie did as she was asked and Kai slipped the thermometer beneath her tongue while she took her pulse.

She turned to Anthony. "Can you turn on the light?"

Anthony clicked on the overhead light from the wall switch.

The digital thermometer beeped almost immediately. Kai checked the reading. "103.2," she said, looking up at Anthony, whose expression was tight as a drum. She searched through her bag and took out a bottle of liquid children's Tylenol, poured it into the measuring cup and helped Jessie to sit up. "Here, sweetie, I want you to drink this. It will help you to feel better."

Jessie sipped down the amber liquid.

"Good girl."

Kai took out her instrument to look in Jessie's ears and her throat. She then listened to her chest and lungs with the stethoscope. She checked the glands under her chin and behind her ears, and then examined her legs and arms. With the initial evaluation completed, she released a soft sigh, offered Jessie a smile and pulled the sheet and light blanket up over her. "I'll be right back. Okay, sweetie? You rest and let the medicine begin to work."

She closed up her bag, got up and indicated to Anthony to follow her outside.

"Well?" he asked the instant they were on the other side of Jessie's door.

"I don't think it's anything too serious. Her chest is clear. Her throat is a bit red, though. The main thing right now is getting her fever down and getting her to drink fluids. Dehydration is more of an issue than anything else. She's coming down with a cold, probably from being out in the damp for so long in nothing more than pajamas."

"At least it's not serious."

She read guilt in his eyes. "No, I don't think so. And don't be so hard on yourself," she said. His gaze jumped to hers. He seemed to recognize the understanding and maybe even forgiveness in her tone.

He pushed out a slow breath. "How long will it take for the medicine to work?"

"Hmm, twenty minutes or so."

He nodded. "I can't thank you enough. At least let me get you something warm to drink."

"Sure. That would be great. I want to check her again before I leave."

"Come on to the kitchen."

She followed him, once again getting an eyeful.

"Do you drink tea?"

"Yep." She took a seat at the island counter.

"I have green, apple cinnamon, and…" he examined the boxes, "chamomile."

"Green is fine."

He poured water in the teapot to boil and placed two mugs on the counter.

"Hmm, something smells good."

"I was roasting a chicken for dinner." He took out a bottle of honey from the pantry.

"My grandmother always said that homemade chicken soup was the cure for everything," she said, laughing lightly at the memory.

"I've always had soup out of the can."

"Oh, Mr. Weston, you don't know what you're missing. And actually, I'm sure Jessie would love some."

He eyed her from over his shoulder. "Care to share the recipe?"

She glanced up at him and her stomach fluttered. She shrugged her right shoulder. "Sure, why not."

"So what do I need besides chicken?" He grinned and dropped a tea bag in each of their mugs.

She angled her body on the stool so that she faced him, folded her arms beneath her breasts and tilted her head to the side. "Well...carrots, potatoes, some celery, onions, a little black pepper and some flour to make dumplings."

Anthony's brows rose with amusement. "All that, huh?"

"Yep, and you simmer it with love. That's the real cure."

His eyes darkened and slowly moved over her face, lighting a match in the pit of her stomach. The warmth spread.

"Let me see what I can pull together. Will you help?"

She swallowed over the dry knot that had settled in her throat. "Sure."

He flashed her a smile that kicked up the flame simmering inside her. She watched his fluid movements while he searched the vegetable bin in the fridge, pulled out the necessary items and placed them on the counter in front of her. Her heart leaped every time he came near her and felt as if it wanted to jump out of her chest.

The teapot's shrill whistle signaled that the hot water was ready and the games had begun. What had she let herself in for?

Chapter 8

"So...what do we do first?"

"Um, we can start cutting up the chicken and then the vegetables."

"I can do the chicken. And what's this dumpling thing you were talking about?"

She laughed. "Simple. Flour and water, milk and a pinch of salt, rolled and boiled."

He made a face.

"I promise, you'll love it."

His gaze held hers for a moment and a tingle ran up and down her spine. "If you say so."

Anthony took a plate from the cabinet and put it on the counter and then found a knife for Kai. She began dicing the vegetables while he cut up the roasted chicken.

"Want to listen to some music while we work?"

"Sure."

"Be right back." He walked toward the open living

space and went to the CD player. "I didn't bring much with me, but I have a few that hopefully you will like." Moments later, KEM's sultry voice floated through the space.

"Oh, wow, one of my favorites."

"Mine, too," he said, coming back into the kitchen. "What else do you like?"

Her hand momentarily froze from dicing the celery and her mind ran in a million directions at once. "Um, you mean music?"

He shrugged. "We can start there."

She continued to chop. "Well, I…" Suddenly her mind went blank with him looking at her…like that. As if he wanted to… She averted her gaze. "Charlie Wilson, Luther Vandross, a lot of jazz artists, Coltrane, Miles, Quinten Parker."

"Good taste in music, doc." He smiled at her and that dimple teased.

She lowered her gaze and focused on the task at hand, while wondering if he could hear her heart racing.

"I met Quinten Parker in New York a couple of years ago. Real cool guy."

"Really?"

He chuckled lightly at the memory. "I was at this club sitting at the bar and he sat right next to me. We got to talking about the Knicks and sports and politics. I finally introduced myself, and when he told me who he was, I nearly fell off the bar stool."

Kai laughed. "I bet."

"We keep in touch from time to time and try to get together when he's in town and I'm not in the middle of a case."

"A case?"

"Yeah, legal stuff."

She frowned.

"I'm chief assistant district attorney for New York," he said.

Her brows rose. "Wow. I had no idea."

"Is that a bad thing?"

"No. I mean… I just never thought… I never met a chief assistant district attorney before," she lamely added. "I guess you must see your share of tough cases."

"That I do. What's next?" he asked, shifting the conversation back to dinner.

"Oh, um…we need a big pot."

He took one out from beneath the sink.

"Two cups of water and then add the chicken. When it starts to boil, I'll add the vegetables."

"Got it. So, what did you do before you became the local doctor on call?"

She rested her hip against the counter and took a sip of her tea. "I was chief of emergency services at New York Presbyterian Hospital."

"Now that is impressive. Why did you leave?"

"Long story."

"I'm not going anywhere."

The heady tone of his voice quickened her pulse. Her hand shook ever so slightly.

She put the cup back down on the counter.

"The hours were demanding. There never seemed to be enough that you could do for all of the people that needed help." She slowly shook her head. "When I got the promotion to chief, the hours were beyond grueling and the constant trauma…day after day. And I knew I couldn't function at that level anymore, but I knew I could never give up medicine. My family had a house here that dates back to when free blacks came to the island. So, here I am." She took the plate with the diced vegetables and scooped them into the simmering pot. "Do you have a cover for this?"

"Yeah, sure."

She was even more amazing than he originally thought. She was smart, hardworking, passionate about her career, independent, sexy as hell and gorgeous. He opened the cabinet beneath the sink next to the stove and when he stood back up there was barely a hairbreadth between them.

Steam from the pot wafted around them. Kai held her breath. She was close enough to see the flecks of dark chocolate in his eyes. His bottom lip was moist and full and the silken curl of his lashes was enviable. His rugged five o'clock shadow stirred something deep and primal within her. She had the overwhelming desire to stroke the hard line of his jaw.

He placed the cover on the pot without taking his eyes off her face. "More tea?" he asked, "or something stronger?"

She blinked back to reality. "Um, maybe some wine if you have it."

"I believe I do." He turned away and she released the breath she'd held.

"Damn," she mouthed.

"There are some wineglasses in the cabinet above you," he said from the interior of the refrigerator.

She took out two glasses and set them on the counter. Anthony used a corkscrew to open the wine. He poured for them both, then raised his glass.

"To wonderful doctors who still make house calls."

She raised her glass and gently tapped it against his. "What made you decide to come out to Sag Harbor?"

"Much like you, it was my job. It's stressful. I wanted

a place away from the city, away from a lot of things really." His gaze drifted off.

"A lot of things?"

The corner of his mouth lifted, then fell. "Bad divorce."

"Oh, I'm sorry."

"Don't be. It happens. Crystal, my ex, said that she could compete with any woman but she couldn't compete with my job, and she wouldn't. So, she left." He lifted his glass and took a long swallow. It was so much more than that but he didn't want to scare her away with the ugly details.

Kai watched the tightness deepen around the corners of his eyes. His jaw flexed.

"How long has it been?" she asked in her best bedside-manner voice.

"Two years in November." He finished off his wine.

Did he still love her? How often did they see each other? Did she want him back? The questions tumbled through her head, but of course she wouldn't dare ask him. It was much too personal. They didn't know each other like that.

"So, I threw myself into my work full force," he said with a derisive chuckle. "She was right. My work was important. It still is. But things were beginning to go wrong before then. We both knew it." He suddenly focused back on her and she felt as if she was hit with a jolt of electricity. "More wine?"

"No. I'm fine. Thanks."

He stared at her for a moment. "I hope you don't take this the wrong way, but you're nothing like I would ever imagine a small-town doctor." His voice had taken on an intimacy that made her feel as if he were undressing her.

"What did you imagine?" she managed.

"Nothing like you, Dr. Kai Randall." He moved a bit closer to her, taking in the satiny brown-sugar complexion, eyes like a young doe's and the riot of natural spiral hair that stood out around her perfect face like a halo. And that body. He swallowed. Nope, not like any house-calling doctor he'd ever imagined.

"Daddy…"

Kai nearly jumped out of her skin.

They both turned toward Jessie who was standing in the middle of the living room.

"Hey, baby…"

The spell was officially broken.

Anthony hurried over to his daughter and picked her up. "How are you feeling, baby?"

"I'm hungry." She rested her head on his shoulder.

Kai laughed. "That's definitely a good sign." She walked over to them and placed her hand on Jessie's forehead. "Cooled down." She stroked Jessie's hair away from her face. "Your dad is fixing you some chicken soup."

Jessie rubbed her eyes.

They stood there together and Kai could feel the bond between father and daughter, and for a moment she wondered…what it would be like…with him…with them.

"I guess I should be getting home. Poor Jasper needs to get out of his carrier and it looks like the rain is finally slowing down."

"Absolutely not. The least I can do is have you join us for dinner. The dinner that you had a hand in preparing, I might add."

"And Jasper," Jessie said at the sound of his barking. Jessie wiggled out of her father's arms and ran over to the carry case that held Jasper. She got down on the floor and put her face up to the mesh opening.

"There's really no reason to rush," he said in a rough whisper. "And you never showed me how to fix those dumpling things you were talking about. So you can't leave." The shadow of a smile played with his mouth.

"If you're sure."

"Without a doubt."

"All right then, I'll stay."

"I'll take Jasper out while you start the dumplings."

"Sure. Oh, do you have any baking powder?"

"Should be some in the pantry." Anthony took Jasper out of his carrier and he yipped and spun around much to Jessie's delight. He came back to the kitchen and washed his hands at the sink. "How can I help?"

By not standing so close to me. "A mixing bowl."

He got the bowl. Kai poured in flour, baking powder, a sprinkle of salt and a half cup of milk, and mixed it together until the mixture was thick but smooth. She scooped out a handful and molded it into a ball. Another she kneaded into an elongated shape.

"Let me try." He reached over her, and as his arm grazed her left breast, she nearly screamed. He took the dough into his large hands and massaged it into shape.

Kai ran her tongue across her lips as she watched him caress the mixture and all manner of images of his hands on her body played hopscotch in her head.

"How's that?" He held a long, thick handful of smooth dough in his palm.

Her throat went bone-dry. Heat seared her cheeks. "Great," she muttered.

"Now what?"

"Umm, when the veggies are good and tender we put them in the pot for about fifteen minutes."

"I can't remember the last time I was in the kitchen cooking with a woman."

He looked painfully shy all of a sudden. Kai's heart ached.

"Feels good."

He said the words so softly that she wasn't sure he'd spoken at all. She didn't know where to look with him staring at her that way.

"I'm sorry, I didn't mean to make you uncomfortable."

"You didn't. I mean…I know the feeling."

His dark eyes flashed. "Do you?"

All she could manage was a nod of her head.

A smile like daybreak slowly lifted the corners of his mouth.

They stood there, staring at each other, neither sure what the next step, the next words should be, but knowing that an invisible line had been crossed.

Kai was the first to look away. "We should put the dumplings in now," she said, barely above a whisper. She took the one he had in his hand and dropped it in the bubbling brew.

Anthony put in the rest. "More wine?"

"All right."

He turned to the counter to pour more wine and realized how quiet it had gotten. He put the bottle down and went into the living room.

Jessie was sitting on the floor, leaning against the couch, dozing with Jasper on her lap.

Kai followed. She lifted Jasper and noticed that Jessie was warm again. "Fever is back. It's only been a couple of hours since she had the Tylenol. It should have lasted at least four hours," she said, concern tightening her voice.

Anthony picked her up. "Let me get her back in the bed."

"She needs fluids."

"Jessie, Jess, wake up, sweetie."

"I'll get some juice. You put her back to bed."

"My throat hurts," she whimpered.

"Okay, sweetheart. We're going to make you feel better." He carried her back to her bedroom.

Kai poured a glass of orange juice and went to Jessie's bedroom. "Let me take her temp again." She got out the thermometer and put it in Jessie's mouth. Within moments the digital thermometer beeped. "Back up to 102."

"What do you think is wrong?"

"It's more than a cold. Probably a virus." She gave her another dose of Tylenol. "If she's not better in the morning, then I suggest we get her over to the hospital and let them check her out. A colleague of mine is a great pediatrician over there. As a matter of fact, I'm going to give him a call." She looked up at Anthony, whose expression was a portrait of anxiety. "I'm sure it's nothing major, but with kids you can never be overcautious," she added, hoping to take some of the worry out of his eyes. "See if you can get her to drink. I'll call Andrew."

Kai got up and went to the front of the house and took her cell phone out of her coat pocket. She typed in Andrew's private number and hoped that he would answer. He finally picked up on the fifth ring. After brief pleasantries that were clearly strained, she ran down the scenario for him and listened to his recommendations.

"Thank you, Andrew. Sorry to bother you. Yes, I will. Thank you." She disconnected the call and returned to the bedroom.

"What did he say?" Anthony asked the instant her body was outlined in the doorway.

"Pretty much what I told you. He said for now to give her the fever meds every two hours, then three, and then four. She has to drink as much fluids as we can get in her. Keep her warm but not too warm. When the fever breaks she'll be damp and sweaty and we don't want her to get a chill. He did say that she was probably coming down with something before she got here and being out in the damp just kicked it into gear."

His cell phone vibrated in his pocket. He pulled it out. For a moment he shut his eyes, got up and walked out before answering the call.

"Hello, Crystal."

"I thought you were going to have Jessie call me."

"I know. She's been sleeping."

"All day? Come on, Tony." She paused. "What's wrong? I know something's wrong and you're not telling me. What is it? Tell me!"

"Relax, Crystal. Jessie isn't feeling very well."

"What the hell does that mean? She was fine when she left me." The accusation was clear as glass.

"She's coming down with a cold. She has a fever."

He heard her muttering a string of curses.

"I knew I shouldn't have left her with you. First you let her wander out of the house and God knows what could have happened and now you tell me she has a fever. I'm coming home. I'll be on the first flight in the morning."

"Crystal!"

Kai jumped at the sound of thunder in his voice.

"Kids get sick. Jessie will be fine. I'm her father! I can take care of my daughter."

"Apparently not."

The barb stung. "Look, you want to come home, fine. That's up to you. I'm done arguing with you about Jessie."

She hesitated. "I want to speak to her. And if she's asleep wake her up. I want to hear her voice."

He gritted his teeth and went back into Jessie's bedroom. For his daughter he put on a smile. "Guess what, baby, Mommy is on the phone. She wants to talk to you." He handed Jessie the phone.

Kai got up and left the room. She went back into the kitchen and checked on the food. She stirred the soup and turned off the flame. Clearly tensions were still high between him and his ex. Whatever vague idea she may have had about herself and Anthony Weston was out of the question.

Jasper sat down at her feet and looked up at her as if he understood her dilemma. "Oh well, boy." She reached down and scratched his ears.

Anthony walked out into the kitchen. Tension radiated around him like an aura. His lean body was coiled and ready to spring.

"The soup is done. I'm going to go on home. I'll leave the thermometer and the Tylenol."

Anthony looked at her as if suddenly realizing she was standing there. "I'll get your coat." His voice was devoid of any emotion and she wondered if that was the way he was when he was prosecuting a case. Cold and detached.

Kai followed him to the front of the house and put Jasper back in his carrier. In silence, he helped her with her coat.

She turned and looked up at him. His eyes burned right through her. Her heart tumbled in her chest. "Every two hours, then three, then four," she said softly.

He nodded and opened the door. "Thank you for coming."

She stepped out into the drizzle, hoisted the straps of Jasper's carrier over her shoulder and walked to her ride.

Just another house call, she told herself. Then why did she feel so crappy?

Anthony watched from the window until the headlights of Kai's vehicle disappeared into the night. Then he turned and walked away.

Chapter 9

Anthony walked toward Jessie's bedroom but stopped at the kitchen. Steam from the pot seeped out from beneath the top. The aromatic scent of the soup filled the kitchen and his head. The past couple of hours were the most comfortable and serene he'd spent in longer than he could remember. There was an ease about Kai that calmed the churning tide that always simmered beneath the surface of his otherwise cool facade. When he was with Kai, working in the kitchen, he felt a lightness in his soul that had been missing for much too long.

It had been that way with him and Crystal in the beginning, the first year or maybe two. She had blamed their disintegrating relationship on his job. That may have been part of it, but the part that she would never own up to was that he worked harder and longer hours to make the life for her that she craved: the town house on the Upper West Side of Manhattan, vacations, clothes, the newest appliances, a nanny for Jessie, hair appointments, weekly massages, flitting from one school to the next trying to find herself—the list was long and endless.

Then he worked longer and harder so that he wouldn't have to come home until he was sure that she was asleep or at least pretending to be asleep. He stayed away so he wouldn't have to listen to her complaints and her ceaseless demands for withdrawals from his trust fund that his parents had left him. He often wondered if that was the dominating part of the attraction for Crystal…the large fortune.

In the beginning, her clinging and girlish delight at the things that he purchased for her boosted his male ego. Her "woman needs her man" persona fed his machismo. He wanted to take care of her, give her what she wanted—all the things she'd missed as a child moving from one foster home to another. He lived to make her life better. In the beginning.

He'd come home one evening after a grueling day in court. He was exhausted, mentally and physically. All he wanted to do was go home to a nice dinner, a hot bath and deep sleep. Instead, he came home to find Crystal surrounded by a mountain of shopping bags on the bed and clothes and shoes all over the room and not a scent of dinner in the air.

He dropped his briefcase on the floor, jolting her from a very animated conversation on her phone. She turned but barely looked at him, whispered something into the phone and disconnected the call.

"Hi," she greeted, not really meeting his eyes.

"What is all this, Crystal?" He waved his arms around at the chaos.

"All what? I went shopping. I needed some new things."

"New things! Are you out of your mind? How many new things can you wear? Have you seen the last credit card statement?"

She folded her arms and pouted. "No. Don't you take care of the bills?"

"You're damned right, I do. I take care of everything, Crystal. This house, the clothes, the cars, the trips, the classes. Everything. What do I get out of the deal? Can I ever come home to dinner with my wife? Can we even have sex without you acting like it's a chore? Can we have a conversation that is more involved than some reality television show crap?"

"Maybe if you paid me some attention instead of that damned job of yours, things could be different!" she snapped back and jumped to her feet.

"Oh, really. And who do you think is going to pay for all of this?" He picked up a shopping bag by the handle and tossed it across the room. "Huh, who? You?"

"You never thought much of me. Never. You always saw me as some unfortunate waif that you had to rescue. You can't rescue me, Tony. Don't you get it?" she said, planting her hands on her hips. Her eyes filled with tears.

Anthony stared at his wife and saw her for the first time. Really saw her. She was right. He couldn't save her. She didn't want to be saved. But whatever it was that she wanted he knew he couldn't give it to her.

Slowly he bobbed his head. "You're right and I'm going to stop trying." He strode across the room, pulled open the closet and took out his suitcase.

"What are you doing?"

"Leaving." He began taking his clothes out of the dresser and some shirts and suits from the closet.

"You can't leave," she said, the fight in her voice replaced with a plea.

He glanced at her over his shoulder as he continued to pack. "I'm leaving. We'll work out the details later."

Crystal grabbed his arm. "You can't leave me."

He straightened and stared hard at her. "It's over. There's nothing between us, at least nothing that money can buy. You're right, I can't save you from whatever is nipping at your heels." He turned back to finish packing.

"I'm pregnant."

His head whipped toward her. His eyes creased to two slits. "What?"

"I'm pregnant."

He looked her up and down. "I don't believe you."

She hurried over to the nightstand and pulled the drawer open. She snatched out a piece of paper and brought it back to him, shoving it at him. "Believe me now?"

He looked down at the grainy black-and-white image. His stomach knotted. His gaze lifted to meet hers.

Now the tears freely flowed down her cheeks.

So he'd stayed and for a while things were good again. Her pregnancy was uncomplicated and he did everything he could to make it as easy as possible for her anyway. And then Jessie was born. His beautiful baby girl who he would lay down his life for. And every day he loved her more and for every day that he loved his daughter, Crystal slowly returned to the woman he'd vowed to walk away from a year earlier. Finally he did.

She believed he didn't know about the man she was seeing. It didn't matter, really. They'd stopped sleeping together before Jessie was born, but at least he'd remained faithful. The hard part was the doubts that sometimes crept up on him in the dark hours of the night. The hushed phone calls. The unexplained hours away. *Was Jessie his daughter?* But then when he looked at her and held her and she called him Daddy, it didn't matter. It didn't.

He drew in a long deep breath and pushed out the past. He walked to the stove and lifted the lid. Time and care had gone into the healing brew. But not even time or care could have saved his marriage. It had been his one megafailure. He'd allowed that soft part of him to rule. What he did know for certain was that he'd never allow himself to be that open and vulnerable again. Ever.

He got a bowl from the cupboard and ladled the soup into it. He prepared a smaller one for Jessie and took them both to her room and was happy to see that she was awake.

"Hey, baby. I brought you some soup." He set the bowls down on the nightstand and pulled a chair up next to her bed. "Hungry?"

She nodded.

"Good. Sit up for me, okay?"

Jessie wiggled her way to an upright position and Anthony began spoon-feeding her. Before either realized it her bowl was empty and so was his.

"Wow. Finished. You want some more?"

"Yes, please."

He grinned wistfully. The chicken soup was even better than Kai promised. And those dumplings weren't too bad, either.

"I'll be right back." He took the empty bowls back to the kitchen and refilled them. What was it that she'd said? *You simmer it with love. That's the real cure.*

Anthony refused to let Jessie sleep in the room by herself so he'd set up an inflatable mattress on the floor so he could hear her if she awoke during the night and be there to give her the medicine. Both of them slept like rocks.

He woke up to Jessie leaning over the side of her bed and wiggling her fingers in his ear. She giggled in delight when he leaped up like a man on fire.

He playfully glared at her. "You must be feeling better." Suddenly he grabbed her, pulled her out of the bed and onto his chest for a bear hug. She squealed with laughter and his heart filled with the kind of joy only loving your child can bring.

"Let's get you cleaned up and dressed, and then I'll fix some breakfast." He ran her a bath and spent the next twenty minutes dodging bubbles and giggles.

After breakfast, Anthony took Jessie's temperature and was glad that it still remained normal. Then he got her settled in the living room with some of her toys and *Dora the Explorer* playing in the background on the television. From his spot in the alcove off the kitchen and living room that he'd carved out as his minioffice, he was close enough to keep an eye on her and get some work done in the process.

He powered on his laptop and opened his office email account. He groaned. In just two days there were more than one hundred unanswered emails. This would take the better part of the morning. It was a job he usually delegated to his secretary. Unfortunately, she was on a well-deserved vacation, too. Shaking his head in resignation, he pushed back from the small desk. He was going to need some coffee before he tackled the mountain of mail.

He walked into the kitchen and again a herd of disjointed emotions poked at him, challenging him to respond. He could still feel her there, almost hear her laughter, see the way that she moved so comfortably in his space as though she could easily belong there.

He lifted his chin as his jaw tightened. Never happen.

Especially not after he behaved like a real ass last night.
He turned on the faucet and filled the carafe with water
for two cups of coffee, measured out the coffee powder
and turned the coffeemaker on. But the least he could
do was call and thank her, let her know that Jessie was
much better. *Right?* Maybe then she wouldn't think he
was a complete jerk.

He took his cell phone out of his pocket and noticed
that he had a message. He frowned. It must have rang
when he was preparing Jessie's bath and he hadn't heard
it. He scrolled to his messages. It was from Crystal. He
muttered a curse. How could he forget? She was planning to come back home today. He forgot because he
wanted to forget.

He pressed the message and listened.

"It's Crystal. After thinking about it, I decided you
were right. It's crazy for me to come all the way back. I
know she's fine with you and kids get colds. All I ask is
that you let me know if something is wrong. Have Jessie give me a call. Thanks."

He didn't know whether to be happy or pissed. Happy
that he wouldn't have to be bothered with his ex for another couple of weeks or pissed for the very same reason.
Crystal didn't have a sudden bout of mommyhood. All of
that righteous indignation that she'd spouted yesterday
was for show. He snorted in disgust. He was sure that
Crystal's "traveling partner" was none too thrilled about
her threat to come back to the United States. That was
the real reason that she so magnanimously concluded
that "he was right."

Yep, his ex-wife was a real piece of work. He inhaled
deeply. He wasn't going to go down that road. Crystal,
even in her absence, had a way of getting under his skin
and irritating the hell out of him. She wasn't going to

ruin his vacation. And on that note, he poured a mug of coffee and went back to begin the task of sorting through his emails.

He placed his cup at his feet and the phone next to the laptop. He stared at his phone. He should call Kai and at least leave a message if she didn't answer. She probably wouldn't answer anyway. She was probably with patients.

He picked up the phone, scrolled to his recent calls and there was her number. Before he could change his mind he pressed "Call back." He was rehearsing in his head what he was going to say when she answered.

"Dr. Randall…"

"Oh, hello. I didn't expect that you'd answer. This is Anthony Weston."

"Hello, Mr. Weston. Is everything all right with Jessie?"

"Please call me Anthony, and yes, everything is fine. She slept well. No more fever…."

The silence drifted down between them.

"That's great," Kai finally said. "Probably a twenty-four-hour virus. Just keep an eye on her. But I'm sure she'll be fine."

"Right… Listen, I wanted to thank you again for yesterday." He paused. "The soup was delicious. The dumplings, too."

"I'm glad."

He was pretty sure he heard the undercurrents of laughter in her voice. "There's plenty left."

"Great. Be sure to give Jessie as much as she can handle. It's the cure for everything."

"Even bad manners?"

"Excuse me?"

"Look, I want to apologize for how I acted yesterday. You didn't deserve that."

"It's not a big deal. Parents of sick kids get testy. I can take it. I'm a big girl. Trust me, I didn't lose any sleep over it."

His brows rose at the backhanded slap. "I still would like to make it up to you."

"It's really not necessary…"

"Lincoln invited me over on Friday…" he said, making it up as he went along. "Up to The Port. Just to hang out. Have dinner." He swallowed. "I'd like you to come with me."

"I—"

"Nothing official. It's not a date…not really." He laughed, more from a sudden bout of nerves than his attempt at humor. He felt her detachment over the phone and it was throwing him off.

"I'll be right there, Mr. Hines," she called out. "Mr. Weston…Anthony, I really have to go. I have patients waiting."

"Sure. Of course."

"Call me on Thursday and let me know what time. Gotta go." The call disconnected.

Anthony's eyes widened in surprise. *Call her on Thursday.* What the… He shook his head and grinned with pleasure. Women!

Chapter 10

Anthony took the towel that was draped around his neck and wiped his sweaty face while slowing his run to a jog. Lincoln came up alongside him. They jogged the rest of the way to the entrance of The Port.

"Still got your stride going, my brother," Lincoln said, as he bent over and breathed deeply. "Sitting behind a desk in the big city hasn't slowed you down." He slowly stood.

"Running after criminals will do that for you," Anthony joked with all sincerity.

Lincoln clapped him on the back. "Coming in or are you heading back to your place?"

"I'll come in for a few. I'll wait until Desi gets back with Jessie."

"Cool." Lincoln pushed open the glass-and-wood door leading to the reception area and strolled through to the lounge. They sauntered over to the bar.

"Two waters, please," Lincoln requested, and took a seat. He turned to Anthony. "Unless you want something stronger."

"Naw, water is fine. A little early in the day for anything stronger for me." He hopped up on the bar stool and redraped the towel around his neck. "I have to do something nice for Desi before I leave, to thank her for hanging out with Jessie."

"Hey, believe me, Desi loves it. She's in second heaven around kids. The first heaven, of course, is being with me."

Anthony snorted a laugh. "Does she know that?"

"Very funny. And speaking of women, what's the deal with Crystal?"

Anthony's expression shifted as if a cloud passed over it. "For the time being, she is far, far away. Mysteriously, she had second thoughts about returning from her trip and asserting her motherly rights."

"Hmm."

The female bartender returned and placed two bottles of Perrier and glasses of ice in front of them. "Can I get you anything else, Mr. Davenport?"

"Thanks. We're good for now."

Anthony filled his glass and took a long, deep swallow. "Speaking of women...how well do you know the good doctor Kai Randall?"

Lincoln arched a questioning brow. He swiveled his chair to face Anthony. "Dr. Randall, huh?" He shrugged slightly. "I don't. Not really, anyway. I mean, she seems nice, easy on the eyes—not that I'm looking," he quickly added with a chuckle. "I hear good things about her from folks in town that have been patients of hers. But Desiree would be a better person to ask. She knows everything about everybody. Why? You interested?"

"Maybe. I sort of asked her out to dinner…with you and Desiree on Friday night. To, uh, thank her for Jessie."

Lincoln tossed his head back and laughed. "Good of you to let me in on the deal. You're doing a lot of thanking here lately."

Anthony bit back a smirk. "You think you can make that happen?"

Lincoln pursed his lips, then lifted his chin in the direction of Desiree and Jessie who were heading their way. "Guess we better clear it with the missus."

"Hey, baby." Lincoln stood, slid an arm around his wife's waist and pulled her close for a kiss.

"Hmm, hey yourself," she whispered against his mouth and stroked his shoulder.

Jessie hopped up into her father's waiting arms even as he took in the brief display of affection between his friends. A flash of envy skipped through him. Lincoln and Desi had been a couple long before he and Crystal and they still had that spark of love and affection that popped between them. He only wished that he would find the same thing one day. He placed a kiss on Jessie's head.

"We had a wonderful afternoon in town," Desiree said, leaning against the hard lines of her husband.

"We saw the boats!" Jessie squealed.

"Really? Were they big?"

"Gigantic." She stretched her arms as far as they would go.

Everyone chuckled.

"Tony and…Dr. Randall are going to join us for dinner on Friday, babe."

She glanced from one man to the other. "Ohhh. Okay." Her eyes twinkled when she smiled. "Umm, I forget, what time is dinner?"

"Eight?" Anthony offered.

"Sounds fine to me." She gave Lincoln a shove in the ribs with her elbow.

"Anthony wanted to 'thank' Dr. Randall for taking care of Jessie." His dark eyes sparked with mischief.

"Of course. It's only right." She angled her head to the side. "I have so many things on my mind... Did we say we were going to have dinner here or in town?"

"Here works for me. I mean, if it's cool with you two," Anthony said.

"I'll have the chef prepare something special."

"Thanks, Desi, I really appreciate it."

"Anytime. Besides, I haven't hung out with Kai in a while. It will be great catching up."

"So you know her pretty well..."

Desiree planted her hand on her waist. "Yes, I do. What would you like to know?" she asked coyly.

"Is she seeing anyone?"

"Right to the big questions." She paused. "Kai has been here about two years. In the time that she's been at the Harbor, I haven't known her to be with anyone in particular. I do know that Dr. Clarke has a thing for her, but nothing has ever come of it."

Anthony nodded as he listened.

"She's hard-working, dedicated to her job and her patients. She comes to some of the parties that Melanie hosts. She's fun to be around. Single..." she added.

"Thanks, Desi."

"Anytime. And the only reason why I'm telling you anything about Kai is because I think the two of you could have something. And heaven knows you need a woman in your life that is *not* Crystal."

Desiree was never shy about her dislike for Crystal and, more important, how she treated Anthony, one of the few goods guys left other than her husband. She pushed out a breath.

"Well, fellas, I'm going to leave this darling girl with her dad and head to the house." She gave Jessie a hug and kissed her husband's cheek. "See you Friday, Tony. Eight sharp."

Anthony grinned. "See you."

"I think I will keep my very accommodating wife company. See you two later. And you behave yourself, little miss."

"I will, Uncle Linc."

"Later, man." Anthony gave Linc a fist tap before the latter darted off after his wife. *One day,* he thought, *that will be me.* "Come on, sweetie, let's get you home. I have a call to make."

Once he'd settled Jessie down for a nap before dinner, he went into his study and pulled his cell phone from his pocket. He scrolled through his contact list, found Kai's number and pressed the call icon. The phone rang several times and Anthony was figuring he'd have to leave a message just as the call was answered.

"Dr. Randall."

"Hey, Dr. Randall. It's Anthony Weston."

"Hello. How are you?"

"Good. Good." He cleared his throat. "I, uh, was calling to see if you'd decided about dinner…with Lincoln and Desiree…and me."

"Sure. It sounds like fun," Kai responded.

"Eight o'clock?"

"Perfect. That'll give me some time after I close the office to get ready."

"I can pick you up about a quarter to…"

"Oh, no worries. I can drive over."

His spirits sank. "Then I'll see you there…at the restaurant."

"Looking forward to it."

"So am I," he said, the words filling him with an inexplicable warmth.

Anthony disconnected the call, leaned back in his chair and smiled.

"Tell me again why you're going out with this man," Tiffany asked from her reclined position on the lounge chair in Kai's bedroom.

Kai glanced over her shoulder from inside her walk-in closet. "It's hard to explain. I feel a connection." She picked a blouse and skirt from her closet and brought them out. "What do you think?" she asked, holding the outfit up against her.

"Hmm. Nice if you're going on a job interview."

Kai huffed and returned them to the closet. "How about this?" She held up a mint-green jersey dress with ruching at the waist and an alluring V cut at the bodice.

"Better. Sophisticated and sexy without giving away too much." She picked up her glass of white wine and took a small sip. "Listen, I don't want to put a damper on your date, but Kai…why even get involved with a man who clearly comes with baggage? He has a daughter and with a daughter there must be a mother. That equals problems. Problems that you don't need."

"I've considered all of that."

"And?"

She turned toward Tiffany. "And…it's not a 'real' date and it's not the rest of my life. He lives in New York with a life that does not include me. I'm fine with that. I have a life here. He seems like a decent guy who will only be here for a few weeks and then both of our lives will return to normal. What's the big deal if we enjoy each other's company in the meantime?"

"I know you, Kai. Remember? You don't do anything halfway. You give one hundred percent in everything that you do. Maybe you think it's serendipity that the man that you photographed months ago turns up on your doorstep, but I don't want to see you get hurt. That's all."

Kai plopped down on the side of the bed and draped the dress across her lap. "I'm a scientist. I deal in facts. I analyze each piece of information and come up with a diagnosis. I've looked at all of the facts regarding Anthony Weston and I've concluded that it's just having dinner with someone that I find attractive and smart and intelligent and whom I want to get to know better, even if it's only for a short period of time. It's just for now, not forever."

Tiffany's right brow rose. She blew out a breath. "Okay," she conceded and a slow smile lifted her mouth. "Then make these the best 'few' weeks of your life." She got up from the lounge. "Now let's finish putting together your knockout outfit. If nothing else, Mr. Right Now is going to remember this nondate."

Chapter 11

Kai pushed the small diamond studs through her lobes, then added a stroke of coral-tinted lip gloss to her mouth. She took a step back, smoothed her dress and assessed herself in the mirror then ran her fingers through her spiral curls to fluff them out.

Nothing left to do now but put on her shoes and wait. That was the hard part. Waiting. She'd been on her share of dates with an assortment of handsome, eligible, sexy men. This was different and she felt as if she were a teenager going out with a boy for the first time. But Anthony Weston was no boy. A flutter rippled through her stomach. He was *all* man. A man that had filled her lens, her thoughts and her dreams for months, and now she was moments away from spending an evening with him, even if it was with friends.

Kai drew in a breath, shook off the jitters and walked out into the living room. Jasper yip-yipped and darted to the door as if he was planning on going with her.

"Relax," she warned. "I'll be back." She ruffled Jasper behind the ears and picked up her purse and keys from the hall table. For an instant she closed her eyes and then pulled the door open and headed to her car. She could have had Anthony come and pick her up, but she didn't want him to think that this was in any way a "real" date. And, more importantly, she wanted to keep her independence and her options open. If and when she was ready to leave, she didn't want to depend on Anthony to take her home.

She turned the key in the ignition and pulled out of her driveway. *Get real, girl,* her little voice whispered. *You are totally not ready to be hemmed up in a car with Anthony Weston*. She chuckled at the dose of reality and pointed the car in the direction of The Port.

It had been a while since she'd been to Lincoln and Desiree's establishment. When she pulled up, she noticed immediately that it had expanded. There was a new wing that boasted the sign *Port Day Spa*. The main entrance featured lavish glass-and-chrome doors that gave a wide view of the stylish interior. She followed the signs to on-site parking, found a space and walked through the main lobby toward the restaurant.

A hostess met her at the door. "Good evening. Welcome to The Port. Dinner or do you want to sit at the bar?"

"I'm meeting some friends. Mr. & Mrs. Davenport…"

"Kai."

She glanced up and saw Anthony coming toward her. Her heart banged in her chest. Damn, he was even more devastatingly handsome than the last time she'd seen him, if that was possible. Clad in all black, he reeked dangerously sexy from every pore. She swallowed over the sudden dry knot in her throat.

Anthony strolled up to her and the heady scent of this all-male specimen flooded her senses. He gently clasped her elbow and a jolt of something electric ripped through them, catching them both off guard. Their gazes jumped and connected and for a moment neither of them spoke or moved. Anthony was the first to recover.

"You look incredible," he murmured, the heavy timbre of his voice rolling toward her like the surf beating against the shore.

She ran the tip of her tongue across her lips. "Thank you," she softly said as the sexy scent of him went straight to her head. "So do you." Inadvertently she moaned.

Anthony squinted at her. "You okay?"

Kai's lashes fluttered. "Fine, just taking in the space."

"It's pretty incredible, isn't it?" he said as his gaze caressed her once again. "Linc and Desi should be here shortly. I was sitting at the bar. Want to have a drink while we wait?"

"Sure." A glass of wine might settle her nerves.

He placed his hand at the dip of her back and guided her into the restaurant, nodding his thanks to the hostess.

The position of Anthony's hand sent hot darts racing up her spine and it took all of her concentration to put one foot in front of the other. This was going to be a long night.

They found two empty seats. Anthony helped her onto her stool and it was akin to a sensual experience; the way he intermittently touched her exposed flesh, the closeness of his body to hers, and the allure of his voice was a total turn-on that kept her pulse racing at a crazy clip.

"What will you have?" He turned toward her from his perch on the stool and those dark brown eyes and killer lashes dipped down into her soul and stirred.

She moistened her lips with the tip of her tongue. "White wine."

Anthony got the bartender's attention and ordered a white wine for Kai and a refill of his Jack Daniel's on the rocks. The bartender placed their drinks in front of them. He lifted his glass.

"To a great evening."

Kai smiled and touched her glass to his before taking a small sip. She set her glass down. "It just hit me. Where's Jessie?"

He chuckled. "My very determined daughter preferred to spend her day with Desiree. She's going to bring her when they come."

Kai smiled even as she wondered, as she often did, why Desiree and Lincoln didn't have children of their own. They would make phenomenal parents. "How long have you known Lincoln?"

Anthony lifted his glass and took a short sip. "Seems like always," he said with a light chuckle. "We met in college and have been friends ever since. We don't get to hang out like we once did, but we stay in touch. It was his idea to get me to come out here." He paused. His gaze moved slowly over her face. "I'm glad he did."

Her stomach fluttered.

"Daddy!"

Anthony turned in his seat as Jessie came running in his direction. He scooped her up onto his lap. "Hey, sweetie." He kissed the top of her head. "Have fun?"

"Yes!"

"She didn't give you too much trouble, did she?"

Desiree laughed. "Absolutely not. We had a great day." She gave Kai a quick hug. "Good to see you."

"You, too."

"Lincoln reserved the private room in back. It should be set up now."

"Great." Anthony helped Kai down from her seat and held her hand for an extra moment.

They were so close, Kai was sure he was going to kiss her until Jessie tugged on his hand. "They're going to leave us," Jessie whimpered and took off behind Desiree. Kai laughed in relief mixed with disappointment that the moment was lost.

"Guess we better hurry," she said on a shaky note.

Anthony squeezed her hand, then guided her out to the private dining room.

Dinner was lively, full of anecdotes, laughter and great food. Kai was able to see another side of Anthony. He could give a jab as good as he could take one. Both Anthony and Lincoln shared stories about their college escapades that had them all doubled over with laughter. Desiree and Lincoln talked about how they almost lost each other years earlier, but it was Lincoln's determination that won her back.

"I was stubborn," Desiree admitted, turning to her husband with love in her eyes. "But he wouldn't take no for an answer. Still doesn't," she added.

Lincoln leaned over and kissed her cheek. "I'd let her get away once. I wasn't going to let that happen again."

"And the rest, as they say, is history," Desiree said with laughter in her voice.

"This place was nothing like this before Desiree came back on the scene," Anthony offered. "It was only about six cottages and a main building."

"True, true." Lincoln chuckled. "It was her vision and her artistic touch that transformed it."

"It was a lot of work and I had a lot of help," she said. She turned to Kai. "Speaking of artists, when are you going to put up some of your photography at the gallery?"

Kai dipped her head.

"Did you know that she is an incredible photographer?" Desiree directed her question to Anthony.

His brows rose. "I had no idea." He zeroed in on Kai. "What kind of photography?"

"Mostly black-and-white. Outdoor shots." She shrugged lightly. "It's just a hobby."

"She's being modest," Desiree said. "The gallery owner has been trying to get her to put on a show of her work for ages."

"A woman of many talents," Anthony said. "I'd love to see your work sometime."

Heat rushed through her veins. She swallowed. "Sure."

The waitress came and began to clear the table.

"Dessert anyone?" Lincoln asked.

"I'm stuffed," Anthony said. He turned to Kai.

"No. Nothing for me. Thanks."

Jessie yawned, her lids fluttering over her eyes as she struggled to stay awake.

"Looks like someone's bedtime," Kai said, lifting her chin in Jessie's direction.

"Yes, it is. I should get her home and to bed." Anthony made a move to pick up Jessie.

"Listen, I can take her," Desiree offered. "You two relax, enjoy the rest of your evening. You can pick her up in the morning."

"Desi, you've done enough. You don't…"

"I want to and it's not a problem. Really." She got up and Lincoln picked up Jessie who quickly snuggled against him.

"See you in the morning," Desi said. "And don't stay away so long," she said to Kai. "This was fun."

"Yes, it was. Thanks so much." She kissed Desi's cheek and squeezed Lincoln's arm.

"Thanks, Desi," Anthony said against her cheek as he kissed her good-night and then his daughter. "See you in the morning, man," he said to Lincoln.

"We'll go for a run."

"Sounds like a plan."

The couple walked off leaving Anthony and Kai.

"So…" Anthony said turning his full attention on Kai. "Would you like some more wine?"

"Okay," she said softly over the thudding of her heart. They were actually alone. Just the two of them.

He refilled her glass from one of the two bottles that Lincoln ordered with dinner.

"Thanks." She took a sip. "Lincoln and Desiree are really great."

"The best. So tell me a bit more about you. You left the big bad city to come here. That must have been culture shock."

She laughed. "It certainly was and took some getting used to, but I wouldn't change it for the world."

Anthony relaxed in his seat. "Really? You don't miss the excitement, the energy of living in New York?"

"Not at all. I visit New York from time to time but I'm always happy to come back home." She took another sip of wine.

"Where did you go to medical school?"

"Cornell. I did my internship at New York Hospital."

"How did you manage to make it to chief of emergency services? That must have been tough."

"Believe me, it was. The hours were inhuman when you were on rotation. Very little sleep and you had to learn to make life-or-death decisions in seconds."

"I'm totally in awe of doctors and medicine. It takes a special person and skills to save lives on a regular basis."

"What about you? I thought I read somewhere that you might run for district attorney."

He pressed his lips together and nodded in agreement. "My boss, Harrison Blumenthal, has been grooming me to take over. He's making a run for governor."

"Did you always want to be involved in law and order?" she asked with an inquisitive grin.

His gaze drifted away as if he was viewing his response from a far-off place. "I don't really think so. I didn't know what I wanted to do with my life." His jaw tightened. "The only thing I was sure of was that I wanted to get as far away from where I was as possible."

Kai studied the hard lines of his profile and then he swung his gaze in her direction. It was like being hit with a jolt of electricity. Her breath caught and she sunk into the bottomless darkness of his eyes that surely held secrets she wanted to uncover. "Where was that?" she tentatively asked.

"Brooklyn." He chuckled. "The Marcy Projects to be exact."

"You're kidding." She slapped her palm on the table. "I grew up not too far from there. On Putnam Avenue."

"What?" He tossed his head back and laughed.

"We probably passed each other dozens of times."

"I was one of those guys that your parents told you to stay away from." He reached out and ran the tip of his finger across her knuckles. A shiver scurried up her arm. "Besides, I know I would have remembered you."

Her thoughts short-circuited for a moment. "I doubt it," she tossed back. "I was pretty unremarkable," she added in the hope of deflecting the direction of the conversation.

Anthony leaned back and glanced at her from beneath his lashes. "Weren't we all." He finished off his drink. "Ready?"

"Sure." She picked up her purse from the table. Now she wished she'd left her car at home.

Chapter 12

The evening was pleasantly warm. A light breeze blew in off the ocean, stirred the leaves on the branches overhead and wrapped around them. They strolled in a comfortable silence in the direction of the parking lot behind the main building.

"I had a great time tonight. Thanks for inviting me."

"I hope this won't be the last."

She glanced over and up at him. "It doesn't have to be." Her heart pounded.

Anthony stopped walking. He took her hand and turned her to face him. He didn't ask. He didn't hesitate. He took what he'd been wanting all night. Her mouth.

The air stopped moving in her lungs. The wind ceased to blow. Everything around her disappeared when she was captured by the sweetness of his mouth. Blood roared in her ears, blocking out everything but the racing of her heart.

Anthony cupped her cheeks in his palms and tenderly worshipped her lips. He hummed in appreciation against her mouth.

Kai's eyes fluttered open. He brushed the pad of his thumb along her bottom lip.

"I would say that I was sorry and I don't know what came over me," he said his voice thick and raspy. "But I'd be lying."

A coy smile moved across her mouth. "We can't have a man of law and order telling lies," she said softly.

Anthony rested his hands on her shoulders and looked down at her. "Then I'd better tell you that I've wanted to kiss you from the moment I saw you standing in the doorway of your house."

Her lips parted ever so slightly.

"I'll only be in town for another week and a half." He paused. "But I'd like to spend as much of that time with you that we can manage. *If* you want to."

"I want to," she said on a breath.

They were suddenly caught in the headlights of a car that was pulling out of the lot.

Anthony chuckled and grabbed her hand. "I guess that's our cue. Let me get you home."

They stopped in front of her car. *Why didn't she let him drive her? She could kick herself.*

"I'll follow you in my car. Make sure you get home safely."

Her insides did the happy dance. "That's not necessary."

"I know it's not. I want to." He opened her car door. She slid in. "I'll be right behind you," he said, before shutting the door.

Kai gripped the wheel and willed her heart to slow down. He was only being a gentleman and making sure that she got home safely, she chanted to herself. She turned the key in the ignition. What if he wanted more? She put the car in gear. What would she do then? She was getting way ahead of herself. Slowly she pulled out, turned onto the lane leading away from The Port. She glanced in her rearview mirror and saw Anthony's SUV headlights. She gripped the wheel tighter and focused on the dimly lit road.

Experience and familiarity were the only things that guided her home because her mind spun faster than she could process the thoughts and images that teased her. She pulled into her driveway and Anthony eased in right behind her. She turned off the ignition. So did he. She drew in a breath, grabbed her purse and stepped out of the car. When she shut the door and turned, Anthony was beside her.

"Thank you for a great evening."

"I'm glad you said yes." He tucked a stray curl behind her ear then lifted his chin toward her front door. "You'd better get inside." His fingertip drifted down the curve of her jaw.

A quick mix of disappointment and relief danced in her stomach. On the one hand she felt let down that he didn't make a move to come inside, yet on the other hand she felt mildly relieved that she wouldn't have to make a decision about what to do if he'd crossed the threshold.

"Maybe we can do something tomorrow."

Her eyes lit up with her smile. "I only have two appointments tomorrow. So…anytime after three is good for me."

"I'll call you." He leaned down and kissed her softly on the lips. "You really need to go inside," he murmured and eased back. "Or I may have to act on my other fantasy."

Her heart thumped. "What fantasy?"

"To take you to bed and make love to you until the sun comes up."

"It doesn't have to be a fantasy," she said, and before she had time to think she turned toward her front door with her hand outstretched behind her. Anthony took her hand and followed her inside.

Chapter 13

Anthony pushed the door closed behind them, turned Kai into his arms and pulled her flush against him, stilling the air in her lungs. The penetration of his gaze dipped down into her soul and weakened her knees and spread heat through her limbs.

The room, only lit by the sliver of moonlight coming in from the slits in the drapes, slowly disappeared from Kai's view as Anthony lowered his head and took full possession of her mouth.

A groan rumbled from the depths of his throat at the first taste of the sweet softness of her lips. Like a man deprived of nourishment, he savored the moment and quickly wanted more. His tongue teased her bottom lip, the corners, the top, and coaxed her mouth open. The burst of sweetness from her tongue to his elevated their need for each other.

The tips of Kai's fingers pressed into the taut muscles

of his back, then relaxed and traveled along his contours, while his large hands and nimble fingers roamed freely along the hills and valleys of her lush body.

With great reluctance, Kai broke away from the kiss, breathless and hot with need. "Not here," she managed to say. Once more she took his hand. This time she led him across the threshold of her bedroom.

It was as if a signal had been given that whatever they wanted, whatever they felt, whatever they needed was there for the taking. Now.

Fingers and hands and mouths were everywhere. Buttons popped and danced across the floor. Belts were ripped from their loops while silky undergarments floated like clouds to their feet. One by one, piece by piece was removed until nothing was between them but air and desire.

"God, you're beautiful," he uttered in a raw whisper as his gaze moved across her naked body. Suddenly, he didn't want to rush. He wanted to burn every moment, every vision into his memory. He wanted to take his time on this trip to discover what turned her on, what made her cry out, what gave her that final push of release. He wanted to know it all for now and every time they were together thereafter.

Anthony reached out, tentatively almost, and ran the tips of his two fingers along the curve of her jaw. A shiver crept up her spine and her eyes fluttered close. The trail of his hand ventured to her neck and along the curve of the slender bone, then across her shoulder and back to traverse the swell of her breasts. Her breath hitched when the pads of his thumbs brushed and taunted her turgid nipples. He began to pay tribute to her butter-soft skin, planting tiny hot kisses that began at her neck and moved like a love ballad down her body.

Kai gripped his shoulders to steady herself as jolts of desire ripped through her. This was what she wanted, what she needed—Anthony—for as long as it would last.

They eased back toward the bed and tumbled down onto the fluffy comforter, wrapped in each other's embrace.

Anthony stretched out alongside her and the look of longing that radiated from her eyes was all the encouragement that he needed. Pure will kept him from simply taking her and demanding that her body be his and his alone. So he took his time, prepared her the way a master chef prepares his signature meal—with care, attention to every detail, mixing and measuring all of the ingredients, lovingly watching as it simmers, waiting for the precise moment when it is ready.

Kai's body hummed beneath his touch. His kisses sizzled on her skin and she wasn't sure how much longer she could endure the exquisite torture. She wanted to touch every inch of him, experience the taste of him, make him feel the same sensations that tripped through her. She captured his mouth, delved into the warmth and the sweet taste of him. Her fingers skimmed across his skin, roamed along the muscles of his back that rippled beneath her fingertips.

The thunderstorm of desire swirled around them. Kai's senses spun. She was on fire. She had to be. It was the only explanation for the fever that lit her body, poured through her veins like lava. Wherever Anthony placed his lips, the skin cooled for a second and then ignited. His tongue stilled the flames, then his hands rekindled it.

"I want you," he breathed deep into her ear. "Tell me you want me," he demanded. His gaze bore down into hers.

"I...want you. Now." Her heart pounded. Her tongue glided slowly across her bottom lip.

The tip of Anthony's finger tucked a loose strand of hair behind her ear. He kissed her lobe, the line of her jaw, grazed her lips with his, teased her throat with his tongue, seared a path down the valley of her breasts, across the flutter of her belly, hovered for a moment between the apex of her thighs before parting them and tasting her there.

Her body arched as if hit with a jolt of electricity. Anthony firmly clasped her hips in his large hands. Kai whimpered. Her essence was an elixir to him lifting him higher, fueling his lust for her. And the more he gave to her, the more she wanted, until her full body shuddered from the points of her toes to the top of her head. Her cry of release hung in her throat, caught in the moment, then it burst forth with such raw intensity that it stiffened the fine hairs along Anthony's neck. He couldn't hold out any longer. He had to feel her wrap around him, grip him, make him come. He quickly retrieved a condom from his wallet in his pant pocket.

Anthony moved slowly up her body, positioning himself between the silk of her thighs until he was directly above her staring down into her eyes. He watched the pulse flutter at the base of her neck.

Kai linked her fingers behind his head and drew him to her. Their mouths locked. She raised her hips, he lowered his and he found his way into the hot valley of her. His groan was a mixture of bliss and utter surrender. For a moment he couldn't move. He didn't want to do anything to disturb the exquisite sensation that hummed through his being in that instant when they connected as one entity for the very first time. He wanted to memorize the feeling, but his body and hers needed to create more memories with every move, every roll, every stroke and every sigh.

They clung to each other. Their mouths and bodies locked together; moving in unison, they awakened each other's souls and sealed an unspoken commitment that exploded, lit up the room and rocked them to their cores.

Damp, hearts banging, limbs entwined, breaths stopping and starting, it all felt like a dream, but it was real. Kai's trembling fingers stroked the curve of Anthony's back, she buried her face into the hollow of his neck, inhaled his scent, matched the rhythm of his heartbeat with her own. This was more than she could have ever imagined. It had been so long since she'd been held and made love to. She didn't want it to end. Not yet. And Anthony was more than willing to give her whatever she wanted.

After some time, they rested, spooned together while Anthony cupped Kai securely against him as if, were he to let her go, she would evaporate into the dream that their lovemaking certainly was for him. Tenderly he kissed the back of her neck and relished the sexy purr that he received.

"This was better than any fantasy," he roughly whispered.

Kai shifted and tried to turn her head to look over her shoulder at him. "Really?"

"Yes, really." He leaned in and kissed her on the lips. He traced the shell of her ear with his fingertip. "I'm going back to New York next week."

Kai's stomach tightened. "I know."

"I'm not sure how…"

"Listen, I'm a big girl. I knew what I was getting myself into. You don't have to try to make it be something that it can't be."

Anthony inwardly flinched. He felt her withdraw from him and he eased his hold on her. He wanted to say something. He wanted *her* to say something—anything that would put them back where they had been only moments ago and not the direction in which they were headed.

Kai bit down on her bottom lip to keep it from trembling. Her throat clenched. What she said was obviously true. He didn't try to challenge what she said or to convince her that she was wrong. She was having a hard time breathing. She curled her body tighter, withdrawing inside herself.

Anthony slowly drew away. He turned onto his back and stared up at the ceiling. Kai pulled the sheet and light comforter up to her neck and snuggled down into her pillow. Anthony would have felt better if she'd simply said to get the hell out.

"I probably should get going," he said quietly and slowly got out of the bed.

"Hmm. Okay."

He gathered up his clothing and walked into the bathroom.

"There are extra towels on the shelf," she called out.

"Thanks." He closed the door behind him.

Kai listened to the water run. She squeezed her eyes shut and pressed her fist to her mouth. There was no reason for her to be upset. *She* was the one that had told him not to make it something it wasn't. She'd all but told him that she didn't expect nor want anything from him.

The water shut off. Kai pulled her sheet closer to her face and feigned sleep. Anthony stepped out of the bathroom. The light went out. She felt him standing over her, but she kept her eyes shut.

"Good night," he whispered.

Kai didn't respond.

Anthony turned and walked out. Moments later Kai heard her front door shut and then the sound of Anthony's car. She lay perfectly still and listened until the sound of his engine disappeared into the night.

Chapter 14

Kai became her own patient the following morning. She spent a restless night, thinking about what had transpired between her and Anthony—how it ended. Her head throbbed.

She stared down at the aspirin in the palm of her hand. She picked up the glass of water, put the pill on her tongue and washed it down. Whatever remnants of her night with Anthony were gone. For good. She drew in a long breath of resolve, put the glass in the sink and grabbed Jasper's leash from the hook by the door and took him for a morning run along the beach. The run and the salt air always helped her to clear her head, and being away from her house would keep her from sitting down and talking to Tiffany, who'd already called three times before noon.

She and Jasper had been jogging for about five minutes when her cell chirped inside the pocket of her jeans.

She slowed to a stop and pulled it out. Tiffany's number and image showed up on the face of the phone. She sighed heavily and pressed the talk icon.

"Hey, Tiff."

"Don't *Hey Tiff* me. How's everything going? You sound out of breath."

She swallowed. "Yes, everything is fine. Was jogging on the beach with Jasper."

"Oh. Weeeell, how did it go? How was your nondate?"

She laughed lightly.

"Fine."

"Really?" she tossed back, the sarcastic tone unmistakable. "You were always such a lousy liar, Kai."

Kai sniffed. "Nothing to lie about."

"Hmm, that means that there's plenty to lie about. What happened? Are you all right?"

"I'm fine." Her voice hitched. "Really."

"I'll be there in ten minutes." Tiffany disconnected the call before Kai could protest.

Kai squeezed her eyes shut for a moment. When she opened them and looked down Jasper was gazing up at her, wagging his tail. "Looks like we're going to have company, J. Come on, let's head back."

Kai and Tiffany stood side by side at the kitchen counter fixing sandwiches for a late lunch.

"Got any pickles?" Tiffany asked.

"Bottom shelf in the fridge." Kai took their plates and walked to the table and sat down. "Can you bring the pitcher of iced green tea?"

Tiffany brought the pitcher and the pickles to the table and sat down opposite her friend who was working very hard not to look her in the eye.

Tiffany took a bite of her tuna sandwich, chewed

slowly. "Hmm, didn't realize how hungry I was." She eyed Kai, who picked up and put down her sandwich.

Kai sipped her green tea. "You were right," she murmured.

Tiffany put her sandwich down on the plate and looked at Kai. "Right? Meaning?"

Kai lowered her gaze. "I shouldn't have gotten involved."

Tiffany reached over and covered Kai's hand. "You want to talk about it?"

Kai pressed her lips together, took another sip of her tea and slowly began.

By the time Kai finished recounting her evening, they had moved to the living room and were curled on the couch and loveseat.

Tiffany was thoughtful for a moment. "Look, this isn't about 'I told you so.' From where I'm sitting what did you expect him to say after what you told him?"

Kai's light brown eyes jerked in Tiffany's direction. "I…expected him to…say it wasn't true."

"Girl, you have been out of the game for so long, you've forgotten how to play. You're both adults. You wanted him and he wanted you. You went into it knowing the deal, but you didn't want to accept it after the fact. Guess he must have really hit that sweet spot," she teased, the beginnings of a smile dancing on her lips. "And changed your whole mind!"

Kai sputtered a laugh and rolled her eyes at her friend.

"You know I'm right!"

Kai slapped her palm on the table and tossed her head back. "Yes, lawd!"

The two friends roared with laughter.

"Shook loose those cobwebs," Tiffany tossed in between spurts of laughing. "It is what it is," Tiffany finally said after the laughter wound down. "Make the most of it while you can."

Kai blew out a breath. "I've sent him on his merry way."

"You have his number, right?"

"Yes, and?"

"Call him if you want to see him, Kai. That's what big girls do."

"I don't know. I'll think about it."

Tiffany uncurled her legs and stood. "Well, don't think too long. He's going back next week. Right?"

"Mmm-hmm."

Tiffany picked up her purse and draped the strap over her shoulder. "Up to you," she added and headed for the door. "Call if you need to."

"Thanks."

Anthony pulled into an available parking space in front of the local market. He didn't really need anything, but he wanted to get out of the house to get his mind off Kai and their night together.

He went over every minute a dozen times. He should have stayed and tried to explain and not let her reaction get in the way. He helped Jessie out of the car and walked into the market.

Anthony picked up a basket, held on to Jessie with his free hand and strolled the aisles with nothing particular in mind. He stopped at the fruit stand and began selecting some apples.

"Hi."

He turned.

"Dr. Kai!" Jessica squealed and ran to her.

"Hey, Jessie." She hugged her against her thigh while

keeping her focus on Anthony, the last person she expected to see.

"Hi, yourself." He placed another apple in the basket. "Doing some shopping?" he asked inanely.

"A little."

Jessica looked up from one to the other. "Are you coming to our house?"

Kai's gaze jumped to Anthony. "I don't…"

"You're more than welcome to join us. I can't match your homemade soup, but I make a mean steak."

"Pleeeasse," Jessica whined. "You can bring Jasper."

Kai laughed. "Jasper might like that." She focused on Anthony. "How about tomorrow night," she said.

"Great. Tomorrow. Say seven?"

"Seven sounds good."

"We'll see you then."

She nodded. "Well, I have to get going. See you tomorrow, Jessie, and I'll bring Jasper."

"Yippee."

"Bye," Anthony said softly.

"Bye." Kai turned and walked out, totally having forgotten what she'd come to the market for. Her thoughts were on tomorrow night and being with Anthony again. Somewhere in those brief moments of seeing him, she'd decided that whatever time they had together would be worth it.

Walking back to her car, an idea for the perfect "coming to dinner" gift came to her. Smiling, she made a quick detour and hurried across the street to make her purchase.

Chapter 15

As soon as she was finished with her last patient for the day, Kai darted to her workroom and gathered up her photography equipment. Her idea was to take a picture of Anthony's home and mount it on the bottle of imported wine that she'd purchased the day before. It would be something for him to always remember their time together.

"Be a good boy until I get back," she warned Jasper as she hurried out of the door. She wanted to make sure to get her shot before the light changed.

Kai parked on the ridge that overlooked Anthony's house. It was the perfect spot and she knew she could get the right composition—the house in the center embraced by the trees on either side.

She set up her tripod and mounted the camera, adding her long-range lens, and then got behind the camera and adjusted the focus. She took a test shot, made some adjustments and was ready to shoot again when a black Lexus pulled into the driveway. She stepped away from the lens for a moment, annoyed that the car had just messed up her shot. The driver's side door opened and a woman stepped out.

Kai blinked and quickly got behind the lens. She zoomed in. The woman was a good look-alike for Layla Lawson, but she knew it wasn't her. Her hair was different and she was taller. The woman took a suitcase out of the car, shut the door and sauntered up to the front door and rang the bell. Moments later, Anthony opened the door. She couldn't quite make out his expression or the words that were exchanged between them because she was too stunned when she saw the woman lean up and kiss him full on the mouth seconds before he ushered her inside.

Kai stood there. Her heart pounded so fast in her chest that it was hard to catch her breath. Hundreds of thoughts ran through her head one after the other but not slowing down long enough for her to get a grip on any of them.

Mindlessly, she packed up her gear, got back in her car and drove home. If she had been a different kind of woman, she would have walked up to the house, rang the bell and pulled a "Housewife of Sag Harbor" move. But she wasn't that kind of woman. The truth was Anthony had every right to see whomever he wanted. She had no claims to him. But still…

Once back at her house, she unpacked her equipment and took it to her workroom. She pulled out the card from her camera and inserted it into her computer. The image of Anthony and the unnamed woman bloomed in front of her in vivid color. A silly part of her had hoped that her eyes were playing tricks on her, but the camera didn't lie. She enlarged the image to try to get a better look at Anthony, but his face was blocked by the woman in front of him.

Downhearted and a bit confused with the unfolding events, she turned off her computer and tucked away the photo card in the desk drawer. She stared off at nothing in particular. Now what?

"What are you doing here, Crystal?" Anthony could barely contain his fury as he paced the living room floor. Even after wiping away her kiss, he still tasted her on his lips.

"Is that how you greet me? Where's Jessie?" She dropped her suitcase on the floor and gave the main room a quick perusal.

"She's taking a nap. Now, answer my question."

Crystal huffed and sat down in an armchair by the window. "I know you don't think much of me most of the time, Tony, but I felt horrible about what happened with *our* daughter. I had to come back." She crossed her long legs.

"Really? How maternal of you." He clenched his jaw.

She angled her head to the side. "You were the one who told me...no, insisted that it wasn't necessary for me to come back early. Remember?"

"I also remember after your rant about coming home on the next flight you called back to say that you'd changed your mind."

She barely flinched. "Well, I'm here now. Isn't that what's important?"

"With you it's always hard to tell."

Crystal uncurled her long, sleek form from her position and slowly stood. Deliberately she closed the distance between them until she was a breath away from her ex-husband. She placed her hand on his chest. "Can't we be civil toward each other?" Her honey-brown eyes moved languidly across his face. "I don't want to fight with you, Tony."

His nostrils flared at her intoxicating scent. He covered her hand with his and brought it down to her side. Her mouth twitched, but she bit back any comment. Anthony moved away to put some distance between them.

"How long are you planning to stay?"

"I plan to stay a few days, get a feel for Sag Harbor since you'll be bringing Jessie here from time to time."

His brows drew together. "A few days? Did you make a hotel reservation?"

"No. I thought I'd stay here." She smiled sweetly.

"Here!" He shook his head. "No, you thought wrong. That's not going to work. I'll make a reservation for you. I'm sure there's something available."

"What sense does that make? I don't know my way around. I'd have to come back and forth to see Jessie… And I thought…that maybe we could do some things as a family."

If he didn't know his ex better, he might believe the sincerity that rippled in her voice. But he knew Crystal and she did nothing if it didn't benefit her in some way. Doing the "family" thing was never high on her list.

"You mean to tell me that what's-his-name has no problem with cutting your vacation short and then staying here…with me?" he taunted. "Where is he, by the way?"

A nerve jumped under her right eye. She drew herself up. "He had business."

"Hmm. In the middle of a cruise?"

"Look, this isn't about him. It's about us."

"There is no us, Crystal." He turned away.

Crystal came up behind him. "But there can be. I want to try."

Anthony tossed his head back and laughed. "You have got to be kidding."

Crystal blinked rapidly as if trying to hold back tears. "I'm not. I want you back, Anthony. I want *us* back."

"That's not going to happen."

"I've changed."

"Good. I'm glad, but it doesn't matter."

"What do I have to do to prove it to you?" She moved closer to him. "We did have good times. I know you remember how it was between us."

His dark eyes flashed on her. "Yeah, I remember. I remember everything. All of it. That's why there's no going back, Crystal."

"There's someone else, isn't it?"

"What? How is that any of your business even if it was true?"

She lowered her gaze. "You're right," she said softly. "I'm sorry. I have no right to ask you that."

"Mommy!" Jessie darted into the room and was swept up into her mother's arms.

"Here's my baby." She squeezed and hugged her, then set her down to take a look at her. She knelt down in front of her. "How are you? All better? I was so worried about you." She stroked her face.

"All better. Daddy and Dr. Kai took care of me."

"Ohhh." She glanced over her daughter's head at Anthony. She kissed her cheek. "I'm glad that you're feeling better."

"Are you going to stay, Mommy? Daddy said Dr. Kai was coming for dinner."

"How nice. I'd love to stay."

"Goodie, goodie, goodie." She clapped her hands and jumped around. Suddenly she stopped and looked at her mother wide-eyed. "Can you sleep in my room? Please, please. I won't kick, I promise."

Crystal laughed. "Only if you promise." She flashed Anthony a short smile.

He slung his hands into his pockets and forced a neutral expression on his face when his daughter beamed at him with joy. He would do anything for his daughter, whatever it took to make her happy and keep her safe, even if he had to put up with Crystal for the evening.

"Come see my room!" Jessie grabbed her mother's hand and tugged her in the direction of her bedroom.

Crystal flashed Anthony a helpless expression.

There was no way that he was having Crystal and Kai in the same room. It would be a nightmare. One night and then Crystal was going to a hotel or home or somewhere. He'd have to postpone dinner with Kai.

He pulled his cell from his pocket and scrolled for Kai's number. Kai picked up on the third ring.

"Hi, Kai, it's Anthony."

"Hi."

"Listen, I'm really sorry, but something came up and I'm going to have to postpone dinner. I—"

"No problem," she managed. "Things happen."

"I don't want to explain over the phone."

"There's no need to explain. Really. Listen, I have a call coming in. I need to take this."

"Uh, okay. Sure. I'll…I'll call you."

The line was disconnected.

Kai squeezed her eyes shut for a moment, put down the phone and walked away.

"Say what?" Tiffany said.

Kai sighed heavily into the phone. "Yeah, some woman. I guess she's still over there now."

"Clearly if he called to cancel. Wow, sis. I'm really sorry. I don't even know what to say other than it's best to find out now rather than later."

"I guess." She tucked her feet beneath her on the couch.

"Listen, don't stress yourself. When I get back from this business trip, we'll have a girls' weekend, maybe go into Manhattan—do the spa thing, see a Broadway show, dinner and stay over. Make a weekend of it."

Kai half smiled. "Sure. When are you leaving?"

"Tomorrow morning. I'm meeting with some of the suppliers. They have a shipment from Nigeria of hand-woven fabrics. Business has been brisk at the boutique and I want to see firsthand what will be available for the upcoming season so that I can put my orders in now."

"Tourist season is right around the corner."

"I know. That's why I want to be ready. Anyway, girl, let me get myself together, throw some things in a suit-case and make some calls."

"Sure. Safe travels."

"And, Kai…"

"Yeah?"

"It's all going to be fine. You'll see."

"Thanks."

"One good thing…"

"What's that?"

"He shook those cobwebs loose!"

Kai burst out laughing. "Shut up and goodbye!" She put the phone down while slowly shaking her head. She exhaled. *That he did.* But now there was some other woman. Would Anthony make her feel the same way he'd made Kai feel? Would he do the same things? Would she cry out his name?

She jumped up from the couch and ran her hand

across her face as if to wipe away the burning images of Anthony making love to that woman. The hell with him. She wasn't going to make herself crazy. Whatever she imagined they'd had between them was just that— all in her imagination. Because obviously Anthony had a different reality.

Chapter 16

"Crystal? At your place? Damn, man. How did that happen?" Lincoln asked.

"You know Crystal. She could do anything at any moment as long as it served her purposes." Anthony looked up at the sky, watching the sun slowly begin to set beyond the umbrella of trees. He slowly paced across the back deck of the house. He could hear the laughter of Jessie and Crystal float to him from inside the house. "Anyway, man, she plans to stay a few days."

"This gets worse by the minute."

"I was supposed to have Kai over for dinner tonight but had to cancel. She all but hung up on me. I wanted to explain, but she didn't give me a chance."

"It really does get worse. Hey, you have to talk to Kai at some point and let her know what the deal is."

"I know. And I have to find someplace for Crystal to stay. She can stay here tonight because it would break

Jessie's heart if she didn't. But tomorrow she's out of here. Any room at the inn?" he asked half jokingly.

"We are booked solid. I can call around for you and see what's available in town."

"Cool. I'd appreciate that. Consider it a 911 emergency."

"I got you. As soon as I hear something I'll give you a holler."

"Thanks, man."

"No problem. Try to keep your cool over there."

"It ain't easy."

Lincoln chuckled lightly. "Later, man."

"Later."

Steeling himself, Anthony opened the back door and returned inside.

Crystal and Kai were snuggled together on the couch watching cartoons. Anyone walking in on this heartwarming picture of maternal bonding would think that Crystal was the perfect mother. He knew that Crystal truly loved Jessie, but she loved herself more. That was the problem—nothing or no one ever came before Crystal's needs or wants. It was the downfall of their marriage. He understood that much of Crystal's issues of self-worth were a result of the life she'd lived before they'd met. But he couldn't fix the past and he couldn't mend her.

"Jessie was telling me some wonderful things about this Dr. Kai. I'm looking forward to meeting her tonight and thanking her for taking such good care of Jessie."

"Unfortunately, she had to cancel." He crossed through the open-layout living room into the kitchen.

"Oh, really? That's too bad. Maybe another time, then."

"Yeah, maybe," he murmured as he took the steaks that he'd preseasoned out of the refrigerator.

Crystal hopped up from the couch and came into the kitchen. "Let me help. Where do you keep your pans?"

Anthony gave her a sidelong look. "Cabinet on the bottom, under the counter."

"What do you want to fix with the steaks—baked potatoes?"

"Sure."

Crystal began moving around and working in the kitchen as if she'd taken lessons from Martha Stewart. Within minutes she'd put the steaks in the oven, washed the potatoes and wrapped them in foil and was stir-frying vegetables in the wok.

Anthony felt as if he was in some kind of bizarre *Twilight Zone* episode. He was waiting for the real Crystal to turn up at his doorstep and want to know what was going on.

Dinner was one for the record books. Crystal talked and laughed and kept them engaged with her stories of the patrons that came to the Museum of Natural History where she worked part-time. Several times Anthony had to blink away the veil that had descended over his eyes and had him seeing them as a family—the three of them. His gut knew that this was nothing but show for Crystal. It would take more than a shortened vacation to turn her from the self-absorbed woman that she was into the one she was posing to be.

After dinner, Anthony cleaned up the kitchen while Crystal gave Jessie her bath and got her ready for bed. All he could think about was explaining all of this craziness to Kai and hoping that she would understand. He wasn't even sure why it mattered to him so much. He would be leaving in a week. He lived in Manhattan. He was a shoo-in for district attorney and his trips to Sag Harbor would be brief and intermittent. That was not the foundation for a relationship and he really couldn't expect Kai to settle for something like that. It would be selfish of him to even consider it.

"Hey, Jessie's fast asleep," Crystal said, walking up behind him. "Need some help?"

"No. I'm fine, thanks."

"You barely ate. Are you feeling okay?"

"Fine."

"Got anything stronger than iced tea around here?" She leaned her hip against the counter.

"There's wine over in the wine cooler." He turned on the dishwasher.

She opened the door to the mini fridge and took out a bottle of pinot grigio and held it up for his approval.

He shrugged. She went to the overhead cabinets and took out two wine goblets and poured for them then took the glasses into the living room and set them on the coffee table. With a bit of trepidation, Anthony joined her but made a point of taking a seat opposite her in the armchair.

Crystal reached for her glass and Anthony did as well.

"To the good times," Crystal said before taking a sip.

Anthony didn't respond. He took a swallow of his wine and put the glass down. "You can sleep in my room. I'll take the couch. There's no way you and Jessie can sleep in that twin bed."

"I couldn't do that to you. If it gets too uncomfortable I can take the couch."

"What's this really all about, Crystal?"

She looked at him with wide-eyed innocence. "What do you mean?"

"I mean *this,*" he said and waved his hand around. "This show, this concern, this tone, this being decent."

She leaned forward. "It's not a show. Why can't you believe that? I've had time to really think, Tony. I've changed. I'm changing…for you…for us. If you would only give it a try."

He stared at her for a moment then looked away. "There are extra towels in the linen closet next to the bathroom." He stood, took his glass of wine and walked out back.

Kai had just returned from a run with Jasper. The cool evening air had done her good and the run had her blood warm and circulating again. She was actually feeling better than she had earlier, and was thankful that she went when she did. The sky had clouded over and the scent of rain hung in the air.

She quickly washed her hands and took a bottle of water from the fridge, downing half of it in four long gulps. She filled Jasper's water bowl with the remainder, then headed off to take a long, hot shower.

Wrapped in her terry robe and feeling totally refreshed after her shower, she decided to order dinner from the Italian restaurant that she and Tiffany liked so much and see what movie she could find on cable.

The restaurant promised delivery within an hour and she was thrilled to find *The Best Man* and *The Best Man Holiday* coming on back to back. She grabbed her throw from the back of the couch, covered up and settled in.

The Best Man movie was up to the part when Taye Diggs comes to the studio and sees Nia Long for the first time in a while when Kai heard the delivery car pull up. She stuck her feet in her slippers, took her wallet from her purse and went to the door just as the bell rang.

She pulled the door open. The rain had already begun. "Wow, that was really quick." She took the bag from the deliveryman, who ducked under the overhang of her doorway while she signed the credit card receipt. She took a ten-dollar bill from her wallet and handed it over. "Thanks for coming out in this weather."

"No problem. Thank you. Good night." He pulled the hood of his jacket up over his head and dashed back to his car.

"Night." She pushed the door closed and took the bag into the kitchen. She got a plate and spooned half of the veal cutlet parmesan onto the plate, sealed the container with the rest of it and added a good helping of the Caesar salad before returning to the movie.

Before she could take her first bite, the doorbell rang again. She looked on the table and realized that she had the restaurant's copy of the credit card receipt. She grabbed it up and went to the door.

She pulled the door open. "Sorry…"

"I know I should have called first, but I didn't think you would pick up." Anthony wiped the rain out of his face.

Her stomach twirled. She leaned her weight on her left leg and casually stared at him. "Why would you think that?" She folded her arms and watched the rain wash over him.

He hunched his shoulders to keep the rain from running down his back. Kai enjoyed watching his discomfort.

"Because of the last-minute cancellation. I wanted to explain, but you didn't give me a chance."

The sound of distant thunder rumbled in the distance.

Kai pushed out a breath. "What is there to explain? Something apparently came up."

"More of a *someone* rather than a *something*. My ex-wife Crystal showed up—unannounced *and* uninvited," he quickly added.

So that was who she saw. "Really."

"Yes."

A streak of lightning flashed, casting him in silhouette against the night. A perfect frame for a photo.

She cleared her throat. "I ordered dinner. It's getting cold."

He lowered his gaze and nodded. "I'll let you get back to it."

"There's plenty…if you want to come in."

He glanced up at the pouring rain, then smiled down at her. "Sure."

Chapter 17

Anthony hung up his wet jacket and took off his shoes.
Kai got him a towel to dry off, then went to fix his plate.
She reheated both hers and his and they settled down in
the living room. The movie was almost over.

For a time they ate in silence, both working hard at
pretending to watch the movie. When the credits rolled
they both spoke at once.

"You first," Anthony conceded.

"I'm glad you told me about…your ex."

He angled his body toward her. "I don't have anything to hide."

"I was there yesterday."

"There?"

"I was at your house yesterday. I wanted to surprise
you with a housewarming gift."

"I…don't understand."

She explained to him what she'd come to his house
to do and then what she saw.

Anthony squeezed his eyes and slowly shook his head, imagining what must have run through Kai's head. He reached out to her. "I am so sorry." He took her hand and brought it to his lips. "Trust me, it's nothing like that at all."

"Maybe you need to tell me what it is like."

He heaved a deep sigh and pressed back against the cushion of the couch. "I met Crystal about ten years ago..."

Anthony didn't leave anything out when he told Kai about his marriage, what it was and what it had become. He talked about how they'd grown apart and why. He even told her that there had been times when he doubted the paternity of his daughter. "Even if I wasn't Jessie's natural father, I wouldn't care. I love that little girl from the pit of my soul."

"I know you do," she said gently. "I can tell just by the way you look at her."

"I tried to make it work. I know that a lot of Crystal's self-centeredness all stems from how she was raised— or wasn't."

"What do you mean?"

"Crystal has no idea who or where her natural mother or her father is. She was given up at birth. Teen parents, she was told. She was adopted by a young, wealthy white couple when she was six months old. They gave her everything—the best food, clothes, toys, schools, trips, and then the couple had a child of their own when Crystal was nine. Nothing was ever the same after that. Her adopted parents doted on their new daughter, and Crystal... Anyway she started acting out, got kicked out of school, got involved in stealing and then her parents did the unthinkable. When Crystal was fourteen, they put her in foster care."

"Oh, my goodness. How awful."

"Yeah," he said, looking off into the distance. "It is." He exhaled slowly. "I guess there was a part of me that thought I could fix her, right the wrongs of the past. I did everything I could. But the betrayals and the lying were more than I was willing to deal with. I had to realize that Crystal was not a case that I could solve. I had to let her go."

Kai studied her entwined fingers on her lap. "Do you still love her?"

Anthony was thoughtful for a moment. "I thought I did even after we broke up and the divorce was finalized. But it wasn't love and, God help me, it may have never been love—at least not the kind to build a life together on. I was on a rescue mission of the beautiful damsel in distress. It fed my ego—her need. But I slowly and eventually realized that's not my role. And it wasn't fair to me, to her and certainly not to Jessie. What I need is a partner, an equal. That's never what I had with Crystal."

Kai's gaze moved slowly over his face, taking in the look of regret, sincerity and hope that played in his eyes. She believed him. She did. But where did that leave the two of them?

"Thank you for telling me that."

"I want to be honest with you. I started to tell you the other night—when we were together." His brows drew together. "Listen, I have no idea how or if this can work between us. All I do know is that I want to give it a shot. It won't be easy. I want to try. I want to see you, spend time with you and let you get to know me. Then…we can see where it goes."

Kai ran her tongue across her bottom lip, then gently tugged it between her teeth.

"*If* you want to…" He reached out and covered her hands with his. "I want you to want to." He grinned.

Her eyes crinkled at the corners as a smile lifted her lips. "I think…I want to."

Anthony moved toward her. His fingers threaded through her hair and eased her toward him.

When his lips touched hers and that spark hit her in the center of her being, it was better than the first time. She gave in to the kiss, let him possess her mouth, taste her, tease her, and she gave him the same and more in return.

The rain pounded against the windows while the thunder rolled through the clouds. There was a loud boom followed by an incredible flash of light and then everything went dark.

They laughed against each other's mouths.

"The backup should kick on in a minute," Kai said as she placed tiny kisses along his jaw.

"How much can we get done in the dark?" he asked, his voice growing thick. He teased her earlobe.

She cupped his face in her hands. "I know my way around a hard body in the dark. I can do plenty."

He leaned her back on the couch. "Is that right?" He kissed her neck and felt her tremble. "And I have a little experience with hugging the curves." He peeled open her robe.

Kai hissed in air through her teeth. His mouth was hot on her bare flesh. He loosened the belt on her robe and pulled it fully open.

"God, you're beautiful," he murmured before lowering his head to feast on the delicacy of her exposed breasts. "I want to do everything to you at once," he ground out and took the hard bud of her nipple between his teeth.

Kai moaned and arched her back. She locked her fingers behind his head and drew him closer. The pleasure that he was putting on her body should be illegal. She wound her way beneath him until she could feel the hard thickness of him pressing between her thighs. He groaned when she rotated her pelvis and draped one of her legs across the back of his thighs.

"It's like that, huh?" He nibbled her bottom lip, licked the top one and hooked his arm beneath her knee and drew her leg up along the length of his back.

"Hmm," she hummed deep in her throat.

Anthony stroked the satin of her hip. He wanted to holler from the delight that touching her brought him. Kai was so much of what he longed for, that person to fill the hole in his soul, the woman that would make him want to come home at night. He was getting way ahead of himself. He couldn't help it. There was something about Kai Randall that made him want to think beyond tomorrow. But her eager body brought him right back to the here and now.

Like two horny teenagers, they made hard, crazy love right there on that couch with the rain slashing and the thunder and lightning beating up the heavens. Their sighs and moans and shouts of pleasure blended in with the cacophony of the night. And when Kai felt the telltale ripple that began at the bottom of her feet, shimmied up the back of her thighs, around to the pit of her stomach and flashed through her limbs, she thrust her hips up at Anthony and then did that thing that made him crazy with her inner walls and it was all over but the shouting.

Eventually they picked themselves up, filled two glasses of wine and wandered into Kai's bedroom.

Kai propped herself up on her elbow while her eyes moved slowly across Anthony's face, which seemed to glow with an inner light. "I'm glad you came and that we talked…"

"So am I." He ran a finger along her cheek. "I'm not sure how often I'm going to be able to get down here…"

She put a finger across his lips to silence him. "We'll figure something out."

"Would you ever consider coming back to New York?"

"Oh, no." She slowly shook her head. "I put that life behind me for good. I don't mind visiting, but I know I could never live there again." She saw the flicker of disappointment in his eyes and lowered her gaze.

He breathed heavily. "I can respect that." He kissed her lightly. "We'll figure it out."

Kai flopped back on the pillow and stared up at the ceiling. "Maybe you should call your house and make sure everything is all right."

He'd been so absorbed with Kai and reconnecting that he'd put thoughts of Crystal in the back of his head. "Trust me, if things weren't all right, she would have been calling my cell phone until it disintegrated. Jessie was fast asleep when I left." Yet for a brief instant a pang of guilt jabbed him in the gut. What if something had gone wrong? No. He had a generator at the house. They had power. It was only a storm. They were fine.

"Sounds like the storm finally stopped," Kai said against his chest.

Anthony caressed her back. "Hmm."

"Can you stay?" she tentatively asked. "Or do you need to get home? I mean, if you do I totally understand."

He propped himself up and looked down into her face. "Do you want me to stay?"

She swallowed. "Honestly, yes, I do. But that would

be selfish. I'd only be thinking of me and what I want. You're a father. You have a houseguest—whether or not she was invited…" The rest went without saying. His gaze warmed her to her core.

"You really are amazing," he said in awe before slowly kissing her with all of the wonder that danced inside of him. "As much as I don't want to admit it, you're right. But I do love being selfish, don't you?" he said before spreading her thighs and loving her one more time.

Chapter 18

The light was on in the living room when Anthony pulled up into the driveway. It was after three in the morning. Inwardly he groaned but promised himself that he would not allow Crystal to steal his joy. He parked and entered the house. Crystal was curled up on the couch beneath a blanket.

For a moment Anthony was tossed back in time to the rare occasion when Crystal would try to wait up for him after he'd had a long day at the office. He blinked back the memories and walked in, closing the door quietly behind him.

"I'm up. No need to tiptoe." Crystal slowly pushed herself into a sitting position. She stretched and yawned. "What time is it?" she asked as if she didn't already know.

"A little after three."

He hung up his jacket in the hall closet.

"Rain finally stopped. The lights went out for a bit but came right back on."

"Generator," he said noncommittally.

"I was worried."

He glanced in her direction. "That's a new emotion for you."

Her expression hardened for a split second. "When you said you were going out…and then the storm came… I didn't know what to think."

"Jessie okay?" he asked, sidestepping her feigned concern.

"Never woke up. Even with all the racket from the storm."

Anthony half grinned. "I'm turning in. Good night." He walked toward his room.

"Good night," she called out sweetly.

Kai languidly stretched her limbs and burrowed deeper under her covers. The storm was long gone and had left nothing but clear skies and bright sunshine in its wake. She pulled the pillow that Anthony had slept on closer to her so that she could inhale his scent. She smiled. Even though she logically knew that getting in too deep with Anthony Weston could never work, her heart and soul said something different.

She'd had her share of short-term relationships, mostly with overstressed, overachieving doctors, which had all been disasters waiting to happen. No matter how great the sex was or how good the mental connection, the chaotic lives that they led left very little time for something lasting. Nothing could develop when all they could offer was a couple of hours per month, if that.

In her last year at Presbyterian, she'd sworn off men and dating, and focused on her career and on healing the lives of others. Relationships were pointless distractions. When she moved to Sag Harbor, all she wanted was solitude and quiet, time to rebuild her inner self. She'd been on a few dates, but nothing much ever came of them; the closest was Andrew.

She hugged the pillow tighter. Now here she was again, up to her neck with budding feelings for the exact type of man she'd determined to stay away from—the driven, career-dominated man. Maybe the very qualities that she feared were the ones that attracted her. Not to mention that this utterly desirable man came with a child and an unpredictable ex-wife. If she were to add up the list of pros and cons, the list was definitely tilting against pursuing this thing between them.

She sighed, tossed the pillow aside and got up. As much as she would have liked to lounge in bed all day pondering the foibles of her love life, she had work to do.

"Please don't tell me what I think you're going to tell me," Anthony said into the phone.

"Sorry, bro. Every place that I checked is booked up through the weekend. How long is she planning to stay?"

Anthony ran a hand across his close-cut hair. "Anytime past right now is too long. Hey, I appreciate the help, Linc. I'll figure something out."

"Holler if you need me."

"Will do. Thanks." He slid his phone into his pocket, just as Crystal and Jessie came into the kitchen.

"I thought we could go into town for lunch and do some sightseeing."

"Please, Daddy."

He smiled at his daughter. He knew what Crystal was trying to do and he wasn't falling for it. "Sure, you and Mommy go into town. Daddy has some work to do. I'll be here when you get back." He glanced up at Crystal over Jessie's head.

"Maybe we'll stop by and say hello to Desiree and Lincoln while we're out."

"Yippee!" Jessie jumped up and down and then ran toward the door.

"We're not going to do this Kumbaya thing that you're trying, Crystal. It's not happening. So spend some time with Jessie and then you need to make plans to go back to New York."

She drew herself up. Her light brown eyes darkened as she lasered in on him. "All I'm trying to do is let you see how it could be between us again. I've changed."

"In less than two weeks you've changed? Tell it to someone who doesn't know you, Crystal."

Her thin nostrils flared. She spun away. "Get your jacket, Jessie. Let's go."

The instant that Crystal crossed the threshold to the outside, the tension dissipated in the house like morning dew. Anthony took a deep breath of relief. If he had to escort Crystal out of town himself, he would. He went to his small kiosk of an office and checked emails and responded to several pressing issues. Although he was off the clock for two weeks, the work never stopped. He downloaded his electronic subscription of the *New York Times,* turned to the political section and brought himself up to date on the New York gubernatorial race. Blumenthal was doing well in the opinion polls, but he was going up against an incumbent with a long family tree in the city. It was anybody's race as trends changed like the weather.

Anthony typed up some notes and emailed them to his secretary for future reference, sent an email to his boss and then signed off. He checked his watch. What he thought would only take an hour had turned into nearly three.

He stretched his tight limbs and stood. He thought Crystal would have gotten bored and come back by now. The last thing he wanted to do with his free mental time was fill it with thoughts of Crystal. Wherever she was, he was certain she was just fine.

He pulled his phone out of his pocket and sent a text message to Kai. Thinking of you. Will call later.

Kai heard the distinct beep of her phone for incoming messages. She put down the patient file that she was updating and picked up her phone. Her stomach did that little flip thing when she read the message from Anthony. Looking forward. She hit Send in concert with the ringing of her office doorbell.

Frowning, she put her phone down and went to the door. She didn't have any more appointments for the day and she really hoped that whatever the ailment was, it would be minor. She put a smile on and opened the door.

"Dr. Kai!" Jessie squealed.

Kai did a double take. "Jessie…what are you doing here?" She looked around for Anthony but instead saw Crystal walking from her car. Her heart banged. She was even more stunning close-up.

"You must be the magical, Dr. Kai," Crystal said and extended her manicured hand.

"Hello. Yes. Dr. Kai Randall."

"I'm Jessie's mother. Crystal Weston." She made a point of emphasizing *Weston*.

"Nice to meet you. How can I help you?"

"May we come in?"

"Oh, of course. Please." She stepped aside to let them pass.

"Where's Jasper, Dr. Kai?"

"Playing in the yard in back."

"Can I see him? Can I?" She looked from one adult face to the other.

"If it's okay with your mother."

"I think that would be fine. It will give Dr. Kai and I a chance to talk."

Kai took Jessie's hand and let her out the back door. She returned to where Crystal regally stood.

"So, how can I help you?"

Crystal looked around taking in the space. "My daughter and my husband seem to have wonderful things to say about you. Since I was here in town, staying with Anthony, I thought it only right that I meet you and thank you personally for what you did for Jessie."

"Thank you, but it wasn't necessary."

Crystal's gaze roamed along Kai's body as if she wanted to pick it apart. "I'm sure it wasn't, but I felt it was the right thing to do. And since we're on the subject of doing the right thing…"

Kai internally braced herself for the "ex-wife scorned" speech.

"Anthony will always be a part of my life. Let's be clear about that. I'm Jessie's mother. Anthony and I will always have a connection, a connection that we are working on rekindling. So you may think you have something brewing with my husband, but let me just say this, Dr. Randall, this country life that you live…Anthony would never survive it. He has a full life in New York, a real life…where Jessie and I live. He is slated to be the next district attorney for the state of New York. Do you really think he will have time for a small-town doctor?"

"Are you done?"

Crystal's brow rose.

"You don't know anything about me. I live my life as

I see fit. And if that fit includes your *ex*-husband then so be it. I'm not desperate for a relationship, *Crystal*...but apparently you are, or you wouldn't be standing in my office posturing about what you *hope* to have once again with Anthony. If he wants you, more power to him, but in the meantime, I have work do to." She smiled sweetly, but her eyes held a coldness.

"Nice to meet you, Dr. Randall." Crystal walked toward the back door, calling out for Jessie. Moments later Kai heard the car pull away.

Kai released the breath she was holding. Her fingers trembled from the outrage that she'd held inside. She stomped back and forth across her office floor. The things that Crystal said reverberated in her head. *How dare she?* As much as Kai didn't want to admit it, much of what Crystal said was true. Anthony did have a life that simply did not mesh with the one she had in Sag Harbor. Was she willing to settle for yet another part-time relationship? Was that what she wanted? Was it what she deserved?

She wrapped her arms around her body. She didn't want to be alone. She really didn't. She would love to have someone in her life, someone to begin and end her day with.

Her cell phone chirped with an incoming call. She glanced at the lighted face. It was him. She pressed Ignore.

That someone could never be Anthony Weston.

Anthony was about to leave a message on Kai's voice mail when he heard the front door open. He disconnected the call, intending to call her back later. He walked to the front room as Jessie burst through door.

"Whoa, little lady, slow down." He scooped her up. "Have a good time?"

"Yes." She rested her head on his shoulder and yawned.

"Two seconds ago you were full of energy. Now you want to go to sleep?"

"She's really exhausted," Crystal said, coming up behind her to place a hand on Jessie's back. "We had a full day. She should probably take a nap before dinner."

"I'll put her down." He walked with Jessie to her bedroom and got her settled down for a nap.

When he came back up front, Crystal was in the kitchen puttering around as if she belonged there. "What are you doing?"

She turned toward him and smiled. "I thought I'd put something together for dinner."

Who was this woman and what had she done with the real Crystal?

"Have you made other arrangements for a place to stay?"

She turned to him with her hand on her hip. "You'll be happy to know that I'm leaving in the morning. I thought I would take Jessie back with me."

"She was supposed to stay with me these two weeks."

"I didn't think you would mind."

His jaw tightened. "Did you say anything to her about going home?"

"She's all for it. She misses her friends." She took out a package of ground turkey from the fridge. "Spaghetti okay?"

"Fine, Crystal." He turned and walked away.

When he returned to his room, he shut the door behind him. At least she was leaving. Although he'd hoped to spend some more time with his daughter, he wasn't in

YOUR PARTICIPATION IS REQUESTED!

Dear Reader,

Since you are a lover of our books – we would like to get to know you!

Inside you will find a short Reader's Survey. Sharing your answers with us will help our editorial staff understand who you are and what activities you enjoy.

To thank you for your participation, we would like to send you 2 books and 2 gifts – **ABSOLUTELY FREE!**

Enjoy your gifts with our appreciation,

Pam Powers

SEE INSIDE FOR READER'S SURVEY

For Your Reading Pleasure...

We'll send you 2 books and 2 gifts
ABSOLUTELY FREE
just for completing our Reader's Survey!

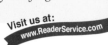

YOUR READER'S SURVEY
"THANK YOU" FREE GIFTS INCLUDE:

▶ **2 FREE books**

▶ **2 lovely surprise gifts**

PLEASE FILL IN THE CIRCLES COMPLETELY TO RESPOND

1) What type of fiction books do you enjoy reading? (Check all that apply)
- ○ Suspense/Thrillers
- ○ Action/Adventure
- ○ Modern-day Romances
- ○ Historical Romance
- ○ Humour
- ○ Paranormal Romance

2) What attracted you most to the last fiction book you purchased on impulse?
- ○ The Title
- ○ The Cover
- ○ The Author
- ○ The Story

3) What is usually the greatest influencer when you <u>plan</u> to buy a book?
- ○ Advertising
- ○ Referral
- ○ Book Review

4) How often do you access the internet?
- ○ Daily
- ○ Weekly
- ○ Monthly
- ○ Rarely or never

5) How many NEW paperback fiction novels have you purchased in the past 3 months?
- ○ 0 - 2
- ○ 3 - 6
- ○ 7 or more

YES! I have completed the Reader's Survey. Please send me the 2 FREE books and 2 FREE gifts (gifts are worth about $10) for which I qualify. I understand that I am under no obligation to purchase any books, as explained on the back of this card.

168/368 XDL GGFG

FIRST NAME	LAST NAME

ADDRESS

APT.#	CITY

STATE/PROV.	ZIP/POSTAL CODE

EMAIL

the frame of mind to debate with Crystal about it. The upside to it all was that Crystal would be gone. He was willing to make the sacrifice.

He took out his phone and called Kai again. Again it went to voice mail. This time he left a message asking her to give him a call when she had a minute.

Chapter 19

Jessie ate her dinner in the living room while she watched one of her favorite cartoons. Anthony and Crystal sat opposite each other at the kitchen counter. He picked at his food wondering why he still had not heard from Kai.

"Not hungry?" Crystal asked, breaking into his thoughts. She refilled his glass of wine.

"Things on my mind." He took a swallow from his glass even as he knew he should eat something to take the edge off the wine.

"I know I'm not the best cook in the world, but you always liked my spaghetti." She smiled sweetly. "Work?"

"Huh?"

"Thinking about work?"

"Yeah." He finished off his wine and she topped him off again.

"How are things going with the campaign? Do you think Blumenthal will win?"

"He has a good shot."

"If he wins, you'd get your dream job. That's a pretty big deal."

"Hmm."

"I know how hard you've worked over the years. You deserve to be D.A."

He glanced across at her. "According to *you,* my job and my ambition was the cause of our marriage falling apart."

She lowered her gaze. "That was the old me, Tony. The selfish me."

"Oh, I forgot you changed."

"Why do you have to be this way?"

"What way?"

"This way—cold and distant."

He pushed back from the counter, taking his drink with him.

She got up and followed him into the living room. "I don't want us to keep fighting," she said. "I know that you don't believe anything that I've told you. All I'm asking is that you at least give me a chance to prove that you're wrong about me."

He turned toward her. "And give me one good reason why I should do that."

She lifted her chin. "I'll give you two." She put her hand on his arm. "Because I still love you. And I want you to love me back the way you once did."

He studied her for a moment, trying to see beyond this fairy-tale facade that she'd constructed. His head swam slightly from the wine and lack of food. He almost believed her. Almost.

"It's over, Crystal. Accept it and move on. We can be civil, but we'll never be an *us* again." He walked away.

* * *

Anthony stretched out across his bed. He could hear the television and Jessie's giggles. Crystal was in the next room. For a moment he imagined what it could have been like without the craziness and the lies and the betrayals. Not for all the money in the world would he put himself through that again. He wasn't sure how or if things would ever work out between him and Kai, but he wanted to try.

Kai was everything that he wanted and needed in his life. It was crazy that in such a short space of time he could come to that conclusion. But if nothing else, he was a man of action. He went after what he wanted with a relentlessness that made him successful in his career. Now it was time to turn those same qualities to his personal life. It wouldn't be easy. He understood that, but if Kai was willing even a little bit to give it a shot, so was he.

He checked his cell phone thinking that he may have missed a call or a text from Kai. Nothing. He stared up at the ceiling and his eyes drifted closed.

Crystal got Jessie settled down for bed, read her a story, then took a long, hot bath. She languidly smoothed her skin with her favorite body lotion and slipped into a nightie that she'd purchased for a very special occasion. She turned out the light in the bathroom and walked down the hall toward Anthony's bedroom.

"She came to your house?" Tiffany asked incredulously.

"Yep. Live and in living color." Kai pointed the remote at the television and mindlessly surfed the stations with the phone propped between her ear and her shoulder.

"Damn, that's bold. So…what is she like?"

Kai took a breath. "Pretty. Tall. Classy dresser."

"Yeah, I figured as much, but what is she *like?*"

"It's hard to say exactly. She comes across as being sincere but there's something just beneath the surface, like she's playing with you. I got the sense that she would do whatever she needed to get what she wanted. And she made it very clear that she has every intention of getting her husband back."

"Hmm. And what do you plan to do about that?"

"I don't plan to do anything. It's more trouble than it's worth."

"Kai. I know you. When have you ever stepped away from a challenge? She all but drew a line in the sand and dared you to cross it."

"What are you saying?"

"I'm saying that I know you like this guy. The first man you've shown the slightest interest in since who knows when. Listen, you're the same woman who managed an entire emergency department in one of the busiest hospitals in the country. You've worked in decimated areas, you've pulled bodies out of rivers, saved lives and soothed grieving relatives. You've seen things and dealt with stuff most of us only imagine in our nightmares. You have heart, but you're tough and you've never let anyone or anything stand in your way. That's the Kai Randall that I know." She paused. "You were willing to give him a shot. What changed?"

"Wait. Are you the same person who told me how crazy it was to get involved with him?"

"No, that was your other friend," she joked. "But seriously. If you want him, go for it. We only live once. Give it a chance. See how it goes. He's told you in no uncertain terms that it's over between them. Do you believe him?"

Kai hesitated. Images of Anthony touching her, kiss-

ing her, making love to her, confessing to her floated
through her head. She saw his face, his eyes, his smile.
She tasted him on her lips. "Yes. I believe him."

"Then you have your answer."

"Yes, I guess I do," she admitted.

Crystal stood in the doorway of Anthony's bedroom.
She'd checked on Jessie to make sure that she was sound
asleep. She stepped quietly inside and closed the door
behind her. She listened to his steady breathing. She
slipped out of her light robe and dropped it on the floor.
Her one-piece negligee was next. She placed it at the
foot of his bed and silently slipped between the sheets.
Her heart raced. Anthony stirred, murmured in his sleep
but didn't wake. She moved closer to him then remained
perfectly still. She waited long enough for her scent to
fill the room and his sheets. She got up and slipped out
as quietly as she'd come in.

Anthony awoke the next morning to a silent house.
His head pounded. He blinked against the sunlight pouring in through the slats in the blinds and listened for
movement. The body oil that Crystal always used drifted
to him. Frowning, he pulled himself out of bed and saw
the black negligee on the foot of his bed. Confused, he
picked it up, then tossed it back down as if it had caught
fire. What the hell was going on? He went to Jessie's
room. Her room was empty.

He walked out front. Crystal was nowhere to be seen.
He looked around and saw a note propped up on the hall
table. He snatched it up.

Tony,
I didn't want to wake you. And I didn't want us to
have to talk about what happened between us last

*night. We're both adults. We have a history. I'm
okay. Once Jessie and I get back and settled, I'll
have her call you. For now, I'd rather if you and
I didn't talk for a while.
Always, Crystal*

He read the note again to make sure he'd seen it cor-
rectly. What in the heck was she talking about? She
didn't want to talk about what happened between them?
His thoughts jumped back to the nightgown on the bed.
He shook his head and tried to get focused.

Impossible. No way in hell did…

He stormed back to his bedroom and tore the cover-
ings off his bed. Her scent wafted up to him. She'd been
in his bed, apparently naked. For how long? He racked
his brain trying to bring an image of him in bed with
Crystal. He couldn't. But obviously she'd been there.
What the hell had she done?

Kai stared at her phone. More than once she'd started
to call Anthony but changed her mind. Since his last
message the day before he hadn't called again. Maybe he
was busy with Crystal and Jessie. Her stomach clenched
at the thought.

Putting her apprehension aside, she called his phone.
"Kai…"

The sound of his voice uttering her name washed
away all of her doubts. "Hi. I'm sorry I didn't get to call
back before now."

"No problem. How are you?"

She hesitated for a moment. There was something in
his voice. "I'm good." She leaned against the wall. "I
was thinking if you weren't busy maybe we could take
Jessie down to the pier for a boat ride."

"Jessie's not here. Her mother took her back to New York this morning."

"Is everything all right? You sound...tense."

"Just some things I need to straighten out. Can I call you a bit later?"

"Sure."

"Thanks. Hey..."

"Yes?"

"Would it be all right if I stopped by rather than call? I mean, I can call when I'm on my way."

"Sure. I'll be here."

"Thanks. I'll see you soon."

The call disconnected.

Kai held the phone. Clearly something was wrong. What made Crystal up and leave? It didn't sound as if Anthony was expecting it and she wondered if it had anything to do with Crystal's impromptu visit to her house. She released a long breath. Seemed like she and Anthony had a lot to talk about.

Chapter 20

Anthony pulled his car into the parking lot of The Port. Guests milled about in the lounge. He went to the reception counter and asked for Lincoln. The receptionist placed a call.

"He's in his office, Mr. Weston. He said come on back."

"Thanks."

Anthony pushed through the swinging glass door and walked down the short corridor to the offices in back. Lincoln's door was open.

"Hey, man, come on in." Lincoln closed a file he was reviewing. "This is a surprise. What's up?"

"I need to talk to you. Get some perspective on something."

"Sure."

Anthony flopped down in an available seat and wiped his face with his hand.

Lincoln sat on the edge of his desk. "What's going on?"

"She's crazy, man, or I am."

"I can only guess that you're talking about Crystal."

"Yeah," he ground out. He shook his head and jumped up from his seat and began to pace.

"What happened?"

Anthony slung his hands in his pockets, then turned to Lincoln. "She was in my bed last night."

"Whoa…say what?"

Anthony heaved a breath and held up his hand. "It's not like that. At least, I don't think it is."

"What? Man, you're not making sense. Start from the beginning."

Anthony slowed his pacing. "She came back from taking Jessie out for the day…"

By the time he was finished with his story, Lincoln was as undone as Anthony.

"Man…" Lincoln's lowered head shook slowly. He looked up at Anthony. "Sounds like she's trying to set you up or something. You're sure nothing went down between you?"

"Hell no! I was a little buzzed, but I wasn't out of it."

"Seems like you were out of it enough that Crystal slipped into your bed and left some evidence behind."

Anthony shot him a look. "Nothing happened."

"All right, all right. I believe you, but it doesn't make sense. And then the note. What's that about?"

"I don't know. I'm going to go back to New York. I've been calling Crystal and only getting voice mail."

Lincoln nodded. "What about you and Kai?"

"I'm going to go see her when I leave here. Tell her what's going on."

"Is it that serious with you two?"

Anthony glanced away. "It could be. I hope that it can be." He paused. "I need to get this mess straight with Crystal."

Lincoln walked over and clapped him on the shoulder. "You'll work it out. Anything you need me to do?"

"Naw. Thanks for listening."

"Anytime."

"Man, I really thought all the drama with Crystal was behind me. Kai is the first woman in forever that has made me feel this way, like I want something more than what I've had. You know?"

"Yeah. It's like that when you meet the right one. Like me and Desi."

Anthony nodded in agreement. "I'm gonna get going."

"Keep me posted on what's happening when you get back to New York."

"Yeah, thanks, man."

They shared the brother hug and Anthony headed back to his car. Once inside he called Kai to let her know he was on his way.

As soon as Kai saw Anthony's face, her suspicion that something was wrong escalated. And she had a strong feeling that whatever it was had to do with Crystal.

"Hey, come on in."

He gave her a light kiss on the cheek and came inside where Jasper enthusiastically greeted him. He ruffled the dog's head and walked into the kitchen. Kai came in behind him.

"Can I get you anything?"

"No. Thanks." He slid onto a stool at the kitchen island. Kai sat opposite him. Anthony remained pensive for a few moments trying to put the words together in his head so that they wouldn't come out sounding as crazy as it actually was. There was no way around it but to get it out.

"One thing that I want you to know is that I want to

be completely honest with you, about what I'm doing, my situation and my intentions."

"Okay," she said, drawing out the word and wondering where this conversation was heading. She linked her fingers together on top of the counter and waited.

He pursed his lips and took a short breath. "Sometime last night…while I was asleep Crystal came into my room…into my bed."

Her pulse beat rose.

"Nothing happened."

"Well, what *did* happen? It must be something or else there wouldn't be a reason to mention it."

He almost smiled at her tactic. It was one that he would have used in court to get to the truth from a witness.

"You're right." He placed his palms down on the countertop. "It's going to sound crazy…" He told her everything: from the dinner, the losing count of the glasses of wine, falling asleep and waking up to an empty house, Crystal's nightgown on his bed, finding her and Jessie gone and the ambiguous note that Crystal had left behind.

"Wow…I don't even know what to say. Why would she do something like that? It makes no sense."

He shook his head in frustration. "I don't know. What I do know is that Crystal never does anything for no reason."

"She obviously wants you to think that the two of you slept together."

Inwardly he flinched. It was the same idea that he had but had yet to voice. "We didn't."

"Then what did she mean by the note?"

"Knowing Crystal, it's all part of her grand plan."

"To get you back."

Anthony's gaze jumped to Kai's and he saw the shadow of disappointment around her eyes.

Kai shifted in her seat. "Since we're opening up, did she mention that she came here to see me?"

"What?"

She nodded her head.

"And? What happened, what did she want?" The heat of anger brewed in his gut and sparked from his eyes.

"She showed up with Jessie…"

The vein in his temple began to pulse. The very idea that she included Jessie in her nonsense was more than he was willing to swallow.

When Kai finished her story, Anthony was so furious he could barely get his thoughts together. He got up from his seat and rounded the counter to stand in front of Kai. He took her face tenderly in his hands.

"I'm so sorry, Kai." He gathered his thoughts. "I know you didn't sign up for this. We're just getting started and I wouldn't blame you if you didn't want to take it any further. No matter what you decide I want you to know without a doubt that there is nothing—nothing—between me and Crystal and can never be. Yes, I have to deal with her because of Jessie, but that's it. Nothing more." He heaved a breath. "And I want you to also know that none of this changes my intentions with you and I. But it's up to you. Whatever you decide…I'll abide by that."

"I don't know, Anthony. You're right. I didn't sign up for this. What we got started—" she sighed "—was so much more than I could have expected. I knew going in that it would be tough if we decided to pursue this. But until you can resolve your issues with Crystal…I don't see how we can make this work on any level."

His chest constricted. He lowered his gaze and nodded. "I understand." He looked into her eyes and his own hurt was reflected there. "Can I ask you something?"

"Sure."

"Don't give up on us just yet."

"I—"

"Not yet." He lowered his head and captured her mouth. The tip of his tongue grazed her lips. He eased back. "Not yet." He stepped away. "I'm going to give you some space. Some time. And if and when you're ready, you'll tell me." He stepped back. "I'm going back to New York in the morning."

Her stomach lurched.

"I need to see Crystal and get back to work. I want to know that it's all right for me to call you…let you know what happened."

Kai drew in a breath. As much as she would like to continue a relationship with Anthony, she didn't see any daylight in this growing storm. Not to mention the distance, their jobs, and of course Crystal.

"I think we need to go our separate ways, Anthony. You need to take care of your issues with Crystal. You have a new job to start thinking about and that alone is going to eat up your time. And that's okay. You worked for it. You deserve it and you don't need the distraction of me."

"What if I want to be distracted by you?" he asked, unwilling to simply give up.

"It's not going to work." Even as she said the words, she wished that they were not true. But they were. She got up and stepped away.

"So that's it?"

Her lips tightened. She nodded. "Yes," she whispered.

He drew himself up. If there was anything he knew about himself and what had added to his success as an attorney, it was his tenaciousness and determination to get what he wanted. He wanted Kai Randall. He'd find a way.

"All right." He moved away and walked to the door, and felt that he was leaving a part of himself behind.

Kai stood on the opposite side of the closed door and listened to his car drive away. She'd made the right decision. The whole thing was too complicated and too messy. It was not what she needed in her life no matter how much she might want Anthony.

It was true that he'd awakened something inside of her that had been dormant. From the moment she'd taken his picture all of those months ago, he'd somehow seeped into her soul and finally finding him, being with him, having him inside of her filled the space that had been empty. She knew all of this. It wasn't rational how she felt, but feelings were rarely rational. She was trained to think and operate logically, to examine the facts and act on those findings, and develop the right course of treatment for the ailment.

The right course of treatment for this ailment was to cut off the part that was not well so that it couldn't damage anything else. That was all she knew to do, and she would.

Chapter 21

By the time Anthony entered Manhattan, it was already twilight. The instant he hit the city, he immediately felt the beat and the electric energy of the city that never sleeps. It was the height of the rush hour, complete with stop-and-go traffic, the blare of car horns, lumbering delivery trucks, city buses, tour buses and speeding yellow cabs.

Sitting at a red light, he watched harried pedestrians race across intersections; others were glued to cell phones as they navigated the jam-packed streets heading to subways and after-work libations. He was home. He'd lived in Manhattan for more than a decade and for the first time he felt out of place, overwhelmed and drained by the very environment that had always energized and fueled him.

A car horn blared behind him, jerking him from his reverie. He blinked and the green light stared back at him. He pulled across the intersection, continued several blocks and made the turn onto E. 67th Street. He drove into his condo's underground garage and parked his car in the reserved space. He gathered his bags from the trunk and took the elevator up to the tenth floor.

Stepping in, his two-bedroom, two-bath condo was his oasis after a grueling day at the office or in the courtroom. Following his divorce, it had taken him more than a year to find a place to call home and set it up the way he wanted. He had his extensive jazz album collection, his wall of books that included everything from law books, biographies to thrillers. His chef's kitchen was the envy of all his friends and he prided himself on the few recipes that he'd mastered. One bedroom was set up for Jessie whenever she came to visit and the master suite, complete with a spa bathroom, had actually been photographed for *New York Style* magazine.

Once he crossed the threshold, he was always able to leave the issues of the day behind him. It was here that he could unwind, renew himself and close out the rest of the world. But today was the first time that he couldn't summon any of those feelings.

He tossed his bag in the closet with the intention of unpacking later. He walked to the front of the apartment and fixed himself a glass of light rum and coke hoping that it would ease the unusual tense and anxious feelings that had seeped into his veins the moment he'd entered the city and had refused to dissipate when he'd come home.

He flipped through the rack of albums and selected a Nancy Wilson classic, hoping that her throaty voice would bring him the calm that he sought. Instead, her voice reminded him of Kai. The inflections, the depth and rawness of it brought Kai into his space.

He lounged on the couch, took a swallow of his drink

and closed his eyes. There she was—her smile, her warmth, and her earthy beauty. He felt the soft curves of her body writhing beneath him, the sensual music of her voice when she cried out his name. A crater of emptiness opened up inside of him. He didn't want to be without her, so he had to find a way to make it work. He would, and the first thing was to deal with Crystal, once and for all. And then he would woo Kai and court her and make love to her until she had no other choice but to say yes.

"When are you getting back? I need a girls' night," Kai said as she checked the baked chicken in the oven.

"Just a couple of more days," Tiffany said. "I still can't believe that chick did that."

"Girl, only me. I swear off relationships and when I finally stick my toe in the water I get swept up by the undertow." She shut the oven door and hopped up on the stool at the counter.

"Are you sure you want to put a halt to everything, sis?"

Kai drew in a long breath. "What choice do I have?"

"Two, according to my count. You can try and see if you can make it work or turn the page on this romance novel."

Kai had to laugh. "It does ring like a romance novel, doesn't it. Boy meets girl, sparks fly, exes show up and the romance is shot to hell."

"Yeah, but you forgot the most important parts."

"What's that?"

"Makeup sex and the happily-ever-after."

"Hmm, I could always go for the makeup sex," she said, giggling wickedly. "But the happily-ever-after…I just don't see it."

"I hear ya. Anyway, as soon as I get back, we'll get together."

"Looking forward. But before you go, how is everything working out?"

"I'm pretty sure that I'll have an investor by the time my visit is over. And then I can expand the shop and open a second one."

"Oh, Tiff, I'm so happy for you!"

"It's pretty exciting. I'm having a business dinner tonight to talk about more details and run some numbers."

"Well, I have my fingers, toes and eyes crossed for you. I know you will nail this thing. We will definitely be celebrating when you get back."

"Yeah, girl, get the champagne ready."

"Will do. See you soon." Kai put the phone down and felt mildly better than she had since Anthony had left the day before.

He'd respected her word and had not tried to contact her. She should be glad about that, but there was that part of her that wished that he had ignored her request and called her anyway. She wanted to hear his voice.

She shook her head, scattering those thoughts. No point in dwelling over what was done. It was finished and she had to move on. It was for the best. Then why did she feel so lousy?

Anthony pushed through the door of the restaurant and looked around. After several attempts he'd finally gotten Crystal on the phone, and she had eventually agreed to meet him at the restaurant instead of her apartment, which was what she'd wanted. Anthony had no intention of being behind closed doors with his ex, not after what she'd already pulled. At least in a public place he hoped that she wouldn't cause a scene.

He went to the bar where they'd agreed to meet and ordered a plain coke with lemon. While he was nursing his drink, a young man sidled up next to him.

"Anthony Weston, right?"

Anthony turned in the man's direction. "Yes."

The man stuck out his hand. "Phillip Wilkins, *Wall Street Journal*."

"Hmm." He sipped his drink.

"Mind if we talk?"

"I'm meeting someone."

"This won't take long. I wanted to get your take on the gubernatorial election. Blumenthal has a good shot, which leaves his job open. You're the favorite. Do you plan to pursue it?" He took out a pad and pen.

"When Blumenthal wins, I have every intention of pursuing the position of D.A."

"Do you plan to follow in Blumenthal's footsteps with his advocating for stop-and-frisk?"

Anthony clenched his jaw. Everyone in the office knew that was a major bone of contention between him and his mentor. However, that was "family" business and he had no intention of airing his family's laundry.

"I'm not in the position and I won't comment on policies that I haven't made."

"Hey, baby." Crystal came up on his other side and placed a kiss on his lips the instant he turned in her direction.

He frowned but refused to get into it with Crystal in front of a reporter.

Crystal stuck her hand out. "Crystal Weston."

"Oh, Mrs. Weston. Phillip Wilkins, *Wall Street Journal*."

Her expression lit up. "Nice to meet you." She put her hand on Anthony's shoulder.

He wanted to shrug her off but thought better of it.

"So, Mrs. Weston, how do you feel about your former husband running for district attorney?"

"I think that whatever Anthony wants he gets. He's the best man for the job."

"How about a picture, Mr. Weston?"

"No, really."

"Go ahead, honey," Crystal said sweetly.

Anthony cut her a look.

"All right."

"Great." Wilkins pulled his digital camera out of his jacket pocket. He took a step back and got a quick shot of Anthony. "Now the two of you together."

Crystal got close to Anthony before he had a chance to say no and leaned her head on his shoulder. Wilkins took the picture. He stuck out his hand. "Thanks for your time, Mr. Weston, and best of luck." He shook Crystal's hand and walked away.

"That was nice," she said.

He could barely contain his anger. "Let's get a table." He got up and Crystal followed him.

A waitress escorted them to a table. Anthony could barely look at Crystal.

"It was nice being called Mrs. Weston," she said while she reached for her glass of water.

Anthony linked his fingers together on top of the table to keep from snatching her by the collar of her blouse and shaking some reality into her.

"Trust me, Crystal, the only reason I didn't correct him was because I didn't want all the follow-up questions that would have come along with it. It has nothing to do with even a hint of your being *Mrs. Weston*."

Her eyes tightened ever so slightly.

He leaned forward and lowered his voice to a hard

whisper. "I'm going to get right to it. I don't know what the hell you thought you were doing the night before you left. But nothing did or will happen between us. It's over. Done. Finished. And your little excursion to Dr. Randall's house! What did you hope to accomplish?"

Crystal blinked back tears.

"Don't even start with the waterworks."

She sniffed. "Why can't you see that I still love you?"

"What you did—you call that love?"

She glanced away. "I…didn't know what else to do." She faced him. "I know that I messed up." She reached for his hand and he snatched it away. "I just wanted you to pay attention to me…to see me." She pressed her hand to her chest. "Me." The muscles in her face twitched. "To let you see how much I want you back."

Anthony drew in a long breath and slowly exhaled. "Crystal, what we had…there is no going back. Too much happened. Too much ugliness and hurt." He paused. "Why? Why now?"

She looked away. "Why can't you just believe me?" she snapped and glared at him. The real Crystal finally appeared.

"Because I know you, remember. It's over, Crystal. All we have between us is Jessie. Whatever she needs I will always be there for her. But you and I…it's not happening."

"It's her, isn't it?" Her voice rose, attracting the attention of the couple at the next table. "She's the reason."

He pointed a finger at her. "Leave Kai out of it. I don't love you, Crystal. That's all there is to it. I'm sorry if you can't understand that, but it's the truth." He touched her hand. "It's time to move on," he said gently.

She bit on her bottom lip and slowly nodded. "I'm going home. The babysitter…" she murmured.

Anthony stood as she rose. She picked up her purse.

"I'm sorry. I won't bother you anymore." She turned, walked out. Anthony let out a breath of relief. Things had been tense for a moment, but it had gone better than he anticipated. He only hoped that Crystal meant what she said, but knowing her... He signaled for the waitress, and even though they never ordered dinner, he gave her a nice tip anyway.

What he wanted to do was call Kai and tell her that he'd straightened things out. Crystal wouldn't be bothering them anymore and they could pick up where they'd left off. But he'd wait and give her the space that he'd promised. However, he wouldn't wait very long.

Chapter 22

"Good to have you back, Mr. Weston," his secretary, Valerie, greeted. "How was your vacation?"

"Eventful." He smiled. "Give me a few minutes to get settled, then come in and bring me up to speed."

"Coffee?"

"Please." He strode into his office and walked toward the window that overlooked the city. That old thrill coursed through his veins. He smiled. The city was his to be had. All he needed to do was be patient.

"Tony!"

Harrison Blumenthal's booming voice jerked him from his survey of his kingdom to be. He turned. His smile was genuine.

"Harrison. How are you?"

"Better now that you're back—a couple of days early, but I'm not complaining." He stepped fully into the room. "Change of plans?"

"Something like that." He picked up a stack of mail that was on his desk and thumbed through it.

"You see this morning's *Wall Street Journal?* You're quite the star—you and Crystal."

He closed his eyes and groaned.

Harrison tossed the paper on Anthony's desk. "Not a bad picture and you were tactful in your answers as always."

Anthony reached for the paper and read the story above the fold. There was his picture with Crystal and they looked like the happy power couple. He gritted his teeth and tossed the paper aside and ran his hand across his head.

"You want to tell me what that's about?"

"The story is too long and complicated. But it's handled."

He held up his hand. "I'm not trying to get in your personal affairs. I'm only mentioning it because I know how you feel about Crystal. It was a shock."

Anthony slung his hands into the pockets of his midnight blue Marc Jacobs slacks. He turned back toward the window. "I met someone…"

"Well, it's about damned time."

Anthony turned back and they both shared a hearty laugh.

"I knew you would pull it off," Kai said, raising her glass in a toast to her friend.

Tiffany beamed with happiness. "Girl, my ship has finally sailed." She threw up her feet and took a sip of champagne.

"So now what?"

"Well, now I can begin construction on the expansion

and start looking for a second location, hire some more staff. But first I need to start getting bids on contractors."

"You're doing the damned thing, Tiff. I'm so proud of you."

Tiffany grinned. "Long time coming. Who knew that my love of one-of-a-kind jewelry, fine fabrics and art would turn into a serious moneymaker and fuel my passion for art and design at the same time?"

"You got that right. We're both blessed to be living our dream."

"I'll drink to that."

"So how was the big bad city?" Kai tucked her bare feet under her.

"Big and bad. Girl, I love me some New York. The men, the clubs, the restaurants, the theater. Did I mention men?" She laughed and slapped her thigh. "Hear from Anthony?"

The light around Kai seemed to fade. She shook her head no. "I didn't expect to. I asked him not to call."

"Then I guess I should tell you."

"Tell me what?"

She got up from the couch and walked over to where she'd left her purse by the door. She came back and pulled the newspaper out of her purse and handed it to Kai.

The image of Anthony cuddled next to Crystal burned her eyes. Her stomach shifted. She barely read the accompanying article before she handed it back to Tiffany and shrugged. "Guess he was lying about nothing going on."

Tiffany touched her shoulder. "I'm sorry."

"Yes," she said softly. "Me, too."

Chapter 23

Anthony had two major cases pending that consumed much of his time and energy. He spent his mornings briefing his legal team and his afternoons in court. In between he had meetings with Harrison on his campaign. There were appearances set up, interviews and countless meetings. By the time he got home at night, exhaustion didn't describe how he felt—that and missing Kai.

He'd been back in New York for nearly three weeks and he had yet to speak with Kai. He'd lost count of how many times he'd picked up the phone to call her and changed his mind. Every night he dreamed of her and the time they'd spent together. The thought of seeing her again was the incentive that kept him going and got him behind the wheel of his car en route to Sag Harbor.

The closer he grew to his destination, the faster his pulse raced. He had so much to tell her, so much that he needed to explain and have her understand. He was still unsure of how he could navigate the distance issue, but if he could convince her to at least give them a chance, he would move heaven and earth to make it happen.

By the time he arrived at his house, it was after eight on Friday night. He got settled quickly, checked the fridge and cabinets and found them both lacking. He'd have to make a run to the market in the morning and simply order in for now.

He pulled out his phone and was as nervous as if he was calling to ask the most popular girl in school to the prom. What if she didn't answer? Worse, what if she wouldn't talk to him? He swallowed down his trepidation. If he didn't call he'd never know. He placed the call to her number and waited.

Kai was in her workroom going through her photos. She'd finally agreed to have some of them on display at the local gallery. It was Tiffany that convinced her to go for it. She had an incredible talent and it was selfish of her to keep it to herself, Tiffany insisted. The world needed to see Kai's work.

As she sifted through the photos, her heart and her hands stopped when her gaze fell on the photo of Anthony that she'd taken all those months ago. Her pulse quickened and tears suddenly stung her eyes. Why couldn't things have been different? She'd felt a connection to him from that very first instant. He'd haunted her thoughts and taken up space in her head long before they'd actually met. And when they did…you couldn't have told her that love at first sight didn't exist. She knew that it did. That's what hurt her so deeply. She'd never admit it, not even to Tiffany, but she'd fallen in love with him from the moment she'd seen him that rainy day. The tragedy of it all was that she didn't realize it until he was gone.

The distant ringing of her phone drew her back. She scanned the top of her desk. She heard the phone but didn't see it. She lifted folders and photos and finally discovered it. She pressed the talk icon without thinking.

"Hello?"

"It's Anthony."

Heat rushed through her, and her heart hammered so hard in her chest she couldn't breathe.

"Hi," she managed.

"How are you?"

"Fine. You?"

"I miss you. I miss you like crazy."

"Anthony, don't—"

"I'm in town for the weekend. I'm at my house. I want to see you, Kai. I need to see you."

Her skin tingled. "I...when?"

He took a breath of relief. "Now. I can be there in ten minutes."

She swallowed over the dry knot in her throat. "Okay."

"I'll see you soon."

She disconnected the call and held the phone to her chest as champagne bubbles of excitement popped through her veins. What had she just done?

The next ten minutes were the longest of her life, but she still didn't have enough time. She ran around straightening up, washed her face, fluffed her hair and brushed her teeth. Jasper was trailing behind her as if she was a puppy treat.

Even though she was expecting it, when the front doorbell rang it shocked her system. Every muscle vibrated. She tugged in a long breath to calm herself and went to the door. Nothing prepared her for the reality of seeing Anthony again. Her soul cried out with joy. And when he smiled at her, crossed the threshold and looked into her eyes…

"Hey," he said in a raw whisper.

Her heart galloped. "Hey." She took a step back to let him in, and her eyes momentarily fluttered closed when she caught a whiff of his scent. She shut the door and followed him inside.

"Have a seat," she said, extending her hand toward the couch. Her gaze quickly swept over his rugged handsomeness: from the late-day stubble on his rich chocolate jaw, to the open collar of the baby-blue cotton shirt, to the thick black belt that hugged his waist, to the washed-out jeans that were butter-soft to the touch and covered a treasure trove of delights beneath.

He slowly sat down and stretched his arm along the back of the couch. Kai sat at the far end.

"Thanks for seeing me."

She didn't respond.

He cleared his throat, suddenly feeling unsure of himself, which always seemed to happen when he was with Kai. He couldn't think straight. "Listen, I know that I promised that I would give you the space that you wanted, and I know that you said it couldn't work. I tried, I really tried to honor your wish…but I can't." He angled his body more in her direction. "One of the big problems between us was Crystal."

Her stomach jumped.

He drew in a breath. "I met with her when I got back to New York…" He told her about their talk, his declaration to Crystal that it was over between them in no uncertain terms. He even told Kai about the reporter and the news article.

She was singing on the inside. He didn't have to tell

her about the article, but now she understood why and how it all happened. He wasn't sneaking around or trying to get back with Crystal. He was trying to end it in a public place to avoid any drama.

"I'm glad you were able to work things out."

"That's it?" He looked at her incredulously.

"What else can I say?"

"At least say that you'll reconsider."

She lowered her head for a moment, then looked directly at him and it was almost her undoing. His eyes went straight to her core.

"I know or at least I understand that what happened with you and Crystal wasn't an easy thing for you to do. You were married. You have a child together and because of that you will always be connected. If…if I were to be a part of your life, I'd have to deal with that aspect of it as well."

"And?"

"You have a life in New York, Anthony, a life that is all-encompassing and will only get more difficult when you step into your new role. I totally accept and respect that." Her eyes pinched at the corners while she spoke. "I know how important it is to you, and I don't know how we could ever be more than a weekend fling when you have time. I don't think I can deal with that part of it."

He took her hand. "You wouldn't be in it alone." He moved closer to her and cupped her face in his hands. "It would be the two of us…trying to figure it out, trying to make it work. I know it wouldn't be your typical relationship. But if we try, if *you* want to we can make it *ours*. Whatever I need to do, I'm willing. Are you?"

Damn, he was good. "I…yes."

Relief flooded through him, and he didn't hold back

a second longer before he took her into his arms and re-confirmed his commitment to her.

Kai heated and then melted in his embrace, and gave herself over to the sweetness of being held and kissed by him. It was better, hotter, steamier than she remembered. His tongue did things to the inside of her mouth that trickled all the way down to her toes. The fine hairs on her arms stood up, electrified, when he touched her. His heart pounded against her breasts and it emboldened her knowing that his want and desire for her reflected her need for him.

"Not here," she murmured against his mouth. She pulled away, stood and led him to her bedroom.

It was as if the bell for the final round had gone off as they went at each other with a hunger that could only be quenched by stripping down until nothing but air was between them, and that simmering need for their bodies to be united was met and fully satisfied.

In a tangle of limbs, hot, wet kisses, moans, sighs and cries of passion, they closed the gap that had separated them, they erased the time they'd lost, and came together in an explosion of emotional and physical release that left them satiated and shaken.

For many moments afterward, Anthony refused to move, to disconnect. He'd always believed that his work, his passion for justice was the only thing that fueled him, that drove him. It was what Crystal always accused him of, and when they were together it was true. His work fulfilled him, not his marriage. Being with Kai helped him to realize that there was so much in his life that he was missing. He wanted to be able to wake with her, see her at the end of his day, make love to her at night. He kissed her temple and she sighed beneath him. But to do that he would have to sacrifice all that he'd worked for or she would have to return to a life that she'd vowed never to do again.

A sacrifice would have to be made if they were to succeed.

For the two days that Anthony was in town, he and Kai spent all of their time together almost as if they believed this ideal would somehow evaporate like a dream if they were ever out of each other's company.

"I finally decided to put up some of my photography at the gallery," she said while they worked side by side preparing a light lunch. She cast him a side look to gauge his reaction.

His expression lit up. "That's what I'm talking about." He hooked his arm around her waist and lightly spun her around. "Congrats. What made you finally change your mind?"

She giggled. "Tiffany. She's relentless."

"Good for Tiffany. Hope I get to meet her next time I come down. But in the meantime, can I at least get a sneak peek?"

She looked at him coyly. "Hmm. Okay. Come on."

Chapter 24

Kai led him to her workroom. There were very few people that she shared her work with. Desiree and Tiffany had been the only two since she'd moved to Sag Harbor, and now Anthony. She was actually nervous about his response.

Several of her pieces were hung on the wall while others were spread out on desks and tabletops. Anthony slowed in front of each one and studied them in silence. The stark black-and-white images of unsuspecting subjects, the magnificence of nature and her ability to capture the nuances of shadow and light as they played across her subject matter were astonishing. He came to a full stop and reached for a photo that was on the desk next to her computer.

Her heart jumped. She tugged on her bottom lip with her teeth.

He turned toward her with a look of wonder in his eyes. "When did you take this?"

"It was a Saturday in early spring. It was an overcast day and I love to capture stormy skies. I went into town and the mist had begun and the sky grew gray. I started shooting." She paused and looked away, recalling the day. "When I got home and printed the pictures I saw that one of you…and something inside of me…"

"Something inside of you what?" he asked softly walking slowly toward her.

"Shifted…as if the earth had moved beneath my feet."

He was right in front of her now. "The same way I felt the first time I saw you standing in your doorway."

The pulse leaped in her throat.

"I haven't stop thinking about you, wanting you since that very first day. If anything it's only gotten more intense, more difficult to ignore." His gaze roamed across her face. "I didn't think it was possible…at least not for me."

"What?" she said on a breath.

"That I could fall in love, really in love, so quickly and so deep."

Her heart pounded so loud and so hard, it felt like it would bolt out of her chest.

"I love you, Kai." He pulled her into his arms. "It's as simple and as complicated as that."

Her fingertips touched his face. "Yes, it's complicated."

His lips touched down on hers with such tender sweetness that she felt her insides give way. She looped her arms around his neck, sank into the moment and turned herself completely over to him.

As with all of the times that they found themselves together, the need for each other blinded them to everything else. His hands were all over her, teasing and tempting and bending her to his need for her. Kai gave as good as she got, tugging his shirt off and tossing it across the room. She swept all of the photos and papers off the desk and onto the floor. It was the only signal that Anthony needed.

They made quick work of discarding clothing that wound up in a tangled pile as he lifted her onto the desk. Kai opened for him, wrapped her legs around his waist and welcomed the burst of hard, hot heat that filled her and pushed the air from her lungs.

She clung to him as he moved deep inside her. She angled her body so that his every stroke tapped the pulsing bud of her sex. Jolt after jolt of fire ripped through her limbs as he grew harder with every dip and dive into her willing wet walls.

Her skin tingled while ripples of sensation flooded her body. She was so close. So was he. She knew from the shift of his breathing, the way he held her, how his strokes grew deeper and faster.

Suddenly, he grabbed her hips, holding her in a vise grip. The muscles in his neck grew tight as he plowed into her over and over and then…

"T…ony! Oh, God. Oh, God."

The world disappeared behind an explosion of light.

"Yessss," he groaned, and swallowed her cries of release with his kiss.

Entwined, they held each other as their breathing slowed to normal. In the distance, the sound of Jasper barking nearly masked the ringing doorbell.

"Expecting someone?"

"No," she said breathlessly.

Reluctantly, Anthony moved away. They stared at each other and broke out into laughter.

"I better get that." She gathered her clothes and

quickly got dressed. She closed the door to the work-room behind her.

"Well, took you long enough," Tiffany said, then stopped and took a good look at her friend who was trying to put her hair in place. Tiffany cleared her throat. "Busy?"

Kai's cheeks heated. "Not anymore." She bit back a smile.

"I can come back."

"No. Come on in." She stepped aside.

Tiffany stepped inside.

"What's up?" Kai asked as they went into the liv-ing room.

"I should be asking you that," she teased. "I just thought I'd stop by and see how you were making out with the photo selection."

An image of her and Anthony getting it on in her workroom flashed through her head.

Tiffany snapped her fingers in front of Kai's face. "Earth to Kai Randall."

Kai blinked. "Sorry."

"You must be Tiffany."

They both turned at the sound of the sexy baritone.

Tiffany's eyes widened.

Anthony walked over to her and extended his hand. "Anthony Weston."

"Tiffany Howard. Nice to finally meet you."

"You as well." He turned all of his attention to Kai. "I'm gonna go," he said. "Let you ladies do what you do," he added with a grin. He kissed her lightly on the lips. "I hope to see you again, Tiffany."

"I'm sure."

Kai walked with him to the door. "Call me if you want to come over later," he said only for Kai to hear.

"I will." She closed the door and turned to Tiffany who was looking at her as if seeing her for the first time.

"When did that happen?" she asked, pointing toward the now-closed door.

Kai drew in a breath. "Since he came back on Friday."

"Girl, and you didn't call me! Guess you were too busy." She walked over to the couch and plopped down. "Well, don't start playing coy now. What happened? I thought you pretty much swore it was over. Done."

"I know." She sat down and tucked her feet beneath her. She sighed and then told Tiffany all that had transpired, the talk they had, what the meeting in New York was about and finally Anthony's declaration of love.

"Wow," was all that Tiffany could manage.

"Exactly."

Tiffany slowly shook her head in amazement. "Guess you just never know." She looked Kai right in the eye. "What about you? How do you feel about him?"

"I know you're going to think I'm crazy. It is so unlike me…but I love him, Tiff. I've loved him before I met him. I know that now. A part of me has always known. I guess that's why the craziness messed with my head so bad. But I do," she added, imploring her friend to understand.

"Look, there's no accounting for the ways of the heart. As long as you're happy. As long as he makes you happy, those are the only things that are important."

Kai pressed her lips together and nodded in agreement. "He does. He makes me so happy that I feel like I could burst."

"Then go for it, girl. Take the happiness where you can find it." She paused a beat. "What are you two going to do about him living in New York and you living here? You planning on going back to the city?"

"I've tossed that idea around every which way but loose. I can't see myself going back."

"Hmm. And he plans to stay there, I take it."

"Looks that way."

Tiffany exhaled a long breath. "I'm sure you two will work something out."

Kai wished that she could agree. It was the one thing she was uncertain of.

Chapter 25

Monday morning, Anthony was right back in the thick of cases and Harrison's campaign. His weekend with Kai still hummed in his veins and it took all of his concentration to stay focused on his tasks at hand. At the end of the day, Harrison pulled him aside.

"Come to my office. We need to talk."

Anthony walked alongside Harrison to his office at the far end of the corridor. Harrison stepped inside. "Close the door, would you."

Anthony closed the door, slid his hands into the pockets of his slacks. "What's on your mind?"

"I think I should be asking you that." He sat down and leaned back in his chair. He folded his arms across his small paunch.

"What do you mean?"

"I mean that your mind is clearly someplace else. I need you at one-hundred-and-fifty percent. I have too much going on not to have you focused. We have a major Rico trial in two weeks. We need to nail these bastards once and for all. That cannot be done if you're not on your game. There is no room for slipups *or* distractions."

Anthony rocked his jaw. "I'm on top of it."

Harrison studied him. "It's that woman, isn't it?"

Anthony's gaze flashed toward his boss and mentor. "I can have a life and a career. I do my job."

Harrison lifted his chin, then leaned forward. "I need to know that you want this as much as I do."

Anthony hesitated—something he'd never done before. "I do."

Harrison slowly nodded. "Good." He lifted a folder from his desk signaling that the meeting was over.

Anthony turned away and walked out, and as he returned to his office and the pile of work that waited for him, it was the first time that he inwardly questioned his journey.

It was nearing midnight when he finally put the key into the door of his apartment. Exhaustion weighed down his steps. He tossed his briefcase on the couch and went to fix himself a drink. No sooner had he taken the first sip than his cell phone rang. He looked at the number on the face of the phone and his exhaustion dissipated.

"Hey, baby."

"Hi. How are you?"

"Better now." He took his drink and walked into his bedroom.

"Sounds like you had a rough day."

He snorted a laugh. "That's putting it mildly, but I'm used to it." He sat on the side of the bed, set down his drink on the nightstand and took off his shoes. "How was your day?"

"Only a few patients today. I went over to the gallery to talk about the show."

"Great. What's the latest?"

"Well…I'm scheduled for my first showing in six weeks," she said, the excitement brimming in her voice.

"What! Fantastic. Are you ready?"

"I will be. A lot of organizing and developing some kind of theme."

"I know it'll be amazing."

"You'll be here for the opening?"

"Of course. I wouldn't miss it for the world."

"Do you think you'll get a chance to get out here before then?" she asked with hesitation.

He paused. The way things were going at work, he was lucky to get off at the end of the day. "I want to. I'll try as often as I can. It's that I have a major case that is ready to be presented to the grand jury. There are mounds of prep work that have to go into—"

"Anthony…it's okay. You don't have to explain. I understand."

"Do you?"

"Sure. Take care of what you need to. It's important."

"So are you."

"Get some rest. I know it's late."

"I love you," he said.

"Love you back. Good night."

"Night."

He disconnected the call and glanced upward. This was only the start of how things would be. Something was going to give.

"When was the last time you saw him?" Desiree asked. She, Tiffany, Layla and Kai were at the gallery to work out the details of the showing and the reception. The gallery had printed fifteen hundred palm cards and there was a big poster in the window announcing the show.

"Two weeks ago." She sighed. "Just overnight. He had to go right back for a campaign event."

They walked through the space where the reception would be held. Kai remembered the night she'd spotted Anthony in the crowd during the book signing. A wave of melancholy swept through her.

"We talk every night at least for a few minutes. He's so exhausted."

"It's not going to get any easier or any better when he becomes district attorney," Layla said. "Are you prepared for that?"

"I hope that I am. I can't be sure of anything until it happens."

Layla nodded. "Believe me, relationships are complicated. No matter how much you may care about someone, they come with baggage. I never thought that I'd be able to break through all the barriers that Maurice had set up around himself. I wanted to give up. So did he. But we didn't. And here we are," she added with a grin and rubbed her very pregnant belly.

"That's true. If it's meant to be, they will work it out. Every relationship has its crosses to bear. I can surely testify to that," Desiree said, holding up her hand.

Kai glanced around at the space and took in the concerned expressions of her friends. "We'll do the best we can. The main thing is that we both want happiness for each other. If his happiness is his career, then that's what I want for him. And the same goes for me. If it comes to a point where we no longer can make each other happy..."

Tiffany looped her arm around Kai's neck as they

strolled. "But in the meantime, you have a show to mount and we're hungry. Right, ladies?"

They all laughed and headed out.

Hiking up the steps to the courthouse was walking the gauntlet. Police struggled to hold back spectators even as the press yelled questions and the flash from the cameras burst like sparklers on the Fourth of July.

"Mr. Weston, Mr. Weston! Do you think you can finally get a conviction?"

"How deep does the organization go?"

"Is this all a big show because your boss is running for governor?"

Anthony kept his eyes on the front door as he made his way up the stairs, braced on either side by his police escort. The days leading up to the trial had been peppered with death threats. Threats that the FBI were taking seriously. He hadn't told Kai. He didn't want to worry her. And as much as he wanted to be with her, he couldn't. He had security following him everywhere that he went and that would mean bringing them to Sag Harbor, something he refused to do. This would all be over soon and then he could get back to his life.

The guard held open the glass-and-chrome door and Anthony crossed the marble-floored entry, and walked down the corridor and into the courtroom. Thankfully, the judge had ruled early on that this would be a closed case. No press allowed. No cameras and no spectators. There was already enough tension for the jury who had to be sequestered from the start of the trial and the witnesses.

The jury had reached a verdict that afternoon, following a week of deliberations, and he'd been called at his office to get right over to the courthouse.

When he entered the courtroom, the three defendants and their attorneys were in place. Anthony's second chair Lawrence Connor was just sitting down. Lawrence was one of the best A.D.A.s that Anthony had ever worked with. He was smart, ruthless and knew the law. They made a formidable team.

"So what do you think?" Anthony asked under his breath as he took his seat.

Lawrence tilted his head toward Anthony. "You put on a helluva case, man. Everything that could have been done was done. No matter which way it goes, you did your job. But personally, I think those young men are going to be very old men by the time they get out."

A shadow of a smile graced Anthony's mouth.

There was some shuffling at the side door as the bailiff announced that the judge was entering the courtroom.

"All rise! Judge Beecham presiding."

The judge stepped up to the bench and sat. "Please be seated."

Judge Alexander Beecham was revered by his peers and feared by attorneys on both sides of the aisle. He was known to make mincemeat out of lawyers who didn't know their stuff and he had no problem implementing the harshest of sentences allowed by law, upon conviction by a jury.

"Bailiff, bring in the jury."

The door opened and the twelve jurors slowly filled the jury box. None of them made eye contact with either the defense or the prosecution table.

Judge Beecham turned to the jury. "Madame forelady, have you reached a verdict?"

"We have, Your Honor."

"On all counts?"

"Yes, Your Honor."

Judge Beecham nodded and extended his hand for the verdict sheet. He studied it for several moments, his expression never changing. The list of charges was long. He handed the verdict sheet back to the bailiff.

One by one Judge Beecham read the charges— thirty-two in all ranging from gun and drug smuggling, to dealing, money-laundering and conspiracy.

"Guilty… Guilty… Guilty."

Anthony could barely contain himself as he heard each and every count and the resounding word "guilty."

"Thank you for your service," Judge Beecham said to the jury. He turned to the defendants. "Sentencing will take place two weeks from today. Until then, the defendants are remanded into the custody of Rikers Island. This court is adjourned." He pounded his gavel once and left the courtroom.

The defendants were taken out of the courtroom. Anthony and Lawrence stood and hugged each other, giving hearty slaps to each other's back.

"You did it, man," Lawrence said.

"*We* did it. I couldn't have pulled it all off without your help."

"Thanks," he said while nodding his head. "I learned everything I know from you."

"Come on." He put his arm around Lawrence's shoulder. "I say we get a drink to celebrate."

Lawrence tossed his head back and laughed. "Sounds good to me."

They packed up their briefcases and headed out to be met by Harrison Blumenthal at the door.

"Good work," he said, looking from one to the other. He clapped Anthony on the back. "Ready for your close-up? The press is waiting."

Anthony clenched his jaw. "Aren't they always."

The trio walked out and onto the steps of the courthouse where they were practically assaulted by the press. Every news outlet was in place.

A set of microphones had been set up for the press conference that was led off by Harrison, who extolled the hard work of his team and their commitment to hunting down crime and criminals in New York City. Of course, he had to discuss his passion for justice which was compelling him to run for governor.

Anthony only half listened. He gazed out into the crowd and the hungry faces of the media. He thought about the relentless hours that this case had consumed with only more to follow. There was a time when he lived for the next case, the spotlight, the win. This case, however, had truly tested his resolve. Just how much of his life was he willing to sacrifice for "the greater good?"

"Now I want to have my chief A.D.A., Anthony Weston, say a few words and answer any questions." Harrison turned with a beaming smile and extended his arm toward Anthony, motioning him toward the microphones.

Anthony stepped up to the microphone and did what he always did, what he was good at—*winning*.

Kai was settled in bed, hoping to hear from Anthony before she dozed off. She'd had a crazy busy day. It seemed as if half of the town was sick with one thing or another and then she had to work to get the images framed for her show in two weeks. She surfed through the channels and stopped on the eleven o'clock news. There was a still picture of Anthony and the reporter was talking. She turned up the volume.

"…shot this afternoon following the jury conviction…"

Kai jumped up from the bed, her heart racing out of control. What was this woman saying? The story moved to the next news item. Kai's hands shook as she switched channels trying to find out what happened.

Her phone suddenly rang and it sent a shock through her system. She snatched up the phone.

"Kai, did you hear on the news about Anthony?"

"Tiff…I only got a piece…that he'd been shot!"

"The news is saying that he was shot. They won't give out any more details. He's in critical condition." She paused. "He's at New York Presbyterian. And before you say another thing, I'm going with you. Throw some stuff together. I'll be there in fifteen minutes."

Kai wanted to weep with relief because she wasn't sure how she would have made it up to New York City alone. But had it come to that, she would have done it.

She grabbed a small carry bag from the closet, threw in some toiletries and a change of clothes. She checked her purse for her keys and her wallet. She dropped her cell phone in her purse.

Jasper sat at the opening of her bedroom door, thumping his tail on the floor. "Oh, gosh, Jasper." She pressed her palm to her head. She couldn't take him with her. Maybe Desiree…she wondered if Lincoln knew. She dug in her purse and took out her phone just as it rang. It was Desiree who was calling to find out if she'd heard about Anthony. She readily agreed to take Jasper and to tell her that Lincoln was going with them.

As promised, Tiffany was at Kai's door in fifteen minutes. Kai told her that Lincoln was going. They swung by The Port. Lincoln was out front.

"We'll take my truck," he said. He stepped up to Kai. "You okay?"

"I don't know," she managed.

"He's going to be fine." He squeezed her shoulder. "Let's go."

Chapter 26

The two-hour drive seemed to take forever. Hundreds of images played havoc in Kai's head. She'd seen more than her share of gunshot wounds and knew sometimes it was the simple shot that could be the most deadly. But she couldn't allow her thoughts to go in that direction. He was in one of the best hospitals in the city and she knew he'd get excellent care.

By the time they arrived, it was nearly one in the morning. The front of the hospital was littered with press and news vans.

"Go around the side to the Emergency entrance," Kai said. "I still have privileges."

Lincoln drove around to the Emergency entrance and found a parking space. Kai was out of the car before it came to a full stop.

The trio pushed in through the Emergency door and Kai went straight to the triage nurse in charge.

"I'm Dr. Randall. There's a patient here, Anthony Weston."

"Dr. Randall," the nurse said in recognition. "Yes, he's been taken to ICU about an hour ago."

"Thank you." She hurried off toward the elevator with Tiffany and Lincoln on her heels.

They took the elevator to the fourth floor. The instant they stepped off, they saw that the corridor was dotted with police. Kai's pulse raced. She went to the front desk.

"I'm Dr. Randall. You have a patient here, Anthony Weston."

The nurse looked at her. "The doctor is with him now. You'll have to wait."

"What is his condition?"

"I'm sorry, Dr. Randall, but I can't give out that information. All I can say is that he made it out of surgery and they are getting him settled. You can wait in the lounge. As soon as the doctor comes out, I'll have him see you."

"Which doctor is treating him?"

"Dr. Lang."

Kai breathed a sigh of relief and almost smiled. Dr. Lang was one of the best trauma surgeons in the business. Anthony was in good hands.

"Thank you." She turned toward the anxious faces of Tiffany and Lincoln. She told them what she knew and they went to the lounge to wait.

Harrison Blumenthal and Lawrence were seated with their heads together, talking in low voices. They both turned when the trio entered.

Harrison stood. Kai recognized him from the news. She walked straight toward him.

"Mr. Blumenthal." She extended her hand.

"You must be Kai."

She angled her head in question.

"He's told me all about you. He's a lucky man."

She lowered her gaze then looked back at him. "Did they catch the shooter?"

"Yes, they did."

"Good. Have you heard anything at all?"

"We've been waiting."

Kai introduced Lincoln and Tiffany and they all found seats to wait.

They'd been there no more than five minutes when Crystal rushed in. She came to a complete halt when she saw Kai and Lincoln and then Harrison.

Lincoln stood. "Crystal."

The muscles in her face fluttered. "Thank you for coming, Lincoln." She turned her gaze on Kai. "I see news spreads all the way to the boonies." She drew in a breath and crossed the room to an available seat, ignoring Harrison.

Kai dismissed the barb and simply tossed Tiffany a look of warning, knowing that her friend would rip Crystal a new one. Tiffany rolled her eyes.

"Have you heard anything?" Crystal asked Lincoln.

"Not yet."

"Dr. Randall…"

Kai looked toward the doorway. Dr. Lang was there with a chart in his hands. She jumped up from her chair.

"Malcolm," she breathed. "How is he?"

"You still have privileges here, correct?"

"Yes."

"Good. Let's step outside."

They stood outside of the waiting room talking in low voices. Kai nodded as she listened to the extent of the injury and what had been done.

"I wouldn't have done anything differently," she said.

"Of course, the main thing now is infection and re-covery, which will take some time. He's very lucky."

"I know. A few inches over…"

"Exactly." He studied her for a moment. "You two must be close. He has you down as his next of kin."

Her head jerked back. "Really?"

He nodded. "I'd better get back to my patient. Give me a few minutes and you can come in and see him. He's a little groggy."

"Of course." She touched his arm. "Thank you."

He smiled and walked away.

Kai slowly turned around and reentered the waiting room. Crystal was on her feet.

"Well, since you seem to have the inside track…when can I see my husband?"

Kai stared her in the eye. "It will be a while."

"What did the doctor say?" Lincoln asked.

"He's going to be okay. The bullet broke his clavicle bone, barely missing a main artery. He's going to be in pain for a while. But he came through the surgery fine."

Tiffany sighed. "Thank God."

"Why did the doctor talk to you and not to me?" Crystal demanded.

Kai turned to her. "I worked here for a number of years as the chief of emergency services. Dr. Lang is a colleague of mine. I still have visiting privileges here." Kai held off on telling Tiffany that Anthony had listed her as the next of kin to be contacted in the event of an emergency. She didn't see how telling Crystal would serve any purpose other than to upset her even more.

Dr. Lang came back to the door. "Dr. Randall, you can come in now."

Kai glanced from one to the other. Crystal looked as

if she would self-combust. "Why don't you come with me, Crystal?"

Crystal blinked in disbelief. Her mouth opened slightly then closed. "Thank you."

Kai and Crystal followed Dr. Lang down the hallway and around a bend. Two officers were stationed outside of Anthony's room. Dr. Lang pushed the door open and they walked inside.

A nurse was checking the fluid drips and the monitors. The bulge of the bandages on his left shoulder looked like an outgrowth. His eyes were closed. His breathing was steady.

Kai stepped over to his bedside. He seemed to sense her presence. His eyes fluttered open, then closed.

"Kai…" he whispered.

"I'm here." She took his hand.

"Don't want you to worry."

"Then you will have to do something other than getting shot on a Tuesday," she said, trying to make light.

He winched even as he smiled. "So tired." His eyes drifted close.

"It's the medicine. Are you in any pain?"

The corner of his mouth turned up. "Nothing I can't handle."

She went to the foot of the bed and flipped open his chart. He'd been given some heavy doses of pain medication and antibiotics. She closed the chart and put it back. "You get some rest."

"Don't leave." He gripped her wrist with surprising strength.

"I'm not going anywhere, but you need to rest. Lincoln is here and so is Tiffany." She glanced over her shoulder and saw Crystal standing forlornly in the doorway. "Crystal wants to see you."

He squeezed his eyes shut. "All right."

Kai leaned down and tenderly kissed his lips. "I'll see you in a little while. Promise." She waved Crystal over.

"I love you," he said, holding her hand.

"I know. I love you, too." She turned away and the look of reluctant acceptance on Crystal's face told her that she'd overheard the exchange. Kai walked outside and returned to the lounge, where she brought everyone up to date.

"We all could use some rest," Lincoln said.

"Do you have someplace to stay?" Harrison asked.

"I hadn't even thought that far," Kai admitted.

"Let me make some calls." He took out his phone and turned away. Several minutes later he came back to the huddled group. "I've booked two rooms over at the Hilton on Central Park West. The rooms are in my name for as long as you need them."

"Mr. Blumenthal, you didn't have to do that," Kai said.

"Oh yes, I did." He smiled. "Tony would have my head if I didn't take care of you."

"Thank you. Really."

"Don't worry about it. Get some rest and come back in the morning."

"I want to let Anthony know that I'm leaving first," Kai said.

"He wants to see you." Crystal stood in the doorway. The arrogant tilt of her brow was gone and a heaviness hung beneath her eyes.

"Thanks." She walked toward the door. Crystal stopped her.

"Can I talk to you for a minute?"

"Of course."

They stepped outside.

Crystal studied the floor, then finally looked Kai in the eyes. "I get it."

"I don't. What do you mean?"

"I finally understand. It's over between me and Anthony. I saw how he looks at you. He never looked at me like that." She emitted a sad laugh. "I'm sure that was more my fault than his. I didn't give him any space to love me like that. I wanted the glitz and the glamour and not the work that it takes to make a marriage or a relationship work. The thing is, I know I haven't changed. I'm still the same self-centered bitch I've always been. And that's okay. There's always someone out there willing to put up with me…at least for a while. I fooled myself into believing that I could get Anthony back. It was stupid." She drew in a long breath. "I guess what I'm saying is, make him happy. He deserves it."

Kai was so taken aback by Crystal's admission that she was at a loss for words as she watched Crystal walk away.

"What was that about?" Tiffany asked.

"You wouldn't believe it."

Chapter 27

"Can I get you anything?"

Anthony crooked his finger to beckon her to his bed-side.

Kai happily complied and gently sat down on the side of the bed.

"You're everything that I want."

She leaned down and kissed him. "Bet you say that to all the girls." She giggled. "I have a couple of patients this morning. Then I'll be back."

"Go. Go. I'll be fine. Jasper can keep me company."

"See you soon." She kissed him again and walked out of her bedroom.

Since his release from the hospital, Anthony had been staying with Kai during his recovery. His wound was healing nicely and he was getting the mobility back in his arm. But he had a few more weeks of rehab ahead of him.

They spent their days talking and walking along the

beach, visiting shops in town, having homemade dinners and making love gently.

He knew that at some point, sooner rather than later, he was going to have to come to a decision about his future, their future together.

Being with Kai like this was something he never expected. He thought he'd be bored out of his mind without the thrill of the chase, the excitement of life in the big bad city. There was still a part of him that fed on the action of his job, but the need for it wasn't the same. Harrison was pressuring him. The election was two weeks away. He'd have to go back soon, but not before Kai's showing at the gallery.

"You excited?" Anthony asked while Kai helped him with his tie.

"Terrified is more like it."

He lifted her chin with the tip of his finger. "You're sensational. Your show is going to be a major success. They will love you…just like I do."

Her heart leaped. "If you say so." She smiled.

"We better get going." He put one arm in his jacket and draped the other side over his shoulder. His arm was still in a sling.

"Even all banged up you're still pretty damned sexy."

"Bet you say that to all your patients."

"Yep!"

He playfully swatted her rear. "Let's go before I get other ideas."

By the time they arrived at the gallery, the guests were already starting to arrive. Kai felt as if she was at the Oscars.

Anthony took her hand. "Ready?"

She drew in a breath. "Ready."

They walked inside and Kai was instantly over-whelmed at seeing her work displayed on the walls. It was really happening.

"There you are." Tiffany hurried over to her friend and kissed her cheek. "This is just too fabulous. Girl... you really did it."

Kai beamed with happiness. "I still can't believe it. And look at all these people."

"Believe it, baby," Anthony whispered in her ear.

Before long, both levels of the gallery were filled to capacity. Drinks flowed in the reception area and every few feet someone came up to Kai to congratulate her on her work. The gallery owner told her that she'd gotten multiple offers to buy her work. It all seemed like a dream.

The one photo that everyone seemed to gravitate to was the blown-up photo of Anthony on that rainy afternoon. The power of it was undeniable. She named it *The Solitary Man.*

Anthony slid his good arm around her waist. "Told you." He kissed her cheek.

She grinned. "Yes, you did."

By the end of the night, twenty of the thirty photos had been sold and the owner wanted to set up another show in the fall. There were multiple bids on *The Solitary Man,* but it was the one that Kai would not sell.

"I am so proud of you, baby," Anthony said as they lay in bed together that night. "You are absolutely amazing."

She turned in his arms to face him. Her eyes moved slowly over the face of the man that she loved, knowing that these weeks of bliss would soon come to an end. He'd have to return to New York City and get on with his life. Just as he wanted her to fulfill her passions, she wanted the same for him. It would be painfully hard, but she'd deal with it. She'd do it for him. That's what love was about.

"I want to talk with you about something," he said into the soft recess of the dimly lit room.

Her stomach tightened. "Sure."

"I've been doing a lot of thinking and soul searching these last few weeks. Being with you, being here wasn't what I expected."

She wanted to tell him that it was okay, that she understood that he needed to get back to his life, but she held her tongue this time.

"Harrison wants me to come back."

Her heart thumped.

"And I've decided that it's not what I want to do."

"What?" She sat up and turned on the light. "What do you mean it's not what you want to do? That's your career, your life. It's what you worked so hard for. It's—"

He put a finger on her lips.

"It doesn't matter if I can't be with you."

"You could commute. You could… We could…"

"No. I know what I want. I think it hit me when I really looked at that photograph you took of me. *The Solitary Man*. That man epitomized loneliness. Lost in a sea of uncertainty. I don't want that man to be me any longer."

"But your career. The district attorney job."

"I'd give it all up for you. I will. Just say that you'll put up with me. Say it."

"I can't let you do that for me."

"Why?"

"Because you'd come to resent it and me."

"Why don't you let me be the judge of that? I'm pretty good at looking at the evidence. And all the evidence points to me loving you from the bottom of my soul and not wanting to spend a day or a night without you."

Tears welled in her eyes. "Are you sure?"

"I've never been more certain of anything in my life. I have a tidy little trust fund and I've made enough money to hold me over for a while until I set up my practice here." He grinned.

"Here? You're going to practice here?"

"Yep. So what do you say? You think you can put up with me everyday for the rest of your life?"

"W-what are you saying?"

"It's not what I'm saying. It's what I'm asking. Be my partner. My friend, my muse, my lover, my wife. Will you?"

She cupped his face in her hands and all the love she had in her heart poured from her eyes. "Yes, for you, I will."

* * * * *

Dear Reader,

Thank you for reading the Harlequin Kimani Arabesque title, *For You I Will* by Donna Hill.

For your consideration, we have included the first four chapters from two of Donna's previous titles: Harlequin Kimani Arabesque's *Touch Me Now,* the prior book in the Sag Harbor Village series, and Harlequin Kimani Romance's *Mistletoe, Baby,* a hot holiday office romance. We do hope this proves to be an enjoyable reading experience for you.

All the best,
The Harlequin Kimani Team

Touch Me Now

Prologue

It was late afternoon. The lunch crowd, what there had been of it, was gone. Business was slow, slower than usual for this time of year. Everyone was hurting, it seemed. She'd been let go from the paper months earlier, but had been lucky enough to pick up a few extra hours at Jack and Jill's, the local lounge and jazz spot in the West Village, and she had begun to build a pretty solid list of clients from her massage business thanks to Brent.

Thoughts of Brent brought a smile to her face and a rush of sensual excitement through her veins. There were times when she still wondered how she'd gotten so lucky. Brent had women running after him like a buy-two-get-one-free sale at Macy's. But she was the one that he wanted. He'd proved it to her time and again, and there wasn't a day that went by that he didn't tell her that he loved her or did something to show her.

She wiped down the tables and glanced with a sense of awe at the dazzling diamond on the third finger of her left hand. In six months she would join the ranks of her girls Melanie and Desiree and become a married woman. She'd picked out her dress. Simple and elegant, Desiree had said. It was going to be a small, intimate wedding—only their really close friends and immediate family. Melanie had offered her place at Sag Harbor for the wedding and reception. Layla couldn't wait to be Mrs. Brent Davis.

"Daydreaming again?" Mona asked, sidling up next to her. Mona Clarke ran Jack and Jill's, and in the six months that Layla had worked there, they'd become more than employer and employee—they'd become friends. Mona completely understood that Layla's job at the lounge was only temporary and that her real love was the art of massage, the power to heal through touch.

Layla turned and a shy smile teased her full lip-glossed mouth. "That bad?"

"Yes, very," Mona said, with her fist on her hip. "Hey, I got this." She took the cloth from Layla's hand. "It's slow as maple syrup in here today. Why don't you go on home to your man, see what he can do about that cheery disposition of yours," she teased.

"You sure?"

"Yeah, go ahead. Unless you really need the tips you're not going to make today. Go, go, practice some of your massage techniques on that fine specimen."

Layla wiggled her brows. "Hmm, maybe I will." She gave Mona a quick kiss on the cheek. "I owe you," she called out as she hurried to the back to get her purse.

"See you on the weekend."

Layla stopped at the local market on her way home

and picked up some fresh vegetables and seasonings for a stir-fry meal and a bottle of Brent's favorite wine. She still had a few hours to prepare everything before Brent got off work. She wanted things to be extra special. In fact she planned to take Mona up on her suggestion and try out a new massage technique on him that she'd been mastering and maybe that new Victoria's Secret lingerie that she'd splurged on. A wicked thought tickled her belly.

With her purchases in hand she strolled the four blocks to her apartment, intermittently stopping to check out the window displays at boutiques and artisanal shops along the way.

She climbed the stairs to her walk-up and came to a dead stop at the front door, momentarily alarmed by the sound of movement inside until she heard Brent's voice. She let go a breath of relief. Calling 911 would have really screwed up her afternoon. Brent home early? The surprise was on her.

Layla turned her key in the door all ready to leap into Brent's arms, but came to a grinding halt when she saw Brent and two suitcases in the middle of the floor.

He slowly turned to her with his cell phone still at his ear. There was a look in his hazel eyes that defied explanation. She'd never seen it before or since—her own terror, disbelief and pain reflected in someone else's eyes.

All he said was that he was sorry. He couldn't do this. He didn't love her. He never wanted to hurt her. He was leaving.

She was certain she'd screamed, thrown things, demanded answers—maybe she'd even begged him not to leave. Who knew? None of it changed anything, anyway. He was gone.

What was she going to do now with the pieces of her heart scattered all over her hardwood floors and her soul on the other side of the door walking into a life without her?

Chapter 1

One Year Later...

Summer came early to New York. Memorial Day was three weeks away and the temperature was already in the low eighties. If this was any indication of what the next three months would bring, it was going to be a long, hot summer in the city.

Layla Brooks sat on the sill of her third-floor walk-up apartment of the prewar building that faced Washington Square Park. She peered out of the smudged window at the entanglement of humanity on the streets below. Absently she fanned herself with the stiff white envelope that boasted a Sag Harbor address—a world away from where she lived in the West Village.

The West Village was known for its eclectic blend of people, styles, food, excitement and entertainment. Those were the things that drew her to this slice of New

York City life, that and her cushy job as a journalist for the *View*. Her beat was New York lifestyles, and in search of the next salacious story, she haunted some of the best and the worst locales in the city.

It was simply ironic how things got twisted all around and she became her own headline: laid off, unemployment running out, and working two nights a week as a hostess at Jack and Jill's, one of the local blues lounges. All things considered, she was better off than a lot of folks. She'd saved her money over the years and invested wisely, thanks to the wise counsel of her godmother Carolyn Harte. The paper had given her a decent severance and in the year that she'd been out of work, she'd finally finished up her classes in massage therapy. It had been an on-again, off-again process for nearly five years. Now she was fully certified in rehabilitation therapy and deep tissue massage, and she had even taken a special course two years earlier in tantric massage, which was how she'd met Brent Davis, her former fiancé.

Brent was the manager of a tantric massage studio tucked away in a three-story town house on the Lower East Side. He'd trained her—*personally*. There was no question that in the right hands the eroticism of the human touch was mind-blowing. Unfortunately, Brent felt the same way—about *everyone*. She'd been naive and in love, engaged to be married to the man of her dreams and too blind to see that Brent didn't only have "hands" for her. It had taken her a while to push that part of her life to the back of her head. But the hurt would rear its ugly head every now and again when she'd see couples hugged up together, whispering to each other, and know that the evening would end with them in bed together— while she would roll around alone on empty sheets.

The upside was that Brent was good at what he did

and he'd taught her everything she needed to know to be just as good a masseuse as him, if not better. She had a few regular clients and the extra income was great. The idea of owning and running a studio became more intriguing day by day. But with the economy still on shaky ground, she wasn't quite ready to take the leap. At least not yet.

She stopped fanning herself and flipped the envelope over. She ran her finger beneath the flap and tore it open, then pulled out the stiff off-white postcard inside.

It was the invitation she'd been expecting, embossed with the Platinum Society logo. It was the kickoff party of the season coupled with Desiree and Lincoln's fifth wedding-anniversary party, hosted by Layla's godsister, Melanie Harte. Although the festivities were more than a month away, Mel always planned way in advance.

Desiree Armstrong was her sorority sister and dear friend. They still laughed about all the fun they used to have as students living in the Big Apple. So when Desiree married Lincoln Davenport and moved out to Sag Harbor to open her art gallery and help out with his bed-and-breakfast establishment, The Port, Layla and Desiree didn't see each other as often as they once did, but Layla could always find a reason to visit Sag Harbor.

She'd spent most of her summers on the Harbor. Her godmother, Carolyn, the cofounder of the Platinum Society—a high-class matchmaking service—made sure that she kept an eye on her precocious daughter, Melanie, and Melanie didn't go far without Layla. They'd grown up rubbing elbows with the people that the average person only saw on television and in the news. Melanie and Layla were trained in the areas of entertainment, money management, travel, fashion and knowing how to mix and mingle with anyone from the man on the street to the president of the United States. Like Melanie, Layla could speak three languages fluently and had traveled to Europe and Africa before she was eighteen. And if Layla had her way, she would have married Melanie's gorgeous brother Alan, even though he always thought of her as the "cute kid" and his little sister's friend.

She smiled as those good memories rushed to the surface. She hopped down from the sill just as a truck backfired below and let off a plume of smoke into the muggy air.

Yes, it would be great to get away. A change of scenery, hanging with her girls and enjoying a blowout party was just what she needed.

"I think you should stay for the summer," Desiree was saying while she held the cell phone between her jaw and shoulder and adjusted a painting on the wall.

"Girl, the whole summer! You have got to be kidding. I have...stuff up here to take care of."

"Yeah, right. What *stuff*—a hostess job?"

"I have clients. They'll miss me," Layla said, trying to sound convincing.

"I have a beach full of clients for you and you know Melanie will hook you up. Besides, when was the last time that the three of us had a chance to spend some real time together?"

Layla thought about the tempting offer. But the truth was, both of her girls were married—Desiree to Lincoln and Melanie to Claude. She would be the proverbial fifth wheel. Her chest tightened as images of what could have been flashed for an instant in front of her.

"I don't know, Desi," she said slowly, teetering on the brink of relenting.

Desiree blew out a puff of frustration. "Well, whatever you decide to do is fine. I think you're blowing a perfectly good vacation."

"Where would I stay for the entire summer?"

"Right here at The Port."

"Desi, come on. What about your guests? The summer is the busiest season. You need all of your guest-houses."

"True, but you wouldn't be a guest."

"What are you talking about?"

"You would be a summer employee."

"I thought you said this was my vacation." Layla chuckled.

"Look, what if you stayed in one of the cottages and paid your way by offering massages to my guests? I've had a spa set up for months with no one to really run it. It would be a major perk. And you get to keep the tips!"

Layla burst out laughing. Desiree always had some kind of plan. "Let me think about it."

"Okay, but don't think too long. I know someone will want to hop on this great opportunity."

"Someone like whom?"

"Doesn't matter. Someone will."

"Girl, you are too crazy."

"Crazy as a fox," Desiree said with a snicker.

"Yeah, okay. Anyhow, I'll see you next weekend. But I'll let you know before then what I'm going to do."

"See you next week. And think about the offer. It's perfect."

"Okay, okay. I'll think about it. I'll see you Friday."

"Smooches."

Layla disconnected the call. *An entire summer on the Harbor? Hmm.* She got up from the side of the bed and walked toward the window. She pushed the off-white curtain aside. Traffic, gray concrete and throngs of rushing people filled her line of sight.

She let the curtain drop back in place. A slow smile lifted the corners of her mouth. Nothing was keeping her in the city beyond her decision to just say yes.

Chapter 2

Maurice Lawson winced when he attempted to push up from the couch and stand. The pain in his leg vibrated through his entire body. He squeezed his eyes shut and gritted his teeth. Slowly, the searing fire ebbed to a dull throb. He inhaled deeply and sat back down.

That night, flying over the Afghanistan mountains, flashed in his head. The skies were clear with just enough cloud cover to camouflage their mission. He and his navy SEAL crew were on a stealth mission. Everything was going according to plan. The target was illuminated on the control panel of the Black Hawk helicopter. And then, without warning, the world seemed to explode. He'd lost two men on that mission and he'd barely survived himself. He'd spent three months in the hospital and the next three months in rehab, learning how to walk again.

The doctors said he'd always have pain…and nightmares. But over time both would diminish. They hadn't.

That was more than a year ago. He still battled the pain and the nightmares…and the guilt. Some days, the guilt was more painful than his injury.

"Maurice…"

He opened his eyes and his gaze settled on Dr. Morrison.

"Are you all right?" She put down her pad.

He nodded. "Yeah." He forced a laugh. "I should be used to it by now."

"How are you sleeping?"

He shrugged. "Some nights are better than others I suppose."

Maurice Lawson had been referred to her through the Veterans Administration. After recovering from his wounds, it was clear that his injuries were more than physical. She'd been working with him for about six months and the psychotherapy was slow, but there were days when she felt they were making progress. Then there were days like this one when that haunted look would come into his eyes.

Dr. Morrison leaned forward. "Maurice, your physical therapy is over, but I can't get you beyond that night if you won't let me help you to help yourself. You're holding on to more than physical pain and that's what's really debilitating."

The corners of his eyes pinched. His full mouth drew into a tight line. "What do you want from me?"

"I want you to accept that what happened that night was not your fault."

"But it was!" he bellowed. "Why can't you understand that? I was in charge. Those men relied on me to get them in and out of there safely. And I didn't."

"What could you have done differently?" she softly asked.

He turned away from her penetrating stare. He'd asked himself that very question a million times. He'd gone over every minute of that flight. Nothing stuck out. It was textbook. But he had to have missed something. And that's what haunted him.

"What?" she asked again.

"I don't know," he finally answered, his voice filled with defeat. "I don't know."

"How about your friends, family—have you been in touch with them?"

"We don't have anything in common. They all want to act as if nothing is wrong or that everything is." His laugh was ragged.

"You can't continue to live in your head, Maurice, disconnected from everything. It's well past the time that you rejoined the world. Begin new relationships."

"Is that right, Doc," he said derisively. "You mean if I join the world, as you put it, I'll be *all* better." This time he fought against the pain and stood.

"I'm saying that you can't continue to punish yourself by shutting everything and everyone out."

"It's not that easy," he said, gritting his teeth against the pain.

"I know it's not. It never is. But if you are ever going to regain some semblance of life, of an existence, you're going to have to try. You're going to have to work at it, just as hard and with just as much passion as you've put into being a decorated fighter pilot."

He stole a look at her. "I don't know how," he admitted.

Dr. Morrison stood up and came to him. "I have a friend who owns a fabulous bed-and-breakfast in Sag Harbor. I think a change of scenery and the relaxation of being by the water would be therapeutic."

"I don't think so, Doc."

"At least think about it, Maurice. And I'll only be a phone call away…when you want to talk."

He pushed out a breath. "Yeah, I'll think about it." She returned to her desk and wrote the information down on a prescription pad, tore off the paper and handed it to him.

He looked at the neat handwriting. "The Port."

"Go, Maurice. A few days, a few weeks." She studied his face. "Give yourself a chance. And think about getting back in touch with Ross."

His gaze jumped to hers.

"You'd mentioned in earlier sessions that the two of you were close, that you even played in a band together. I'm sure he would be glad to hear from you. Have you spoken to him since you've been home?"

He lowered his head. "No." Then he folded the paper and shoved it in his pants pocket. "Time up?"

She moistened her lips. "Yes."

He bobbed his head and clenched his jaw as he turned toward the door. "See you next week, Doc."

Maurice opened the door to his one-bedroom condo apartment. He'd lucked out and was able to purchase the condo from his veterans benefits in one of the most sought-after communities in the quickly gentrifying neighborhood of Fort Greene. *One of the perks of fighting for your country,* he thought derisively.

He'd been in the space for nearly a year after leaving rehab and it was still sparsely furnished, only the basic necessities. It didn't matter much to him. It was only him. He didn't have company, there was no woman in his life, and all he needed was a place to sleep, eat and bathe.

He tossed his keys into a plastic bowl on the kitchen

counter and limped over to the window. He drew in a long, slow breath. Never in a million years would he have imagined his life coming to this point. His breathing echoed in the cavernous space. *Alone. Broken.*

Dr. Morrison's words bounced around in his head.

If you are ever going to regain some semblance of life, of an existence, you're going to have to try. You're going to have to work at it, just as hard and with just as much passion as you've put into being a decorated fighter pilot.... And think about getting back in touch with Ross.

Ross. He almost smiled. Ross McDaniels was his best buddy all through high school and into college. They discovered their love of music together and that it was a surefire way to charm the ladies. Ross was the sax man, he the piano. The two of them together were a lethal combination. Ross had been in his corner when he lost his father and never once came down on him for cutting himself off from his family, even if he didn't agree. They'd stayed in touch throughout his years in the service and it was not until the accident that Maurice cut off all contact. He didn't think he could stand to see the look of sympathy in Ross's eyes. That, he knew, he could not take.

He slung his hands into his pockets. Ross didn't deserve that. His stomach muscles tensed. Was his number still the same? He pulled his cell phone from his pocket and scrolled through his contact list.

Ross McDaniels. What could he possibly say to him after all this time?

Maurice swallowed over the tight knot in his throat. Ross had a birthday coming up. His was a month earlier to the day and Ross used to always tease him about being "the oldest."

He stared at the number, debated a million reasons why and why not, and finally pressed Call before he could change his mind.

The line rang three times before it was picked up. "Hello?"

"Hey, Ross, it's me...Maurice."

For a moment the line went completely silent. "Mo..." he finally said. "Don't B.S. me, man, is this really you?"

The tight knot in his gut burst loose and a tentative smile tugged at his lips. "Yeah, man, it's me. You usually have impersonators calling you?"

Ross laughed from deep down in his belly, a sound so welcome and familiar. Maurice's eyes stung.

"Not usually. I... Where the hell are you?"

"In Brooklyn."

"Brooklyn? You're back? Why haven't you called? I tried to find you for months. The navy wouldn't tell me shit. What happened? How long have you been home, man?"

Maurice waited a beat. "I've been home a little over a year," he said quietly.

He could almost see the waves of confusion pass over Ross's face as he tried to process what he'd just been told.

"Say what?"

"It's a long story. I...would have... I should have called..."

"I'm gonna forget that I should be pissed as hell right now. Brother, I thought... We all thought you were dead, man."

Maurice heard Ross's voice crack and that nearly broke him. "Look, I had my reasons."

"I'm listening. No, as a matter of fact, this is not for a phone conversation. I want to put my eyes on you. Where are you in Brooklyn?"

"Fort Greene. Why?"

"You driving?"

"Yeah."

"Janet is throwing me a little birthday party tonight. I want you here."

"Ross...man..."

"I'll text you the address. Eight o'clock. Not taking no for an answer. Besides, I spent enough birthdays without my man at my side."

He thought about it. "Things are different. I'm different."

"We all are," Ross said softly. "Eight o'clock."

"All right. Eight."

Chapter 3

Layla was never one for sitting in traffic and knew that city dwellers would be packing up to head to the shores come Friday afternoon. The idea of bumper-to-bumper cars, noise and horn blowing put her spine in a vice grip. She decided to hit the road on Thursday at midday. Getting around the winding streets of lower Manhattan was half the battle. Once she hit the William Floyd Parkway toward Shirley, Long Island, it got easier. She put her foot down on the gas and didn't let up.

The two-and-a-half-hour drive took just about two hours, and before she had a chance to get tired, she saw the signs for the Sag Harbor turnoff up ahead.

She pressed the button on the armrest to lower the windows and took a deep inhale of the ocean-tinged air. The scents of salt, sand and sea were carried along by the balmy breeze. Layla inhaled deeply. Her grip loosened on the steering wheel and her shoulders slowly lowered from their sentinel position near her neck. She had no idea how tightly wound her body was until she felt the embrace of the leather cushion of the seat.

Her clients had been lukewarm about her departure and one woman had even begun to whine about how Layla's leaving was interfering with her calendar. Mona told her that her job at Jack and Jill's would be waiting for her when she got back and not to worry about a thing. Mona had lent a strong shoulder after the utter devastation of her engagement to Brent, spending many an hour with her drinking countless mimosas and listening to Layla pour out her heartache and fury, and assuring her that it was Brent who was the asshole, that it was his loss not hers and that a real man was out there waiting for her—when she was ready. She was certain she would never be ready. She couldn't survive another hurt like that and the only way to get hurt like that was to love someone. That was something she had no intention of ever doing again. She was going to build her business, travel, enjoy her friends and maybe even write a book one day about the art of healing through touch. But love…she was done.

She'd paid up her rent for three months, had her utilities and cable temporarily suspended, packed her bags and hit the road. Taking in the magnificent view and allowing the tranquility of the shore to seep into her limbs, she knew she'd made the right decision.

Her foot eased off the accelerator as she entered the town proper. The cobblestone streets were lined with bright-colored canopies and shiny glass windows advertising the array of shops, restaurants, bakeries, specialty stores and art galleries. The waters along the pier were home to everything from basic fishing boats to outboards to large yachts and party boats that lolled atop the soft waves.

The Port was beyond the center of town, across a wide swath of beach and soft rolling hills. Lincoln had built the place up from two small cabins to a dozen, complete with the kind of amenities expected at high-price hotels—a bar, sit-down restaurant, exercise room, a lounge and room service. And now The Port had its own masseuse.

Layla followed the winding streets out of the main part of town until the shops began to recede in her rear-view mirror. The summer homes and, for some, year-long homes began to dot the landscape with pops of color against the sandy shores and green slopes.

Twenty minutes later she was driving onto The Port property. She pulled into an available parking space and got out. She arched her back and stretched her arms high over her head, then took a look around.

Not much had changed that she could determine since the last time she'd visited. But knowing Desiree and Lincoln, *Mr. and Mrs. DIY,* she was sure that there were many new changes yet to be discovered.

Layla grabbed her oversize purse from the passenger seat, shut the car door and walked into the reception area.

A gorgeous young woman who looked as if she'd been carved out of polished ebony wood greeted her. "Welcome to The Port. My name is Gina. Do you have a reservation or would you like a tour?"

"Hello, Gina. Umm, I'm actually a friend of Desi and Lincoln. I'm going to be doing massage therapy for the summer."

Gina's brows lifted and her lush mouth widened into a brilliant smile, displaying two rows of even white teeth. "Of course. Mrs. Davenport told me to expect you. Let me tell her you're here." She picked up a phone on the desk, spoke briefly, then glanced up at Layla. "Follow me, Ms. Brooks."

Much of what Layla remembered since her last visit was the same. The Port was still a classy place, from the high-end furnishings to the sense of elegance, style and professionalism that seemed to ooze from the staff. She did notice some new artwork, and a humongous flat-screen television that both served as an entertainment medium and provided updates about The Port and the town of Sag Harbor.

Layla followed Gina down the short hallway to where she remembered Desiree's office to be. Gina tapped lightly on the partially opened door.

"Come in," rang out the cheery voice.

"Your friend Ms. Brooks is here." Gina headed back to the front.

Before Layla could put one foot in front of the other, the door swung fully open and Desiree burst out like sunshine after a storm.

"Layla!" Desiree swept her friend up in a tight hug, then stepped back and held her at arm's length. "How was the drive?"

"A breeze. You look fabulous. And happy." Desiree had opted for a short, natural spiral hairstyle and her complexion fairly glowed from the inside out.

"Thanks, and I am." She beamed, then a frown tightened her brow. She glanced around the space where Layla stood. "Where are your bags?"

"In the car."

"Oh," she breathed in relief, pressing her hand to her chest. "For a minute I thought you weren't planning to stay." She hooked her arm through Layla's. "Let's get your bags and I'll show you where you'll be staying."

"I'm not sure for how long, but I have enough clothes and accessories to last me a minute."

Desiree laughed. "Now that's what I'm talking about."

They walked arm in arm out of the main building and across the landscaped front. Desiree had one of the staff gather Layla's bags from her car and bring them to her room.

"I'm so glad that you decided to come," Desiree said while she turned the key in the cottage door lock. "You're going to love it and my guests are going to love you." She swung the door open and they stepped inside.

As Layla expected, the space was beautiful. Pale walls and whitewashed floors gave the rooms an expansive, open-air feeling, and the rattan furnishings, glass accessories and bay windows topped it off. Although The Port had a full-service restaurant and bar as well as room service, each cabin came with its own fully functional kitchen.

Layla's cabin looked out onto the beach and down the pathway that branched right and left with a cabin on each side of comparable size to hers.

She dropped her purse on the kitchen counter and turned toward Desiree with a broad smile on her face. "Beautiful."

Desiree took a mock bow. "And you're going to have a ball. I'll leave you to get settled. When you're ready come on over to the main building. Lincoln can't wait to see you."

"Okay. Give me about an hour."

"See you then."

Desiree let herself out and Layla took her bags to the bedroom and began to unpack. She laid out an outfit, then went into the bathroom for a quick shower.

Wrapped in a thick pale peach towel, Layla padded

around her new digs and she had to admit, from the moment that she'd stepped onto the property and inhaled the ocean-washed air and spectacular views, she felt lighter inside. All of the worry and stress of everything related to home evaporated. She went into the seating area and turned on the stereo, and then two-stepped to the beat back into her bedroom.

Totally refreshed, and dressed for the sultry spring afternoon, Layla followed the path back to the main building and took in the sights along the way.

Maurice Lawson lounged beneath the shade of the blue-and-white-striped canopy that hung above his back deck. His injured leg was elevated on a pillow. Absently, he rubbed his upper thigh while he watched the waves gently move in and out from the shore. The temperature was perfect, and the light breeze blowing off the water combined for a near-hypnotic effect. Although he'd been reluctant to take his therapist's advice, he was glad that he'd come. The past few nights were the first in months that he wasn't awakened by the nightmares. Simply being able to rest through the night was beginning to have a positive effect on his spirit.

It was hooking up with Ross that finally changed his mind.

There'd been several moments of panic when he'd pulled up in front of Ross's Long Island home. He'd sat in his car debating on whether to get out and go inside. But then the front door to the house opened and Ross stepped out and all the time apart slipped away. It didn't matter to Ross and Janet that he'd been hurt or that he'd cut them off for so long or that he was seeing a shrink to try to get his head right. All that mattered was that their friend was alive and he was back.

He and Ross talked long after the last guest went home. They talked until the sun rose, and when he returned to his apartment in Brooklyn he felt almost human. Human enough to take Ross and Janet and Dr. Morrison's advice and go to Sag Harbor. Do some thinking and some soul searching. And whatever he decided, they would be there for him when he returned.

He rested his head against the back of the chair and was just about to close his eyes and let the pain medication settle in when movement to his right drew his attention. At first he thought that perhaps it was an apparition, a vision like the ones he would see at the end of the tunnel of light—beckoning him through those painful nights of recovery. That light and the ethereal image at the end of it were the only things that gave him hope and the will to go on. He hadn't seen the vision since he'd left the military hospital in Afghanistan, until now.

But it wasn't his imagination and the image wasn't a result of hallucinations from the pain. She was real and she moved as if walking on air. The lightweight white clothing that she wore gently floated around her, lifted by the gentle breeze.

Maurice sat up a bit to see where she was going, and to convince himself that she was real. She turned a corner and disappeared behind one of the houses. He stared at the space where she'd been until his vision blurred. He shook his head and blinked his eyes several times to clear them. A strange, unsettling sensation rippled in the center of his stomach.

"Crazy," he muttered to himself and tried to push the moment aside. He closed his eyes, leaned back and let the medication do its work. He dozed lightly and the one thing that he remembered when he awoke and found the sun setting down beyond the horizon was that he'd dreamed of the illuminated image again.

Chapter 4

"Are all the cabins full?" Layla asked, sipping on her mojito.

Desiree, her husband, Lincoln, and Layla were seated at the on-site bar, relaxing and catching up while listening to the backdrop of soft jazz and calypso floating in from some unseen source.

"We have three vacancies, for now. But they're already booked. Of course, everyone isn't staying for the entire season. The majority are here for about two weeks," Desiree said, then popped some peanuts into her mouth.

"Surprisingly, business has remained pretty good, even in the off-season," Lincoln said.

"During hard times people need some kind of escape, even if it's only temporary," Layla added.

"True, that's why we work really hard to keep the prices down and the service up," Desiree said. "And at least once every quarter, we have a half-price weekend special with all amenities included."

"That must really help to draw in the business and make people want to come back."

"It does. And, of course, Melanie recommends all of her clients to come and visit. When she has functions up at her place and clients want to stay over, some of her guests will stay here."

"Can't wait to see Mel. I haven't seen her since the wedding," Layla said.

"She's out of town, but she should be back early next week. She insisted on hosting our anniversary party, so I know she will have plenty to do when she gets back. And she has a long list of very eligible men she wants you to meet."

"Meeting men is not on my list of things to do. I came here to get away from the city, help you out and get some sun in. That's it."

Desiree and Lincoln shared a quick "sure, you're right" look between them.

Layla pushed out a breath and slowly gazed around at the tranquil setting. Singles and couples walked along the beach, gathered beneath umbrella-covered tables or swam in the pool. Several guests were entering the restaurant and the sound of happy voices filled the air. She could easily get used to living like this. The whole notion of not having to think about where she was going to park her car every day was more than worth the price of admission.

"Did you show Layla her place?" Lincoln asked.

"Yes."

"Love it," Layla said. "I get the feeling that the two of you have intentions of me being around for a while." She looked from one guilty face to the other.

"We just want you to be happy and comfortable," Desiree offered, putting on her sweet as syrup voice. Lincoln draped his arm around his wife's shoulder. "And if you decided to stay," he hedged, "you'd be all set up already. As a businessman I have to always think ahead."

Layla deadpanned the two of them and then laughed. "You two are a mess."

"We try," they said in unison.

"Listen." Lincoln pushed back from his seat. "I'm going to leave you ladies to do whatever it is that you do and I'm going to check on some inventory." He leaned over and gave his wife a slow, sweet kiss and whispered something against her lips that Layla couldn't make out, but whatever it was, it had Desiree's face flushed with heat.

Desiree's gaze followed Lincoln until he was out of sight. She sighed deeply. A light smile softened her lips.

"You two are still as hot for each other as boiling oil."

"Is it that obvious?" Desiree teased. She reached for her glass of white wine.

"Uh, yeah."

The friends laughed.

"So when did you want me to start? Did you let your guests know about the new massage therapy services yet?"

"I've been working on a small flyer to hand out, but I wanted your input first to make sure I had all the details right, and I wanted you to have a couple of days to unwind and relax."

"Girl, around here, I could get too relaxed and you wouldn't get any work out of me!"

"I know the feeling. But that's the kind of atmosphere Lincoln and I want at The Port. A real getaway, you know what I mean. If you look around, you don't see anyone hunched over laptops and checking BlackBerrys and iPhones every five minutes. They're actually here to enjoy themselves. At least, that's what I see when they come out of their rooms," she added as a caveat.

Layla nodded in agreement. "In that case—" she raised her hand to get the attention of the bartender "—another mojito please."

Layla couldn't stay in bed a minute longer. And as much as she wanted to simply loll around on the sandy shores like a careless beach bum, the urge to be busy grabbed hold of her. She was actually anxious to get her massage room ready and her fingers moving. All night she'd dreamed of how she was going to set up her space and the atmosphere she would create. This would actually be the first time that a work space would truly be all hers and not the vision of whomever she was working for. A twinge of memory tried to pull her back to those times with Brent, with him teaching her the techniques that had made her successful, that they practiced on each other late at night. She shook off the vision. That was the past, she reminded herself once again.

It was barely 7:00 a.m. and she was bathed and dressed. She tucked her iPad into her tote bag and headed out.

The morning was simply exquisite. The sun was at a perfect pitch. The sky was clear enough to see for miles and the gentle warmth that blew in from the ocean was invigorating. She spotted several guests jogging along the shoreline and there were already a few out for an early morning swim in the pale blue ocean.

Layla drew in a long breath and smiled. Whatever reservations she may have had about packing up and leaving the city were fading fast.

Desiree had given Layla the key to the massage suite the previous evening after their cursory tour. It was during the night that her wheels had started spinning and she'd woken up knowing exactly what she wanted.

She let herself in and stood in the center of the room and looked around. She took out her iPad and opened it to the Notepad icon and began jotting down a list of the things that she would need, from thick towels to oils, literature on massage therapy, robes, slippers, lighting and music. She would also need cases of water and a place to keep them cold.

Lincoln and Desiree hadn't cut corners on design layout or expense. Connected to the therapy room were shower stalls and a sauna room.

Layla guessed that what Desiree had said was true—that if she didn't take this spot someone else would. And she would be right. It was perfect and she couldn't wait to get started.

She could already envision the space as a full-time operation with a staff. She grinned, knowing that she was getting way ahead of herself. The first thing she needed to do was make a list and then go shopping for supplies before she started reviewing résumés.

Layla switched off the lights and locked up, her mind on the task ahead as she came around the short corner and came face-to-face with Maurice Lawson.

She came up short and started to apologize for nearly causing a collision, but the words hung somewhere in the back of her throat, stuck there with all the air that refused to move out of her lungs and fuel her brain.

Her center ignited and she could feel the fine hairs on her arms and along the back of her neck begin to rise. Good Lord, the man was…was…

It was her. The woman that he'd spotted yesterday. She was real. "Sorry," he said.

The two-syllable word sounded like a love song in her ears.

"No, you're fine… It's fine. Really." *Did she just say that?* "I'm always in a hurry," she babbled. She couldn't think straight, not with those haunting dark eyes staring at her and that chiseled upper body encased in a sleeveless white T-shirt that outlined every muscle that begged to be touched.

Maurice shifted his walking cane from his right hand to his left and shook hers. "Maurice."

Her hand was enveloped in the warmth of his. "Nice… to meet you, I mean. You're a guest?"

"Yes. You?"

"Yes and no. I'm a working guest. I'm the new massage therapist. Layla Brooks."

"Hmm." He nodded his head.

They stood there momentarily frozen in that "what now" moment that was mercifully broken by another guest needing to squeeze by in the narrow corridor.

"Nice meeting you," Maurice said.

"You, too."

He moved past her and tried to ignore the pain in his leg and limped away with as much dignity as he could summon. He wanted to vanish and not have her watch him as he tried to pretend that he was as whole as any other man.

Layla didn't realize that she'd stopped breathing until a burst of air rushed from her chest. Her heart was beating triple time, and although she was much too young for hot flashes, her entire body was flushed with heat.

"Humph, humph, humph. That is one specimen of a man, cane and all," she whispered. She definitely wanted him to sign up to be on her client list so that she could see for herself just how hard those muscles really were. She gave a short shake of her head to clear it.

It was still a little too early to drive into town. She took a slow stroll around the property, reacquainting herself with the layout, and then around to the back of the main building to the outdoor lounge, drawn by the aroma of breakfast. Her stomach responded.

A few of the white circular tables were occupied and the waitresses were busy filling juice glasses and coffee cups. She found a table that was near the buffet, put down her bag and walked over to check out the breakfast offerings. She started down the length of the table and filled her plate with fresh fruit, eggs and wheat toast. She walked back to her table and was thinking about her close encounter with tall, dark and handsome Maurice when the plate in her hand rattled. He was on the other side of the buffet table.

Maurice was settling down in his seat. Alone. He braced his cane against the table and she could see from where she stood the relief wash over his expression as he took the weight off his leg.

She wondered what had happened to him. Was it an accident? Surgery? She watched the expression on his face tighten. For a moment he closed his eyes while he massaged his thigh. What would that thigh feel like under her expert fingers? She knew she could take the pain away.

"Umm, excuse me."

Layla blinked. A smile flickered across her mouth. "Oh, sorry. I'm daydreaming," she said to the couple standing behind her who were waiting for her to move along. She walked with her plate back to her table, taking furtive glances in Maurice's direction.

He was reading the paper and sipping on a cup of coffee. Maybe she should go and join him. No sense in the both of them eating alone, she thought. A dozen different scenarios played in her head on how she should approach him and what she should say and what he would say to her in return. The minutes ticked away.

Maurice put down his coffee cup and turned slightly in her direction, then away before doing a short double take and looking back again. He lifted his chin in salute. Layla waved. Her heart pounded. Maybe he would come over. Maybe he would ask her to join him. Should she go over and sit down? What if he was waiting for someone and she looked silly?

Maurice folded the paper, finished off his coffee and reached for his cane.

He was going to come over. She could hardly breathe. She swallowed over the tightness in her throat.

Maurice stood slowly, offered her a brief smile and walked out.

Layla felt as if she'd been pumped full of air and then suddenly stabbed with an ice pick. As the air in her balloon dissipated, so did her appetite. She pushed her food around on her plate until it was sufficiently cold, then gathered up her things and went out to get her car for the drive into town.

Maurice returned to his room. He'd wanted to say something more to Layla. But what was the point? He tossed his cane into a corner and plopped down on the couch. Even if he was attracted to her, what would she want with him? She probably felt pity for him just like everyone else.

He stretched out his injured leg and absently massaged the never-ending ache.

It had been longer than he would have liked since he'd been with a woman, through choice as well as circumstance. After his injury and then rehab, he continued to struggle with what had happened that night. The guilt was almost as painful if not more so than the injury that ended his career. The therapy sessions helped, but only so much. He still could not get beyond the feeling that had he done something differently, lives would have been saved and he would be 100 percent man. Without his career as a navy SEAL, the job he'd worked so hard for, trained for, lived for—all of that was gone. Being a SEAL had defined who he was. The loss of that combined with his debilitating injury was almost more than he could stand. He didn't feel like a man anymore. And if he didn't feel it, what woman would feel it? He leaned his head back against the cushion of the couch and closed his eyes against his inescapable realities.

Layla spent the better part of the morning shopping for supplies for the suite. Her car's trunk was loaded and it took several trips back and forth to unload and get everything inside the suite. She'd purchased plants, artwork, oils, lotions, CDs, mats, small bowls, oil burners, hand sanitizers, disinfectant, cases of fruit juice and water, and soft lightbulbs. She'd placed an order for a dozen terry-cloth robes and shower slippers. The boutique where she'd made her purchases promised that her items would be delivered within the next two days.

She spent the next couple of hours organizing her supplies and rolling towels to be stacked. She hung pictures and poured the aromatic oils into the burners. Aromatherapy was just as important in creating the perfect atmosphere as the treatments.

Layla took a look around and was finally satisfied

with what she'd accomplished. She took some pictures of the space for the flyers, then locked up and walked back to the main building in search of Desiree.

"It looks fabulous," Desiree said when she saw the pictures. "Let me download them to my computer."

Layla touched a few icons on her iPad and sent the images to Desiree.

Within moments Desiree was loading them into her graphics program. "You've been busy," she said while she worked.

Layla laughed. "To keep my mind off other things."

Desiree looked up at her friend for a moment. "Other things like what? Don't tell me New York."

Layla sat on the edge of Desiree's desk and folded her arms. "No. Not New York." She leaned closer. "Do you know that guy...with the limp?"

Desiree frowned in concentration. "Limp?"

"Yes and gorgeous."

Desiree grinned. "Oh, Maurice Lawson."

"Him."

Desiree crossed her legs. Her right brow rose with her question. "What about him?"

"What do you know about him?"

"Hmm, not much. He checked in about three days ago. Booked his cottage for six weeks. That's about it really. I see him around from time to time." A slow smile moved across her mouth. "And you want to know all this because..."

Layla blew out a breath. "I wish I knew. Well, maybe I do know. It's hard to explain. I mean, I only saw him for a minute a couple of times...but..." She looked away as if searching for the answers somewhere in the corners of the room. Finally, she shrugged. "No big deal. Forget it. He looked like he'd rather be alone."

Desiree stared at Layla's profile. "Hey, this is the twenty-first century, girl. If a woman is interested in a man, she doesn't have to stand on protocol and wait for the man to make the first move anymore."

Layla slowly shook her head. "That is so not me. In my head, I'm bold and aggressive. But then reality sets in."

Desiree reached out and touched Layla's hand. "Bold and not standing on protocol *is* you. Brent screwed up a perfectly good relationship. But you can't let what he did diminish you. Every man is not like Brent."

Layla hopped down off the desk. "I know that. I'm over Brent."

"Are you? Really? I'm not saying that you still have feelings for him, but I am saying that what he did messed with your confidence, challenged your womanhood."

Layla snapped her head away. She tightened her arms around her waist. The words to refute Desiree's assertion were on her lips. They lingered on her tongue. She couldn't say them. What Desiree said was true. It was painfully true. It had been a year since she'd come home to have him tell her that he was leaving, that he no longer loved her. But there wasn't a day that had gone by when she didn't remember how small and insignificant she'd felt. How could he so easily stop loving her? It wasn't until months later that she found out why.

She'd gone over that night a million times. In some versions she threw a lamp at Brent and then dumped all of his clothes out of the window. In another he came running after her, begging her to forgive him. But in all the versions, in the end, she was alone. Probably what stung the most was that she'd heard from their mutual acquaintances that Brent and Grace—his assistant, the woman he'd stopped loving her for—were still together and there was talk of *them* getting married ing spring.

There was no way that she could get around the feeling that it was something she'd done or didn't do or that she wasn't appealing enough. *Something.* The feeling of inadequacy was not as bad as it had been, but it hovered and sat on her shoulder, waiting patiently to whisper in her ear.

"I remember the Layla Brooks that would walk into a minefield with high heels and a smile on her face, who could step into a room and every head would turn, who could have a conversation with the secretary of state as easily as the woman who owns the dry cleaner on the corner. *That's* the Layla that I know."

Layla lowered her head for a moment. Had she really changed that much? She looked at Desiree. "So I should just walk up to him and what?"

"Hand him one of your flyers for starters," she said, pressing the print button on the computer. Moments later a color-printed flyer announcing the new massage therapy services slid out of the printer. Desiree lifted it from the tray and handed it to Layla with a "now what's your excuse" look on her face.

Layla tilted her head slightly to the left and eyed the flyer. "Not bad. I'll see what I can do with it," she said with a lift of her chin before turning away and waving goodbye on her way out.

Mistletoe, Baby

Chapter 1

Her farewell party was in full swing. The kisses and hugs had been given, the toasts made and the tears shed. Now it was on to the business of drinking and eating—in that order. Her staff had managed to commandeer the very dignified presidential conference suite and transform it into an "after five" lounge that was complete with bartenders, waiters and a DJ.

Even as she looked around at the people that she'd considered family for the past five years and knew that she would miss them dearly, there was an undeniable bubble of excitement that wanted the day to be over, her bags packed and the jet taking off from Hartsfield-Jackson International Airport en route to New York City. Atlanta was a great place. It was her home. She'd built a stellar career in academia rising up in the ranks at Atlanta College to her current position as Dean of Academic Affairs, but as the old saying went: "Always leave them wanting more."

She was at the top of her game. The name Alexis Montgomery was always spoken of in the highest regard. Word had gotten around that she excelled at what she did and she'd been made an offer that she couldn't refuse.

During the past six months she'd been flown out to New York to meet with the board of directors at R.E.A.L., toured their Midtown Manhattan office and talked terms. After weeks of negotiation, she'd signed off on her five-year contract.

Alexis brought the glass of champagne to her lips and smiled at the throng of faces. She'd left the college in better shape than when she'd stepped in. She had much to be proud of and she had every intention of making her mark in New York the same way she'd done it in Atlanta. A thrill of anticipation coursed through her. In a little more than a week, her new life would begin. *Look out, New York—this Southern belle is on her way.*

"You realize there's really no one to fill those high heels of yours," came a rugged whisper in her ear.

Alexis casually angled her head to the right. A secret smile moved across her mouth and a light of something more than "we're only colleagues" lit the dark embers of her brown eyes. "I'm sure you only mean that in the most professional sense." The corner of her mouth flickered in a barely there grin.

"If you say so." He lifted his chin in the direction of her almost-empty glass. "Refill?"

She shrugged her bare shoulder. "Sure. It's my party, right?"

"Be right back."

Alexis watched him walk away and smiled to herself as several of her female colleagues scoped him out, as well. Ian Matthews was without a doubt a very eligible bachelor. He was the whole package: six feet plus, well built, with a walk like Denzel, a mind like Einstein, sweet milk chocolate all over, funny, well-endowed and an expert at using his "equipment," a tenured professor, chair of his department, and actually an all-around decent guy to boot. They'd been discreetly seeing each other off and on for nearly a year. But something kept Alexis from committing, although Ian said that he wanted to. She honestly cared about him. She was close to being addicted to the crazy sex that they had, but something was missing.

That missing something was the thing that had allowed her to sign on the dotted line. With her mother's passing, her best friend Naomi Clarke all happily married and relocated to Virginia, and that spark she was looking for in a relationship still out of reach, there was nothing more to keep her in Atlanta.

Ian returned with her drink. "Thank you."

Ian's voice rose above the hum of conversation. "Can I have everyone's attention for a moment?"

By degrees the room quieted and the guests all turned in his direction.

"What are you doing?" Alexis whispered through clenched teeth that doubled as a smile.

He gave her a long, stirring look and her heart nearly jumped out of her chest. Her face heated.

"I want to make a toast to the most brilliant, beautiful, decent woman that I know. Her departure is going to leave a big gap here at Atlanta College and a bigger one in my heart." He pressed his hand dramatically on his chest.

There was a collective gasp of wide-eyed surprise for some and a "knew it all along" expression on the faces of a few.

Ian turned to her with a smile that could steal her

heart if she let it. For a moment she doubted her decision. He raised his glass and the rest of the guests did the same. "To Alexis. Wishing you much success and happiness, and here's hoping that you take a big bite out of the Big Apple. Cheers!"

"Cheers!"

Alexis mouthed her thank-yous and sipped from her glass.

"I meant what I said."

Alexis gazed up at him. "Ian…"

They were mere inches apart. Their voices were low and intimate.

"No need to take it any further. I wanted you to know that what I feel for you isn't only in the bedroom." He grinned. "I'm not going to lie and tell you I'll wait, but I will say that I'm not in a hurry to look."

She pushed out a breath. "You are determined not to make this easy for me."

"When has anything between us been easy?"

She lifted her glass. "Touché."

"I'm so sorry I couldn't be there for your send-off."

Alexis adjusted the phone between her ear and shoulder while she put the last few items in her suitcase. "Naomi, the last place I expected you to be was at my going-away party."

"I know, but still. You came to see me last week."

"That's different. You just had a baby last week. And I had to see my brand-new goddaughter before I left and make sure my bestie was all right."

"I'm exhausted and achy, but every time I look at April my heart swells. I still can't believe that she's here and she's mine and Brice's."

Alexis listened to the awe and joy in her friend's

Chapter 2

Alexis had to give props to R.E.A.L. The organization—Realize Excellence Achievement Leadership—had arranged to have her furniture and clothing moved, they'd found her an apartment in New York, and they'd gotten her a first-class ticket. She could easily get used to this kind of treatment.

The moment she stepped off the airplane and into the JFK terminal, she could feel the energy that always seemed to hum beneath the surface in New York. It was hard to explain to anyone who had not experienced it, but it was similar to turning up the volume on your life, or walking into a dark room and someone flipping on the bright lights.

She rode along with the other arriving passengers on the Down escalator to the baggage claim area. As soon as she stepped off the escalator, she was stunned to see a navy-blue-suited young man holding up a sign with her name on it. She grinned. R.E.A.L. was pulling out all the stops. She was totally impressed.

She walked up to the driver. "Hi, I'm Alexis Montgomery."

"Ms. Montgomery." He gave a short nod. "Michael. I'm your driver. I'll help you with your bags and then I'll go and get the car."

"Great. Hopefully it won't take too long." She headed in the direction of carousel three with Michael at her side.

"How was your flight?"

"Very nice, thanks to a first-class ticket. The organization treats its employees very well."

They stopped in front of the carousel that had already begun to fill with luggage.

"Yes, it does."

Shortly her bags came around on the belt. Michael took them and walked to the exit. "If you wouldn't mind waiting a moment, I'll bring the car."

"I can walk with you to the car."

"No worries. I'll be right back."

She inwardly shrugged. *Fine with me.* She walked over to a nearby bench, sat down and watched arriving travelers run into the arms of waiting loved ones. She experienced a momentary twinge of melancholy, knowing there were no open arms to greet her, just a furnished apartment in an unfamiliar city. She sniffed, opened her purse in search of her cigarettes, and then remembered that she'd recently quit and suddenly wished that she hadn't and took out a stick of gum instead. She glanced around, took in the sights and sounds. Although it was early May, it was a balmy seventy-five degrees. *Almost like home,* she thought.

Just then a black Lincoln pulled up in front of her

and Michael quickly got out. He reached for her carry-on and opened the passenger door. Alexis slid into the roomy interior and gasped in alarm.

"Sorry, I didn't mean to startle you. Please. Sit." Alexis's pulse raced. She settled herself opposite her surprise guest.

"Graham Stone." He extended his hand.

Her eyes widened. "Graham Stone, CEO of R.E.A.L.?" Her hand, of its own volition, found its way into his. His long fingers wrapped around her hand and it was as if he'd cut off the oxygen to her brain.

He grinned and even in the dim interior she could see his eyes sparkle. Her stomach fluttered. She pressed her knees together to silence the lady that had jumped up and started to purr.

"Guilty as charged. My flight from London came in just before yours. I told Michael to find you. Much more efficient for him to take the both of us than to have you take a cab in a strange city."

"I...appreciate that."

Graham leaned back against the plush leather of the car. His steel-gray suit was in that new slender cut and it clearly outlined the long lean lines of his body. He looked her over in slow motion. "I have to apologize for this impromptu meeting," he said, and she caught the barely there British accent. "It was unfortunate that I was out of town when you came in to meet with the board last month. And that we couldn't 'meet' on the conference call."

"I was beginning to think that maybe you were only a voice or a figment of everyone's imagination."

Graham chuckled, the kind of deep robust sound that made one all warm inside.

"Not the first time I've heard that. Unfortunately, my focus is on building the organization and getting the kids of the inner city into the kind of schools that they deserve. I don't always have time for the elbow rubbing and schmoozing. I prefer to remain behind the scenes as much as possible, in addition to which the work involves a great deal of travel." As he spoke he stared directly at her, never averting his gaze. It was mesmerizing as much as it was unsettling.

Alexis cleared her throat. "And that's why you hired me?"

"Yes. I want you to be the face of R.E.A.L. and I need your expertise."

Want and need had never sounded so erotic. She shifted in her seat and linked her long fingers together and rested them on her lap. The pure surprise of stepping into a car and meeting her very gorgeous boss for the first time had completely thrown her for a loop. She was accustomed to being in control of a situation and certainly in control of her thoughts—but not now. And what was that intoxicating scent he was wearing?

"At least you have the weekend to get comfortable—a little." He grinned.

"I'm looking forward to getting started," she managed.

He slowly nodded his head without taking his eyes off her. "Good. I have several new projects waiting for you on your desk. You'll have to hit the ground running."

"I'm ready." The instant the words were out of her mouth she wanted to pull them back. She knew what she'd said was simple and direct, but in her head they held a completely different meaning.

He stroked his clean-shaven chin with his thumb and forefinger and Alexis had the overwhelming need to open the window. It was as if someone had struck a match in her belly.

"Would you like something to drink?" he asked, jumping into her head.

She blinked and smiled. "That would be great. Thank you."

He reached into the minibar. "Water, juice, soda or something stronger?" He gazed across at her from beneath his lashes.

"Uh, water is fine."

He produced a bottle of water and plucked a glass from the holder, and handed both to her.

"Thank you." Somehow she managed to get the bottle open and pour it into her glass without making a mess and a fool out of herself. She was quite amazed actually, as her fingers usually wavered between being board-stiff or weak as wet noodles. When she lifted her head from the minor task, she was rattled to see Graham looking at her with a bemused expression on his face.

"Are you always so intense?"

She straightened. "Intense?"

"Yes. You were working on that bottle as if it was the most important job you'd ever undertaken."

Her cheeks flushed. She lifted her chin. "You haven't seen me intense," she said, the hint of a taunt on her tongue.

Graham made a humming murmur in his throat. He angled his head to the side and his eyes creased ever so slightly at the corners. "Have they found a replacement for you at the college?"

"Not yet. The position has been posted. I'm sure they'll find someone reasonably soon."

"I'm sure they feel your loss already. You made a lot of important changes over there. Several of the departments missed the ax because of you."

At that moment she wasn't sure if she was seriously

impressed or annoyed. The fact that she'd been able to work with the board and the department chairs to restructure without losing students or teachers was not common knowledge beyond the boardroom of Atlanta College. "How did you know all of that?"

"I make it my business to know everything there is to know about the people that get hired at your level. I also want to make certain that there is real substance behind the fancy words on a résumé and cover letter."

"I see." She now knew she was annoyed. What else did he know about her that wasn't on her résumé and didn't come out in the phone interview? Clearly it didn't matter if he was around to ask direct questions or not. He still got answers.

And then as if reading her mind he asked, "How did Ian take your leaving?"

Her eyes widened. "I beg your pardon?"

"Ian…Matthews. Isn't it?"

Her heart began to race. "Yes." Her response was as much a question as an answer.

"He was one of your references," he said as if in answer to the question that hovered on the tip of her tongue. "He had wonderful things to say about you and gave the impression that…you would be missed."

Her cheeks were on fire. A tight line formed between her brows. "I don't recall giving Ian Matthews as a reference."

"You didn't. Whenever I'm interested in a potential candidate for the organization at the management level, I look into their surrounding circle of colleagues."

"So basically, screw what's on the reference letters."

The corner of his mouth lifted into a slight grin. "Well, let's be honest, what person who really wants a job would get reference letters or use references from someone who wouldn't say that they were wonderful?" Her right brow arched. She almost laughed but didn't.

He was actually right, but she'd never tell him that. "So who made these calls? You?"

"Yes. I generally do, but I felt it was even more important since I didn't have the pleasure of meeting you in person during your visit. You'll come to see in the days and months and hopefully years ahead that I'm a very hands-on person."

Her gaze dropped to his hands that rested casually on his thighs. She swallowed and nearly choked over the dry knot in her throat. She coughed and took a sip of water.

Graham moved forward, halfway reaching for her. "Are you all right?"

She nodded her head. "Yes," she managed. "Throat got really dry." She took another sip of water. She made herself look at him and forced a confident smile. "Fine. Really."

He leaned back in his seat, eyed her for a moment, and then took out a pair of glasses from the inside breast pocket of his jacket, slipped them on and picked up a folder that was next to him on the seat. He flipped it open and began to read.

Glasses. Nice touch, she thought absently. He had that whole *GQ* look down to an art form. He scanned through the papers in the folder and then handed them across to her, taking her a bit by surprise.

"Some easy weekend reading so that you won't come in cold on Monday." He lifted his chin in the direction of the folder. "Those are the plans for the upcoming projects. Some of the details were hammered out while I was in London. No one has seen them as yet. I'd like to get your take on it."

Alexis cleared her throat. "I'll let you know."

He gave a short nod just as the Lincoln cruised to a halt. "We're here."

Michael rounded the car and opened the door. He extended a hand to help her to her feet. Alexis stepped out onto Sutton Place. She glanced upward at the four- and five-story town houses that ran between Fifty-Seventh and Fifty-Eighth Streets, oozed style and sophistication, and paid homage to the bygone era of the roaring '20s. The building boasted a long list of who's who from the financial world like the Vanderbilts and the Morgans of J.P. Morgan fame, and celebrities such as Marilyn Monroe, actress Sigourney Weaver, designer Kenneth Cole and architect I. M. Pei.

"I know originally that we were to set you up in Midtown," Graham was saying as he stepped out of the car to stand beside her. "A good friend of mine owns one of the apartments at 10 Sutton and he's never here. R.E.A.L. leased it from him. I hope you'll like it."

Okay, now she was speechless. She'd heard about Sutton Place, read about it and saw pictures of the stately homes and co-ops. Never in her wildest dreams had she imagined living there. She wanted to do the happy dance but was sure it would be inappropriate.

"Very nice. I'm sure it'll be fine," she said, with a slight wave of her hand as if she lived in million-dollar homes on a regular basis.

Michael retrieved her bags from the car and was met at the curb by the red-vested doorman complete with a luggage cart.

"Welcome back, Mr. Stone. How was your trip?"

"Very productive, Glen. Thanks. How've you been? Did your wife have the baby yet?"

"Any minute now," the young man said with a beaming smile. "And I really want to thank you for writing the scholarship letter for my niece."

Graham clapped Glen on the shoulder. "Not a problem. You just tell Misty to make us all proud."

"Oh, she will. I know she will."

Alexis took this all in as Michael and Glen loaded the suitcases onto the cart. Did Graham Stone live here or did he just know the doorman? She could hear her voice rising in her head. Michael took Graham's bags and added them with the others, answering her unspoken question. "I want you to look out for Ms. Montgomery. She'll be taking over Vernon's apartment on three. Alexis Montgomery, Glen Johnson."

"Nice to meet you." Alexis shook his hand.

"Ms. Montgomery." He gave her a short nod and a smile. "Well, that explains the cleaning company and all the moving. I thought Mr. Vernon was finally coming back," Glen said as he began pushing the cart to the entrance.

"Hopefully they did a good job," Graham said as he strode forward. He stopped at the front desk and shook hands with the man behind the counter, took a set of keys and waved Alexis over.

"Alexis Montgomery, this is Milton, the building's concierge. Whatever you need, he'll help you." He placed the keys in Alexis's hand.

"Welcome to 10, Ms. Montgomery." He produced a brochure from beneath the desk and handed it to her. "It contains a list of amenities as well as information on local services."

"Thank you."

Graham had walked off and was in conversation with a woman who'd just gotten off the elevator. He kissed her cheek and held the elevator door for Michael and Glen, who stepped aside to let Alexis board.

The door swooshed closed behind them. Alexis was working hard at being cool, but it was becoming more difficult by the minute.

Michael pressed the button. Within moments the doors opened onto her floor. The corridor was as exquisite and lush as a staged photograph. The cool spearmint-colored carpet made the hallway virtually soundproof and exuded a sensation of tranquility. Michael and Glen led the way toward the front door. Alexis's heartbeat escalated with each step. Graham lingered a few steps behind. He was busy texting on his phone.

Alexis stood in front of apartment three. She fiddled with the keys until she located the correct one and then inserted it into the lock and turned.

The front door opened onto a spacious living space flanked by floor-to-ceiling windows that rose to meet cathedral ceilings. She slowly walked in, feeling as if she were entering someone else's life. It was ultramodern with splashes of noir chic. The wood floors sparkled. The open floor plan showcased a chef's kitchen complete with an oversize stainless-steel refrigerator, dishwasher, double oven, and a center island with a sink in the center and seating for four. The overhead cabinets wrapped around the kitchen and were inset with opaque glass. At the far end of the living room was a metal spiral staircase that led downstairs.

"Where would you like your bags, Ms. Montgomery?" Glen asked.

Alexis blinked rapidly, gave her head a slight shake and turned to face the three men who stood behind her.

"Umm." She looked around quickly.

"The bedrooms are downstairs," Graham offered, briefly glancing up from his cell phone.

She looked at him with a raised brow of question. "My apartment is similar," he said by way of an answer. "I'm on top of you."

Her insides quivered. *On top of me.* Her thoughts galloped off at breakneck speed and nearly dragged her along with them. She drew in a breath. "Downstairs, then," she said. "Thanks."

Glen and Michael unloaded the cart and began taking the bags to the lower level.

"This apartment is fabulous."

"They've upgraded all of the units in the past five years." He looked casually around. "Vernon did a nice job with the space."

"How long have you lived here?"

"Almost eight years."

Glen and Michael returned. "Your bags are in the master bedroom," Glen offered.

"Thank you so much."

He nodded his head and hurried out, shutting the door softly behind him.

"We'll let you get settled," Graham said and was walking to the door before all of the words were out of his mouth. Michael reached the door before him and opened it.

"Thank you again," Alexis called out.

Graham raised a hand in acknowledgment just before the door closed behind them.

Alexis released a breath of pure, giddy delight. She grabbed the handrail and hurried downstairs, stopping in her tracks when she reached the bottom. The bottom of the stairs opened onto a sitting room. The walls had built-in shelves with cabinets underneath. Beyond the sitting room was a full bathroom on the other side of the stairs. Down the narrow hallway was another kitchen— smaller than the one upstairs but just as finely detailed and equipped. Opposite the kitchen was a formal dining room. The next room over was a good-size bedroom and around a short corner was the master bedroom with a cedar walk-in closet complete with en suite.

Now this is off the charts. She opened and closed doors and explored all the nooks and crannies. *Wait until I tell Naomi.* She had definitely hit pay dirt. Dream job, dream apartment in the city that never slept and a boss that… Her breath caught in her chest. She wouldn't think about that. Couldn't think about it. Instinctively her eyes rose and she imagined Graham walking through his apartment—on top of her.

Chapter 3

Graham loosened his tie and shrugged out of his jacket while he walked from the entrance straight to his bedroom. He'd opted to keep his bedroom on the lower level as well, with the main level reserved for dining and entertaining. He'd purchased the apartment almost eight years earlier, but he was still unaccustomed to the luxury of it all. His former life was a far cry from the one he lived now, and even though the battle scars weren't visible they remained.

He hung his jacket on the hook behind his bedroom door, opened his walk-in closet and slid his suitcase inside, only taking out his shaving kit. He'd deal with unpacking later. He tugged his tie all the way off and hung it on the tie rack, stepped out of his shoes and placed them on the shelf with the others, then shut the closet door. Two rows of shoes. Sometimes he had to look more than once to believe it.

What he wanted was a cold beer, to stretch out on the couch and catch a Knicks game. He stripped out of his shirt, tossed it in the laundry bag and hung his slacks up with his jacket on the back of the door. He'd have Milton send everything over to the dry cleaner in the morning along with his other suit and the shirts from his trip.

He grabbed a white T-shirt from the middle drawer of his dresser and a pair of navy blue sweatpants that were faded and as soft as a baby's blanket from years of washing and wearing. The U.S. Navy insignia on the right pocket was barely visible. He headed back upstairs with the hope that there was at least one beer in the fridge. He lucked out.

He plucked the bottle of Coors from the shelf and took a quick look at the contents inside the fridge and then the deep freezer, packed tight with meats, fish and chicken. A ball of tension knotted in his stomach. He walked over to the pantry and pulled the door open and then the cabinets one by one. His heart thundered in his chest. Not enough. There wasn't enough. For a moment his right hand trembled ever so slightly as he ran it across the rows of canned goods, boxed items, bags of pastas, jars of sauces and columns of spices. What he saw was half-full, not abundance. Rationally he understood that, but emotionally he saw empty. He felt pangs of hunger and an unreasonable fear that made his heart race.

He forced himself to close the cabinet door. He twisted off the cap on the beer bottle and took a long, calming swallow. He squeezed his eyes shut and willed his pulse to slow. By degrees he began to relax and the images of his past slowly receded.

Graham crossed the room, picked up the remote from the coffee table and aimed it at the wall-mounted flat-screen television. He surfed until he found the game before setting down the remote. Second quarter. The Knicks were down by ten. He shook his head, chuckled and stretched out on the couch.

When a commercial played across the screen, showcasing a quartet of beautiful women celebrating with a night out on the town, he thought of Alexis Montgomery and wondered how she would fit in with his team and the pace of the New York lifestyle.

He'd read her résumé. It was impressive to say the least. She had an MBA in finance and a doctorate in education. She spoke fluent Spanish and French and was competent in Mandarin. She was well traveled, well-read and well respected, and she was definitely easy on the eyes. He was eager to hear her thoughts on the proposal that he'd given her to review. He liked the sound of her voice, the even throatiness of it and the way she looked directly at him. And even the way she'd tackled opening that bottle of water. He smiled and took another long swallow of beer just as the game resumed.

In a little under two hours, Alexis had unpacked and began to familiarize herself with her new digs. She'd set up her laptop in the smaller of the two bedrooms that she would use as her office. She'd verified that the cable was on and the internet was working—all courtesy of R.E.A.L. There were the basic staples in the fridge and pantry, but she needed to go food shopping, especially to pick up some of the things that she liked. She had no idea where to go, but maybe Milton could tell her where the nearest supermarket was.

She shoved her feet into her sneakers, grabbed her purse and dropped her cell phone inside. She palmed the weight of her new keys and grinned as she wrapped her fingers around them and her new life. She took another look around before heading out of the door.

Milton was reading the *New York Times* when she approached the front desk. "Ms. Montgomery." He rested the paper on the desk. "How can I help you?"

"I was wondering if you could tell me where I could find the nearest supermarket."

His right brow rose momentarily. "Certainly." He frowned. "Should I get you a car service?"

"How far is it?"

"Several blocks."

She smiled. "I'll be fine. I could use a good walk and get a chance to see the neighborhood."

He didn't look convinced and gave a slight shrug. He came from behind the desk with the intention of walking with her outside and pointing her in the right direction, just as the elevator bell tinged and Graham stepped off. His dark eyes widened. A half smile teased his mouth as he approached the desk.

"Everything okay with your flat?"

Flat. That made her smile. "Fine. Everything is great. I was asking Milton about the supermarkets in the area. I want to pick up a few things."

Graham placed the linen laundry bag with the building's logo on the desk. "Can you send these out for me? The usual. Light starch on the shirts."

"Sure thing, Mr. Stone."

"If you don't mind some company, I'll walk with you," Graham offered.

"Great."

Graham extended his arm toward the front door.

The early evening weather was still warm. Couples walked hand in hand and families strolled along the avenues pushing baby strollers, while others jogged to the rhythm of the tunes coming from their headsets and ear-buds. The towering trees had begun to bloom, filling the air with the sweet scent of awakening.

"Great neighborhood," Alexis said as they made the turn onto First Avenue.

"Yes, it is."

She tilted her head to look at him. "You don't sound convinced."

He laughed lightly. "Oh, I'm convinced." His eyes quickly roamed the street. "Who wouldn't be?"

Alexis studied his profile for a moment, watching his countenance stiffen and then relax as if he'd seen something he wished he hadn't.

Graham pushed out a breath and turned his megawatt smile on her just as they approached Gristedes. He pulled open the heavy glass-and-chrome door. Alexis walked in ahead of him. Every aisle was lined with shoppers, and the incredible assortment of goods was beyond imagination. It was a food lovers' paradise.

"Take as much time as you need," Graham said. "I have a few things to pick up myself and we can share a cab back."

"Great. Thanks."

"I'll meet you up front when you're done."

She nodded in agreement, grabbed a shopping cart and started off. She probably should have eaten a full meal before setting foot in this emporium. She was tempted to purchase everything that she laid her eyes on and wished she'd brought a list. She selected a case of imported water, fresh vegetables and baked bread, fish, chicken and seasonings, sorbet, yogurt, fruit, and mixings for salads. She could easily spend the day here, but her cart was nearly full. She pushed her cart to the checkout line and watched the numbers add up. New York prices were enough to send her into a sticker shock.

Alexis took out her credit card and reluctantly swiped it. *Good thing this job pays well.* She watched the groceries being bagged. Graham was standing at the store's exit talking on his phone when she pushed her loaded cart next to him.

His eyes skipped over her purchases and hers were agape at his. He had two carts filled to the rim and she could only conclude that he hadn't shopped in months.

Graham ended his call. "Get everything you need?"

"I sure hope so." She lifted her chin in the direction of his carts. "I see you must have gotten one of everything."

His eyes crinkled in the corners. "A few things." He stepped away toward a cab that was lined up at the curb.

The driver got out and opened the trunk.

"You think there will be enough room?" Alexis asked with a laugh.

"We'll make it fit. Won't we?"

Her eyes leaped to his face, but he was concentrating on getting the bags into the trunk. The muscles of his arms and back flexed as he lifted and deposited each sack. A lick of heat flamed in the center of her stomach. She swallowed.

"All in," he said, turning toward her with a glimmer in his eyes. "Off we go, eh?" He shut the trunk and opened the cab door for her. Alexis slid in and moved over to make room for Graham.

Gone was the scent of his enticing cologne. It was replaced with a lighter fragrance that was even more alluring in its subtlety. She licked her lips.

"Liking the flat so far?"

She blinked rapidly and focused on him. "It's fabulous. More than I could have ever imagined. I can't thank you enough for arranging it."

"You do a good job for R.E.A.L. and that will be thanks enough." He smiled ever so slightly.

Alexis linked her fingers together on her lap while her gaze flicked across his face.

Within moments the taxi was pulling up in front of their building. Glen hurried toward the cab with a luggage cart and helped to unload the bags of groceries and wheeled them inside.

"Don't know whose is whose," Alexis said. "We can sort it all out upstairs."

They followed Glen onto the elevator. "Where to first?"

"Stop by my flat first, then you can help Ms. Montgomery."

"Sure thing, Mr. Stone."

They rode the elevator to Graham's floor while Glen whistled some off-tune melody. Exiting, Alexis followed the two men down the hall to Graham's apartment. He opened the door, but Alexis lingered at the threshold.

"Come on in. You can help sort through."

Alexis came in and looked around. The setup was similar to hers, but the decor was decidedly different. Graham's furnishings were in a deep chocolate. A leather sectional that could easily seat ten dominated the living space. At least she thought it did until her gaze landed on the mammoth television. She held back a laugh. Boys and their toys. One wall was covered from floor to ceiling with a bookcase that held at least two hundred books. Impressive. She wondered if he'd read them all. The tabletops held framed photos of Graham in a variety of situations. Most were with people who she believed were students, in others he was at banquets, and there were several with senators and one with President Obama.

Graham and Glen sifted through the bags and deposited all that belonged to Graham on the kitchen floor and on the counters.

"All done," Graham announced by the time Alexis made her way to the unloading zone. "Glen will take yours down to your place."

"Thanks. When did you get to meet with the president?" she asked while Glen wheeled her groceries to the door.

"I was on his education committee during his first term. That particular photo was taken during a fundraising dinner for his second term."

"You travel in pretty high circles. I had no idea you were part of the education committee."

"It's not something that I broadcast."

"Why not during his second term?"

"As much as I wanted to help President Obama further his agenda, it took me away from mine. My focus needed to return to R.E.A.L."

She nodded her head in understanding. "Good choice."

He grinned. "I'm glad you think so."

"Good night."

"Good night."

Graham stood in his doorway and waited until the elevator door swished closed. He slowly shut his door and hoped that he hadn't made an awful mistake in hiring Alexis Montgomery.

Alexis had finished putting away her groceries, seasoned a piece of salmon and was waiting for it to finish broiling when her doorbell chimed. She frowned, wiped her hands on a towel, and went to the door and pulled it open.

"Graham. Mr. Stone."

"Graham is fine." He held up one of the Gristedes bags. "This was mixed in with mine." He extended the bag that was filled with salad greens.

"I thought it might be with your things. Thank you. I could have come up and gotten it."

"Not a problem. Mmm, something smells good."

"I have some salmon broiling." She paused. "You're welcome to join me if you want. There's plenty."

"Thank you, but I'd probably fall asleep. Jet lag is beginning to catch up with me."

She wanted to run her fingers across the expanse of his chest...just to see if it was as hard as she imagined. She smiled instead. "I totally understand. Get some rest." She took the bag. "Thanks."

"Enjoy the rest of your weekend."

"You, too."

Alexis slowly closed her apartment door, then rested her head against it and shut her eyes. They were going to wind up in bed together, and there was nothing that either of them could do about it. That she knew for sure. What she didn't know was if she'd be able to keep her job the morning after.

Chapter 4

"Finer than Ian?" Naomi squeaked in disbelief.

"Yes. They haven't invented the word to describe the man." Alexis put her feet up on the couch and snuggled into girl-talk mode. She reached for her glass of wine and took a sip.

"Details, details. Let me live vicariously."

Alexis giggled and then began to fill Naomi in from the moment they met in the car to his dropping off her misplaced groceries.

"Sounds yummy, and a Brit accent, too. Got a little Idris Elba thing going on. Is he single? No, forget that question. You know that mixing business with pleasure is always a disaster."

Alexis sighed. "I know. Bad business for all concerned. Great if it works, a nightmare when it doesn't." She finished off her wine. "But a girl can dream."

"Make sure it's *only* a dream, Lexi," Naomi warned.

"This is a phenomenal career move for you—don't sabotage it. Besides, if he is as fine as you say he is, then he probably has a string of women nipping at his heels anyway."

"You're probably right. But I still have my dreams," she said on a playful note. Naomi had always been the more provincial, live-by-the-rules, don't-rock-the-boat kind of girl. She was her conscience, and Alexis knew in the months to come that she was going to need Naomi's good sense to whisper in her ear when it came to Graham Stone.

At eight forty-five on Monday morning, Alexis walked through the doors of R.E.A.L. The offices were located on the fifteenth and sixteenth floors of what was once part of the ABC Television offices on Avenue of the Americas and Fifty-Third Street in Manhattan. Everything looked pretty much the way she remembered from her last visit.

The receptionist looked up from her computer screen and smiled. "Good morning. How can I help you?"

"Good morning. I'm Alexis Montgomery. I start work today."

The young woman's eyes widened. "Oh, Ms. Montgomery." She hopped up from her seat. She extended her hand across the horseshoe-shaped desk, and Alexis shook it. "Mr. Stone told me to send you straight to his office when you arrived."

Alexis's pulse quickened at the mention of his name. "Certainly."

"Let me advise him that you're here." She quickly pressed a button on the multiline phone and spoke into her headset. "Yes. Of course." She looked across the desk at Alexis. "Straight down the hall, make the first right and his office is on the left."

"Thank you."

Alexis followed the directions and passed several employees in the hallway and others who were getting settled into their offices. She made the turn and slowed her step. The door was partially open. She could hear his distinctive voice but couldn't make out the words. Alexis approached the door and knocked.

"Yes. Come in."

Alexis pushed the door open and stepped inside. Graham stood up from behind his desk. A stunning woman with large, luminous dark eyes and a short pixie haircut turned from her seat to look at Alexis from over her shoulder. She had on a soft pink skirt suit. Most women couldn't get away with wearing pink without looking like Barbie. But this woman could.

Graham came from around the rather large desk. "Alexis. Good morning." He turned to the seated woman. "Tracy Carter, this is Alexis Montgomery."

Tracy extended her hand but didn't get up. "I've heard a great deal about you."

Alexis shook her proffered hand and was drawn to Tracy's green eyes that reflected like hidden jewels against her sandy-brown complexion. "Nice to meet you."

Tracy's softly tinted lips barely lifted into a smile. "Welcome aboard."

The two women held each other's gaze. Tracy was the first to turn away.

"Tracy is my executive director and probably knows more about how this business runs than I do. She'll bring you up to speed and get you set up in your office." His phone rang. He reached for it and gave them a brief look that the meeting was over.

Tracy retrieved her iPad from the desk and stood. "I'll direct you to your office," she said, swinging past Alexis. Alexis offered Graham a tight smile that he completely missed before leaving with Tracy.

"So how long have you been with the organization?" Alexis asked while they walked down the hall and back to the elevators.

Tracy tucked her iPad under her left arm and pressed the up button on the panel. "Since we opened," she said without any further elaboration.

Alexis's right brow flickered upward. She slid a look at Tracy from the corner of her eye. This was going to be interesting.

They got off on the sixteenth floor and Tracy silently led the way to the corner office at the end of the wide hallway. She took out a key card from the pocket of her jacket and slid it through the slot like a hotel room. The lock clicked open. Tracy opened the door and stood aside to let Alexis go in. Her first gracious overture since they met.

Alexis looked around. A genuine corner office. Wow. She turned to Tracy. "Thank you."

"I.T. will be up in about—" she checked her watch "—twenty minutes to get your computer set up, and give you a company cell and iPad. I'll send in Claire. She'll be your assistant. Graham... Mr. Stone has you on his schedule for eleven-thirty in his office."

"Thank you, Tracy."

"I'll send Claire right in." She handed Alexis the key card, walked out and closed the door behind her.

Alexis stared at the door for a moment. Tracy Carter clearly had a bug up her behind. Alexis wasn't quite sure how she fit into the equation, but she wasn't going to let Tracy's cold shoulder rub off on her. She walked to the window that overlooked the city. In the distance she could see the treetops of Central Park, and felt the buzz and electricity of the city speeding by below. It was like looking at a magnificent movie with the sound muted.

Her heartbeat escalated. She was here—New York City, with a six-figure job and an apartment on Sutton Place. She had the opportunity to make major changes in education on a global scale. It was everything she could possibly hope for. And then, of course, there was the Graham Stone factor that made the package perfect.

She turned away from the window at the sound of a knock on the door.

"Yes, come in."

The door eased open and a young woman peeked her head in.

"Claire?"

"Yes."

Alexis crossed the room as she spoke. "Please come in."

Claire stepped fully inside. "Good morning, Ms. Montgomery. Claire Davis."

Alexis extended her hand. "My pleasure. I understand we'll be working together."

"Yes, ma'am. Whatever you need."

"How long have you been working here, Claire?"

"Two years."

Alexis bobbed her head. "Good." She blew out a breath. "I.T. will be up shortly. But until they get here, why don't you give me your perspective of R.E.A.L., the who's who and where you see yourself in five years."

Claire blinked back her surprise. "Well…"

Alexis sat down on one of the club chairs and indicated that Claire should sit, as well.

"Before you say anything, I want you to understand that as my assistant I will be entrusting you with keeping me on task, from something as simple as taking a phone message to scheduling appointments, maintaining my calendar, navigating me through the minefield of R.E.A.L. We are a team. That means we work together as a unit. I depend on you and you depend on me to help you do your job. When I'm lagging, I want you to let me know. I can be demanding and get an awful case of tunnel vision when I'm immersed in a project. I give one hundred and fifty percent, and I expect no less from anyone that I work with. I make sure that hard work is rewarded."

Claire sat up straighter in her seat. "As I said, I've been here for two years. I worked for Mr. Martin. He had the position before you arrived." She paused a moment. "Actually, we all thought that this position would go to Tracy."

That explained the attitude. Alexis nodded and let Claire continue.

"I have a master's degree in educational leadership. I spent four years with Teach For America, teaching fifth grade in Bedford-Stuyvesant in Brooklyn. I'm good at what I do. I'm married and have a two-year-old son. I'm dedicated to my job, but I will be honest—my family comes first."

Alexis smiled. "That was the most impressive thing you said…about your family." That little ache that echoed in her belly was still there, not as powerful or as painful as when her mom first passed away, but there nonetheless. She knew the importance of family. She was sure that if her mom were still here she would have never left Atlanta, no matter how good this deal was. She cleared her throat. "I think we're going to make a formidable pair."

Claire smiled and appeared to physically relax. The knock diverted their attention.

"I.T.," a voice announced.

"Come in," Alexis said, standing. Claire followed suit.

"Morning, I'm Jason. I'm gonna connect all of your equipment and set up your accounts."

"I'll get out of your way."

"It should only take about fifteen minutes." He sat down at the desk, booted up his laptop and turned on her computer. He got set up and went to work.

"Where can I get a cup of coffee?" Alexis asked.

"Come on, I'll show you the employee lounge and my office...and—" she added with a grin "—the ladies' room."

By the time Alexis and Claire returned to her office, Jason was just finishing up. He showed Alexis how to sign into her email account, and had her sign for an iPad and a company cell phone.

"Thanks, Jason."

"Sure thing. Any problems or questions, we're at extension 2100."

Alexis and Claire sat down to finish their coffee. "While you're at the meeting with Mr. Stone, I'll get your files set up on your computer and check your supplies to see what you may need."

"Perfect."

Claire got up. "If you need anything before your meeting, I'm on speed dial."

Alexis grinned. "That's definitely good to know."

"And I'll email you my cell so that you can program it into your phone," she added on her way out of the door.

Claire quietly shut the door and Alexis released a long breath. The combination of excitement and nerves ran rampant through her veins. She was eager to get started. She'd had the opportunity to review Graham's plan and she had some ideas on how to make it happen, as well as a suggestion that she hoped he'd agree to. After studying the company's objectives and their projects already in operation, she found one area that had been overlooked and, if implemented, could elevate R.E.A.L. on yet another level.

She turned on her computer and took her jump drive from her purse and popped it into the computer's USB port. Once the notes that she'd made appeared on her computer screen, she reviewed them, made a few corrections and additions and then sent them to a secure folder. Just to be on the safe side, she printed two copies of her report.

She jumped at the sudden ring of her desk phone. She picked it up. Claire was calling to inform her that Mr. Stone wanted to move up their meeting to "right now." She added that it was something Alexis would have to get used to as he often changed meeting times when he was juggling several projects.

"Thanks. I'm on my way." She collected her notes, laptop and cell, and took the elevator down. It occurred to her as she stepped off that it was odd that Graham, as the founder and CEO, should be on the lower floor.

But from everything that she'd gleaned about Graham Stone, he was anything but status quo.

Alexis took a moment to get her bearings. She caught a glimpse of soft pink at the end of the corridor, moments before the slender figure crossed a threshold and was out of view. She wondered if Tracy would be attending the meeting. Hopefully she would. It would give Alexis an opportunity to see up close and quickly how Tracy operated and the dynamics between Tracy and Graham.

The rhythmic click of her long-legged stride was absorbed by the dove-gray carpet. Graham's door was open. Several people were in the office. She walked in.

Graham sensed her before he actually saw her. The short hairs on the back of his neck tingled. He turned from the conversation he was in with one of his staff members and his gaze zeroed in on Alexis. The tingling sensation spread down the center of his spine. His jaw clenched.

"Ms. Montgomery, please come in." Graham waved her in and the other four people in the room stopped in midsentence and looked at her.

Alexis felt as if she was on the runway at Fashion Week and was being appraised by potential buyers. Graham made the introductions.

"All of you are aware that R.E.A.L. has a new VP of Development. I would like to formerly introduce Alexis Montgomery."

Alexis's gaze swept the small assembly and graced them with a warm but professional smile. "Good morning."

Graham continued the introductions that included Anthony Harrelson, Vivian Small, Kwame Knight and Jae Jennings. They were all heads of each of the following departments: Finance, Corporate Communications, Marketing, and Social Media. They would all report to Alexis.

"It's a pleasure to meet all of you. I'm looking forward to us working together and me getting to know you."

"You can set up your individual meetings with the

department heads and they can bring you up to speed," Graham said with a briskness that indicated this would not be the place for chitchat and small talk. Everyone took their cue and moved to the rectangular conference table and sat down.

Graham undid the single button on his suit jacket before he took his seat at the head of the table. Alexis found herself between Jae and Vivian. Jae was head of Social Media, and Alexis was sure the evolving digital platforms kept her challenged. She reminded Alexis of a lightning bug in a bottle, buzzing and flashing pinpoints of light and biding its time until the lid was opened and it could escape. Vivian was the diametric opposite. There was a calming aura about her. The strands of silver that ran through her intricately twisted upswept locks belied the buttery smoothness of her skin. Alexis placed the head of Corporate Communications in her early to mid-forties, and noted she wore a striking wedding band encrusted with diamonds.

Anthony Harrelson and Kwame Knight, heads of Finance and Marketing respectively, sat on the opposite side of the table. They could have easily stood in for magazine cover models—gorgeous from head to toe. Alexis absently wondered if good looks were a part of the hiring criteria.

Then much to Alexis's surprise Tracy strutted in and joined them, taking the seat nearest Graham.

"Let's begin," Graham said, turning to Tracy.

"The first agenda item is from Finance." She gave a short nod to Anthony and placed her iPad on the table. She took notes as each executive outlined issues of concern in their departments and gave updates on pending projects.

Alexis remained an observer, which allowed her to get

a good sense of the staff members' styles and personalities, as well as the dynamic between Graham and Tracy.

It was clear that he relied on her and she knew it. Alexis had to give Tracy her props, though. She knew her stuff. She was up on every nuance in every department and if she didn't understand what was being conveyed, she had no problem challenging the information.

Alexis was surprised at how laid-back Graham appeared to be. She perceived him to be one who relished control, but what she slowly realized was that Graham controlled everyone in the room without uttering a word. It was in a look, a subtle shift of his body in his seat, the sound of a low hum in his throat. Each person in that room deferred to Graham Stone.

The meeting lasted for exactly forty-five minutes. Tracy announced that everyone would have the details of the meeting uploaded to the corporate shared drive by the end of the day.

Everyone except for Tracy and Graham gravitated toward Alexis at the conclusion of the meeting, offering warm words of welcome and promises to contact Claire to set up a one-on-one. Even as she shook hands and smiled and nodded, she managed to catch glimpses of Graham and Tracy nearly head-to-head at the conference table, talking in low whispers.

Alexis was at the door when Graham's voice stopped her. "Would you wait a few minutes, Alexis? I'd like to have a word."

Alexis would have sworn on a stack of hotel Bibles that Tracy's perfectly made-up face contorted. But it happened so quickly. Maybe she was wrong.

"Of course." She moved back into the room. Tracy took a seat.

Graham's gaze dropped down to her. "No need for you to stay."

This time Alexis didn't mistake the shift in Tracy's expression. It was lightning quick, but it happened.

Tracy grabbed up her iPad and phone. "Oh, of course. I have some calls to make. Don't forget about your three o'clock." She breezed by Alexis as if she didn't exist.

Inwardly Alexis rolled her eyes at Tracy's immature behavior and took a seat at the table.

"How has the morning been so far?"

Alexis smiled. "A whirlwind. But not more than I expected. Claire is wonderful and everyone seems friendly and good at their jobs."

Graham nodded while she spoke and Alexis had the feeling that Graham wasn't really listening, not from the way he was looking at her. His unfaltering gaze and the way he would periodically run his tongue across his bottom lip ignited a slow heat inside her belly, akin to a pot of water put on the stove to simmer.

"I'd like to hear your thoughts on the proposal that I gave you to read."

Alexis swallowed and shifted a bit in her seat. She crossed her legs. Graham's gaze momentarily tracked the movement, then returned to her face.

"The proposal is solid, which I'm sure you already know. I did a bit of research and I couldn't find any other urban model that resembled it. I know we can sell the idea to charter and independent schools."

"I want to begin with the public school system."

Alexis flicked a brow. "Okay. If we select a school and set up a model…"

Graham slowly rocked his jaw and pressed his body forward. "My goal is to give every inner-city child—particularly children of color—the educational opportunities that the kids Uptown and in suburbia get. The Pub-lic-Private Partnership Initiative will bring in successful people from every area of discipline to conduct classes on how they did it. Ten months of school, ten separate sessions. We work it into the curriculum."

She was mesmerized by his intensity. The way he presented the proposal was so definitive, so clear, so do-able. Except she knew the NYC Department of Education was a sea of bureaucratic red tape. It might take her the length of her five-year contract to pull it off.

"I'll get working on making the contacts at DOE. I take it you have a list of investors."

"I do. I'll get you the list. I want you out front on this." He leaned back a bit and the heat that he ema-nated lessened. His eyes moved lazily across her face. "You'll need to set up individual meetings with each of the potential investors, pitch them the idea and get them on board. Once you and I knock out all the details—this will be tight," he added, tapping his long finger on the table. "And then we'll have Legal draft a contract for the investors. I need you to complete this phase of the project in three days."

Alexis nodded. "I'll get right on it." *Right on it. I won-der how that would feel?*

The corner of his mouth curved ever so slightly as if he'd read her wicked little thoughts. Her face heated.

She stood and smoothed her skirt. "If there's noth-ing else…"

"I'd like us to meet again on Thursday to discuss your progress. I have to go out of town on Friday."

"Oh." A twinge of disappointment pinched her. "Of course. I'll get as much done as I can."

"All of the organization's resources are at your disposal. All of the department heads report to you. Don't hesitate to use them."

"Yes, thank you." She walked to the door.

"Enjoy the rest of your day," Graham said.

The murmur of his voice slid up her spine and tickled the hairs at the nape of her neck, and the tiniest of moans escaped from her lips. She glanced over her shoulder. "You, too."

Alexis headed back to her office, acutely aware of the dampness between her legs. Was she going to have to carry around an extra pair of panties in order to be in the same room with Graham? *Damn.*

The best thing to get her mind and body off him was work and she had plenty of it. Yet even as she returned to her corner office she wondered what was going to be more challenging: completing the details of his complex proposal in three days or staying in her right mind around him.

*She had only herself to rely on...until a wounded
soldier offered his friendship...and ecstasy
beyond her dreams.*

JERICHO

GINGER JAMISON

Georgia Williams has traveled a hard road from sheltered
preacher's daughter to struggling single mother. As a night nurse at
Jericho Military Hospital, she meets Lieutenant Christian Howard—a
man of duty, honor and deep desires. Something about the scarred
war hero touches Georgia, awakening feelings she's tried to keep
hidden. But one passionate night changes everything, erupting with
consequences neither could have foreseen.

"Complex, engrossing novel." —*RT Book Reviews* on *Liberty*

Available September 2014 wherever books are sold!

www.Harlequin.com

KPGJI660914

Can he convince her to take another chance on love?

ESSENCE **BESTSELLING AUTHOR**

GWYNNE FORSTER

McNEIL'S *MATCH*

After a bitter divorce, twenty-nine-year-old Lynne Thurston is faced with the prospect of not knowing what to do with the rest of her life. Once a highly ranked pro tennis player, she gave it all up six years ago when she got married. Now with nothing else to lose, can she make a comeback on the tennis circuit? Sloan McNeil is a businessman who wants to convince Lynne that she still has what it takes... both on *and* off the court!

"Caring and sensitive...FLYING HIGH is a moving
story fit for any keeper shelf."
—*RT Book Reviews*

Available September 2014 wherever books are sold!

KPGF1590914

He was the one who got away....

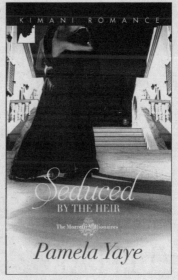

Seduced
BY THE HEIR

Pamela Yaye

Years ago, Paris St. Clair was Rafael Morretti's college sweetheart, and the career woman is still haunted by the passion they shared. Maybe meeting Rafael again is a sign that their love is meant to be. As they give in to desire at a private villa, will a sudden web of blackmail destroy Rafael's good name and sabotage their precious second chance?

The Morretti Millionaires

www.Harlequin.com

Available September 2014
wherever books are sold!

KPPY3690914

They are political rivals...until the doors are closed!

SECRET SILVER *Nights*

ZURI DAY

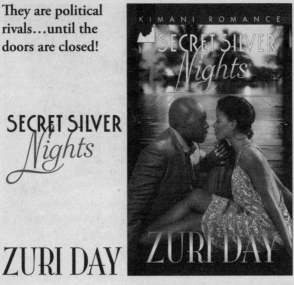

Nico Drake dreams of one day becoming governor of his state. First item on his agenda? Beating his newest mayoral challenger, Monique Slater. She has big plans for their small town, and they don't include falling for her sexy political rival. Keeping their sizzling relationship under wraps while running against each other is a tightrope act, but can Monique convince Nico that there are no losers when it comes to love?

The Drakes of California

www.Harlequin.com

Available September 2014 wherever books are sold!

KPZD3700914